THE TIGER AND THE BEAR

ТИГР И МЕДВЕДЬ

PHILIP LAZAR

an imprint of Sunbury Press, Inc.
Mechanicsburg, PA USA

an imprint of Sunbury Press, Inc.
Mechanicsburg, PA USA

For information about special discounts for bulk purchases, please contact Sunbury Press Orders Dept. at (855) 338-8359 or orders@sunburypress.com.

To request one of our authors for speaking engagements or book signings, please contact Sunbury Press Publicity Dept. at publicity@sunburypress.com.

FIRST AGENCY BOOKS EDITION: March 2025

Set in Adobe Garamond Pro | Interior design by Crystal Devine | Cover by Lawrence Knorr | Edited by Gabrielle Kirk.

Publisher's Cataloging-in-Publication Data
Names: Lazar, Philip, author.
Title: The tiger and the bear / Philip Lazar.
Description: First trade paperback edition. | Mechanicsburg, PA : The Agency Books, 2025.
Summary: A tense thriller set in contemporary Washington, Europe and Southeast Asia, as well as the Soviet Union during the Gorbachev years, depicting the imagined discovery by U.S. journalists of Moscow's attempt to influence the 2016 U.S. election and covert efforts to stop their quest. Reminiscent of John le Carré and Charles McCarry.
Identifiers: ISBN : 979-8-88819-278-8 (paperback).
Subjects: FICTION / Thrillers / Espionage | FICTION / Thrillers / Political | FICTION / Thrillers / Suspense.

Designed in the USA
0 1 1 2 3 5 8 13 21 34 55

For the Love of Books!

To my wife, I couldn't have done this without you.

CONTENTS

AN INCIDENT IN THE CORRIDOR

The blood had been the frightening part. So much of it.

It was late night. Having spent the day serving coffee to tourists in the lobby bar, as usual, she was shaken. She was recounting the story to a desk clerk she knew from back home as they walked out of the hotel after their shifts. Both were glad to have jobs in the hotel and sent money back to their parents upcountry, but she was now wondering whether she should quit and go back home.

She had stumbled onto the body in a corridor, she said. The throat was slit and the man, European of some sort, was staring up at the ceiling with dead eyes. His dead hands were clutching his dead throat.

There was blood everywhere.

She quickly called the manager, who called the police, and soon, the corridor was swarming with them. It seemed, from what she overheard before she was shooed out, that the man was not registered in the hotel, maybe a guest's visitor. One of the policemen said there seemed to be some sort of problem with his passport. Someone from his embassy, shaking his head, was staring at the passport and consulting his iPhone.

Where was this, the desk clerk asked. When she told him, he remembered the woman with the snoring husband and wondered.

The next day, though, when he began his shift, he discovered that the woman and her husband had checked out suddenly.

CHAPTER ONE

THE ENVELOPE

Washington, 2014

The boldfaced red Cyrillic warning was what jumped out at Paul Girard when he slipped the document out of the envelope for just a moment.

Очень секретно. Не распространять!

It would have been threatening, even if he had not been able to read the words. They were printed across the top of the first and every succeeding page in the sheaf of about forty papers. They were otherwise covered with dense, menacing, single-spaced Russian script.

Очень секретно. Не распространять!

A warning, obviously, Paul said now, sitting in the dining room. *Ochen' sekretno. Ne rasprostranyat'!*—very secret, do not distribute, something like that, he said. That was mainly for the benefit of Elise sitting across the table in her customary spot. Gunther Schroeder, who had arrived shortly before, had no customary spot but, like Paul, spoke Russian from their time covering Moscow, and he nodded his agreement with Paul's description. He sat in one of the guest chairs at one end of the table.

Очень секретно. Не распространять!

Elise stared at nothing for a moment. Can we go over how you got this again, she asked.

He had told her the story, but clearly, something was bothering her. OK, Paul said.

Очень секретно. Не распространять!

* * *

It had been that afternoon, he said. He had been at a think tank conference digging around among the graybeards for a report he'd been contracted to do. Nothing earthshaking, a small job that would take him a week, tops, he said. Good money, easily earned. His post-journalism career—telling consultants, NGOs, U.N. agencies, and the like what they needed to know in crisp, unadorned reports for which they paid good, and sometimes very good, money.

He had been in the audience, toward the back, out of the way, listening to an academic in from Australia and taking notes, when this congressional staffer—Paul now consulted the business card he'd had sitting on the table in front of him—Archibald, or Archie, Richter had sat down next to him. The last folding seat in the row.

Elise slid the business card over, looked at it, and passed it to Gunther, who then passed it back. It looked like a million other U.S. government business cards with Archibald Richter's name, contact information set in raised letters in a bland, if dignified font, and the standard engraved gold U.S. seal in the top left corner. Nothing to write home about.

Paul hadn't taken much notice, he said, he was listening to the speaker and working out how he would finish up the project in the next couple of days so he and Elise would have a few days together, maybe get away. It seemed, he thought, that the staffer was watching him out of the corner of his eye.

At the end of the presentation, Paul picked up his papers to leave. As he got up, Richter turned to him and handed him the card—call me "Archie," he said—and asked if they might chat for a moment, maybe over there in the corner where there was still some coffee. It will be worth it to you, he'd said.

A little film noir, Gunther said. Elise looked at him, but Paul continued.

Richter looked to be about thirty or so, Paul said, with a pronounced Southern drawl. He had a good ol' boy smile and a haircut that looked like it had been done in the dark. He wore a blazer, button-down blue oxford cloth shirt, striped tie, and khakis, an ensemble that might have come from J. Press, or maybe the knockoff version found in a strip mall.

He wore an American flag pin on his lapel and tortoise-shell glasses. No wedding ring but some sort of class ring on his left hand. Like the business card, standard young Washington up-and-comer issue. He carried a canvas briefcase that looked like a giveaway, from a National Rifle Association gathering of some sort. Everyone in Washington now wore their heart on their sleeve, Paul thought.

"Sure," Paul told Archie. He'd looked briefly at the card and saw that Archie was a staffer for a House member Paul was vaguely aware of, a first-term conservative from the South, who hadn't attracted much attention since arriving on the Hill. He headed toward the corner Archie had pointed to.

Archie followed Paul to the corner, next to the coffee. It was the final session of the all-day gathering, and the marquee speaker, a visiting official from one of the newly Western-aligned central European countries, had spoken at lunch and gone. Most of the audience had left after the meal and Paul and Archie were alone by the cooling, half-empty urns.

Archie fumbled in his NRA briefcase for a moment before pulling out a large envelope and handing it to Paul. You should take a look at this, he said. His smile seemed a little forced, Paul thought. As if he wanted to get this over with.

Paul took the envelope and flipped open the flap, glancing inside. That was when he got his first glimpse of the document and its Russian-language warning.

He looked up at Archie, who gazed back at him impassively, the grin flagging only slightly.

Paul looked around, making sure they were alone before pulling the document partway out of the envelope. He quickly read the first paragraph of Russian script and looked up at Archie, who was still watching him.

"What is this," he asked.

Archie told him, briefly, in hushed, clipped sentences. When he was through, he looked at his watch. As if maybe he had a date he had to meet.

"Why are you giving me this?" he asked Archie.

Archie paused, as if he wanted to measure his answer before giving it.

"You have connections, you speak Russian," he said, his country-boy smile returning.

"Did some reading up on you," he added. Smile still pasted on.

Unsurprisingly, journalists' profiles were all over the net.

"You want to get this out?" Paul asked.

"Yes. Well, the congresswoman does."

Out of the corner of his eye, Paul saw a George Washington University professor he'd been hoping to buttonhole leave. He turned back to Archie.

"I'm not a journalist anymore," he said, "I do contract work for think tanks and consultants."

"Right," Archie said, "but you still have your connections."

Paul looked at him for a moment. He wondered whether Archie might not be quite the rube he appeared to be.

"You're a congressional staffer," he said, "don't you think this would more appropriately go to someone in the government? Defense or one of the intelligence agencies?"

Archie paused again, mulling over his answer. A cloud seemed to pass over his face.

"Paul—do you mind if I call you Paul?" he started. Paul gestured for him to continue.

"Paul," he resumed, "we're a junior member in the back benches of the opposition party. No one gives a shit what we think and if I call up the CIA, they'll put me on hold until some intern gets around to picking up the phone to thank me for calling and to tell me to drive over to Langley and drop whatever we have at the front gate or send it by mail. Or maybe by CIA courier if they happen to have one in the neighborhood for something important, but I'll never hear back from them."

Paul wasn't sure about all of that, but he'd had to ask and, frankly, he'd never worked for Congress, only covered it, so maybe Archie was right. He was also becoming convinced Archie wasn't as dumb as he looked.

For his part, Archie seemed to be working to control his nervousness. He wanted to get this over with.

"OK," Paul said. He looked around, no one was nearby so he risked pulling the sheaf of papers out to look at them. Archie glanced over Paul's shoulder.

"But still, why me?" he asked, "There are working reporters who speak Russian or could get this translated."

"Well," Archie said, suddenly, unexpectedly, the big good ol' boy smile reappeared as if Paul had tumbled onto the joke, "look at the last page." He glanced around. "Go ahead," he said, "there's no one around to see you."

Paul turned to the last page. He looked at it for a moment before putting it back in the envelope.

"I see," he said.

Archie looked at him, the smile still on his face.

Paul said nothing, his mind turning.

"You'll let me know what you find out?" Archie asked.

"Of course," Paul said, still thinking.

He thanked Archie and walked out the front door of the hotel where the session had been held and hailed a cab home. He didn't want to take the Metro suddenly. His mind was back in Moscow as he watched Washington pass by the windows on the ride home.

* * *

The house was empty when Paul got back.

Elise wasn't home yet. Their townhouse was a few decades old but designed to fit in with the authentic nineteenth-century neighborhood, without the authentic resulting twenty-first-century decay. It was nicely furnished with a combination of modern European styles, not pretentious but attractive. Crate and Barrel and West Elm furniture. Nice art that showed some taste and flair. Knick-knacks from around the world— a samovar here, something Buddhist there, but nothing too ostentatious.

Paul made some coffee and sat down in the office he and Elise shared with the envelope.

On his side of the room, the shelves were filled with books and notebooks, photos, and souvenirs from his journalistic career—coffee cups from deservedly defunct Third-World airlines, matchbooks, a set of opium weights, some military challenge coins, a sign warning of landmines in Khmer, a wooden carving of a house that was actually a cigarette box from the Russian gulag. Old-reporter crap. An ancient Nikon F camera with a lot of brass showing through the black watched from a top shelf. The other side of the room, Elise's province, held another desk, but the shelves were filled with carefully arranged law books and neatly stacked binders and folders. There was a picture of an attractive young woman in an eighties-style perm in front of what looked like a government building. Elise, as a young lawyer. Her appointment as an investigator, framed, next to her canceled federal investigator's credentials and badge, perched on the wall.

Paul cleared some space on his desk for the coffee and took the papers out of the envelope to read, taking notes on a legal pad. As he finished, he heard Elise come in downstairs and shouted down to her. As she responded, he picked up his cell phone and called Gunther.

* * *

The document now sat on his dining room table in front of Gunther. He and Paul had served in Moscow together years back, during Gorbachev's time, and had serviceable Russian. He had taken twenty minutes to read the document, occasionally consulting a Russian-English dictionary Paul had pulled down from a shelf, while Paul and Elise sipped coffee. Gunther had been as alarmed as both Paul and then Elise had been. Elise and Paul had married after Russia; she spoke no Russian but knew from Paul what was in the document.

The room was quiet except for the sound of an old-fashioned clock ticking. Like a bomb, Elise thought. There were drink fixings on the sideboard, but no one had touched them.

Gunther passed the paper back to Paul, who looked down at it for a moment.

Not an official classification, Gunther said. Paul nodded in agreement. This, Gunther continued, looks like something someone put together on their own, not in a government agency. That would have been more like *Sovershenno sekretno/osoboy vazhnosti*, top secret, special importance.

What is the title, Elise asked, pointing to it, *Тигр и Медведь*, on the front page.

"*Tigr i medved'*—*The Tiger and the Bear*," Paul said. Elise thought for a moment, then nodded, understanding the reference. It was not reassuring.

Paul turned the sheaf over in his hands. In the 1980s, while reporting in Moscow, as things were opening up, it would not have been unusual for a Russian paper on an interesting issue to come over the transom for a reporter like Paul or Gunther. Even then, though, nothing like this would have been likely to drop into their laps, or any but the most highly cleared laps, for that matter. That was certainly less likely now. Nevertheless, here it was.

He looked at Elise and Gunther for a moment before speaking.

"Just so we're all clear," he said, "this seems to be a report on a movement for secession by the Russian Far East—which is a massive part of the country—from Russia.

"The fact that it is labeled as a secret document but not in an official way indicates that is not a government document, but something prepared by someone outside the government who doesn't want it widely circulated.

"Here's what I think we have," he said.

He scanned the first couple of pages.

"It is a pretty well-developed movement, according to this document. It describes detailed operational plans, appraisals of local officials and which way they'd go. It contains proposed contacts with foreign officials in the region and references to potential communications with Western powers, even with the CIA—which is pretty impressive. It has what purport to be CIA station direct numbers and cover email addresses in several U.S. embassies and consulates in neighboring countries. It also has what it claims are the names, or at least working aliases, of CIA officers there. Same with some other Western intelligence agencies who might be interested in what they're planning or useful in providing support. We have the Brits, the Australians, Canadians, South Koreans, a few others. This is a complete job. It has information on defense and other officials in nearby countries, and contacts with the U.S. Pacific Command in Honolulu. Some of this is public, but not much of it, and some of it, if true, is nowhere near public.

"The people behind the movement, if there is such a movement, have very high access to very closely held files in Russia's intelligence services or other, equally inaccessible sources.

"More to the point, though," Paul said, "this report looks like one that was prepared for very high-level Russian government officials or some other high-level audience."

"Like who?" Elise asked.

"I don't know," Paul said, "maybe oligarchs, maybe sympathizers elsewhere in the country. It's in Russian without an English or other translation except for the Western names, so far as we know, so there's no indication it's intended for foreign eyes."

"How plausible does it seem?" she asked. She looked out the window. She had worked for the government chasing people and companies flogging weapons and arms technology to terrorists and adversaries, so she knew something about Russia if not as much as Paul and Gunther. She and Paul had met when he had been writing about one of her cases.

"Well, we can't be sure," Paul said, "it could be made up, it could be real. Some of it is the kind of information that no reporter could confirm or disprove."

"It is, though," Gunther said, "something we should follow up."

"I agree," Paul said.

"I don't think," he said, "that I can think of too many other events right now that would have as major a global effect. This is a powder keg that could start a series of events leading to a major catastrophe, by which I mean war, and not some little bullshit bush war, the real deal. Think of the assassination of Archduke Franz Ferdinand or the Cuban Missile Crisis.

"This would be seen by Moscow, and not unreasonably, as an existential threat to Russia and to the continued power of the current regime there. It would not just threaten to rip away a big part of the country, it would spur and give hope to other such movements in Russia and to the opposition in Moscow itself elsewhere, I'd guess. The last thing Putin and the current Russian leadership want to see. It would spur an intervention by Russian troops, in effect a civil war in Russia, that could spread or spark off other conflicts elsewhere in Russia. It could be the collapse of the Soviet Union all over again.

"Plus," he said, "there would be military intervention or at least assistance coming in from governments, exile groups, and who knows who else coming in, threatening to turn this into more than just a Russian civil war, as bad as that itself would be."

"And that's just Russia," Gunther said.

"This sort of cataclysmic event," Gunther said, "if it were to succeed, would throw all of East Asia into tumult. We don't know how China, which is doing its best to be the region's dominant power, would react, but it would be a major crisis for them to deal with. Other countries, such as Japan, would be drooling over the enormous economic potential of a newly separated Far East. They want those natural resources and the market, for starters. Same with, I don't know, the South Koreans, maybe the Indians, not to mention U.S. and other Western companies.

"It would change the whole geopolitical picture in Asia, giving China, Japan, and North Korea a new situation to think about, not to mention the U.S., which remains a Pacific power. The West is going to jump at the prospect of pulling the former Russian Far East into its orbit, the way it has done in Eastern Europe. Which, aside from more separatist movements growing up in Russia and NATO creeping up on its Western borders, is the absolute last thing the Kremlin wants to see.

"That prospect, a reordering of the situation in the Far East," he said, "would not only loom large in the minds in Moscow, but it's going to be on the mind of all those spooks listed in the memo ten seconds after they first get wind of this.

"Not to mention all the classified Russian goodies they might suddenly be able to put their hands on," Elise said. Our instincts are always honed by our jobs, or former jobs.

"OK," she said, "but is this real?" The question had been nagging at her since Paul had first told her about the document.

"I mean," she said, "this part of Russia could be full of crackpots cooking up schemes to break away every full moon. Is there any indication they've actually reached out to any Western governments or intelligence agencies at this point?"

"No," Paul said, "it seems as if they've done their homework and have either found out the real identities of the officers who they should contact, or at least names those officers use while stationed in an embassy, but there's no way to tell whether they've actually made any approaches yet."

"Listen," Gunther said, "this isn't a movie, so let's take a realistic look at what we have—we might have—here and what we don't.

"If this is fake, if this is some sort of hoax, like the Howard Hughes diaries, and we get caught out, we'll be the laughingstock of Washington, not to mention probably causing a major diplomatic incident or worse.

"What I'm saying," he said, "is that we need to tread carefully and not be dazzled by the prospect of celebrity into taking shortcuts."

"Do we know how Archie got this?" Elise asked.

Paul didn't.

"And he seemed in a rush to get it to you," she said.

"Well, it's pretty hot stuff," Paul said.

She thought for a moment.

"Why did he pick you?" she asked, "you said he told you to look at the last page."

She flipped to the last page but, like most of the rest of the document, it was in indecipherable Russian.

"Look at the bottom part," Paul said.

At the end of the text was what looked like a name. Олег Борисович Макаров.

"The author?" Elise asked. She hadn't been expecting this.

"Yes. Makarov, Oleg Makarov," Gunther told her. "Oleg Borisovich Makarov," he added. He shot a glance at Paul.

Through a window, over Gunther's shoulder, Elise saw a presidential motorcade race by in the distance on the Southeast-Southwest Freeway, piercing the quiet and the darkness for a moment with its flashing lights and cacophony of sirens.

"And who is Makarov?" she asked.

"An old friend," Paul said.

He looked at a painting behind Elise for a moment.

"From the Russian Far East," he said, "back in the Eighties."

The clock in the hall suddenly chimed the hour.

"Or, as we used to call it," Paul added, "the Soviet Far East."

Then he told Elise a story.

CHAPTER TWO

OLEG BORISOVICH MAKAROV

Soviet Far East, 1988

Through the stopped train car window, Paul Girard paused from his newspaper to notice a Red Army soldier glancing up from the platform as the first light of Pacific dawn broke. As if in coordination, the train suddenly started again, the final leg of its trip down the coast from Khabarovsk toward Nakhodka, as near to the closed city of Vladivostok as an American was likely to get.

It was good to get out of grey, dreary Moscow, he thought, sipping some cooling tea.

The city was relatively pleasant in the warm summer months and livelier than it had been before Gorbachev, but it was still, to Western eyes, an oppressive-feeling place. Paul welcomed the break from the uniform drabness of the people and buildings, the half-empty streets, and the poverty.

Like most of his colleagues, as well as the Soviet friends he had made, Paul was pulling for Mikhail Sergeyevich Gorbachev. Whatever the dreams in 1917 had been of a workers' paradise, it was plain that the Soviet Union was now a creaking, inefficient, corrupt country that couldn't feed its people—whom, by the way, it feared so much it kept them in the dark about what was going in the world. The country would have been an international laughingstock if it weren't so big and powerful and didn't have nukes.

Paul had seen too many teenagers with atrocious teeth from years of malnutrition and too many desperate lines in front of barren shops for stale bread and bad potatoes to believe otherwise. No amount of harkening back to the prerevolutionary evils of the tsars or invocations of the Great Patriotic War—World War II to the rest of the world—could hide that in Paul's mind. He thought Gorbachev understood the weaknesses of the system and was taking a stab at fixing them. Maybe that meant capitalism, maybe not, in Paul's mind. As far as he was concerned, if this appealing son of peasants who was now the party's general secretary could do so and save the U.S.S.R. as a socialist state, more power to him, if not, so be it.

Paul wondered, though, about the unreasonable expectations that Gorbachev's reforms were stirring. On an overnight train to Leningrad from Moscow one night, an engineer had shared with Paul his expectations that within a year, thanks to Gorbachev, Soviets would be living exactly the way Americans did. He meant by this the way the Americans on the newly available U.S. television shows did. Paul had patiently tried to explain that that was not what America was really like, but the engineer dismissed Paul's denials as Soviet propaganda. He knew what he knew. Paul wondered what would happen when the hopes of Soviets like the engineer did not pan out.

Paul also knew, though, what most people outside the Soviet Union did not. Gorbachev and his reformers were facing headwinds within the corridors of power, and there was resistance among hardliners who were happy with things just the way they were. The KGB and the Gulag hadn't gone away. There were critics within the government, the military, and the party, as well as among ordinary people, who were convinced that Gorbachev was maliciously killing the glorious Soviet Union that had supplanted the tsars and vanquished the Nazi hordes. We don't need all this *perestroika* and *glasnost* nonsense, we need a strong leader, a leader like Stalin, to set things right again, they thought.

He watched the countryside pass through the train window.

He thought about the increasing swarms of Westerners who, smelling a quick buck as cracks began to appear in the Kremlin's stranglehold on society, were swooping in for a kill and how they looked through Russian eyes.

Many, Paul thought, were blatant opportunists, clothing their greed in the language of détente and a new global cooperation, gaining as much expertise in Russia as they could from seminars back home in the Western capitals and reading travel guides on their first-class flights from New York or London. Now they sipped expensive drinks in hard-currency bars and draped their arms around the waists of young slim new Moscow acquaintances who found them irresistible.

Paul, who spoke good Russian and had a good grounding in Russian and Soviet history, stayed away from the well-trodden Moscow correspondent tracks. He avoided embassy gatherings where most of his colleagues went to be spoon-fed worthless nuggets they passed off as news and worked hard to talk with ordinary Soviets—not just in Moscow and cosmopolitan Leningrad, but elsewhere, in places like Kiev and Kishinev, respectively in the Ukrainian and Moldavian Soviet socialist republics.

That wasn't easy. The U.S.S.R. was a xenophobic place, full of distrust of foreigners, as he had found early in his posting one summer day in June.

No one likes sunny days more than Muscovites, and this day was no exception. The city was full of couples walking and parents pushing strollers. Paul saw dozens of girls in bikinis tanning themselves on the banks of the Moskva River.

It was a slow day at work, so he went to a park. There was a crowd there, he discovered, surrounding a poet who was reading his work aloud.

As Paul watched and listened to the poet, an old woman standing nearby turned to him. He was unremarkable in the crowd, at least at first glance, wearing a short-sleeved sport shirt, jeans, and running shoes.

"*Kto chitayet?*" she asked Paul—who is reading?

"*Izvinite, ne znayu,*" he said. I'm sorry, I don't know.

As he started to speak, she gazed at him intently for a moment. His Russian was good if not his accent. She realized she was talking to a foreigner, maybe even an *amerikanets*. Her eyes grew wide, and she turned, fearfully fleeing the scene.

* * *

Moscow was a hard place to cover, but this trip to the Far East had popped up as if Fate had heard his thoughts.

He was traveling with a group of young American professionals attending some sort of mushy, international cooperation-inspired conference in Nakhodka on "Pacific Rim" issues, a subject much in vogue that year among nerdy policy wonks. The Americans would be there with a Soviet delegation and others from various fellow socialist countries. It would be an easy trip, he thought. He'd do a couple of light features, relax, and probably watch the Americans get their asses kicked when they discovered the Soviets and their East Bloc pals weren't all in on everybody suddenly being buddies.

Now, bleary from the endless Aeroflot flight from Moscow and a quick stop in Khabarovsk for a nap and a shower before boarding the train for the final, overnight leg of the trip, Paul sipped his tea, looking out the train window. Two of the Americans smiled at him as they passed by. They were talking about how excited they were to be on this trip.

A moment later, a thin red-haired guy approached him. He wore the universal Soviet uniform of the day, sneakers, jeans, and a T-shirt from a U.S. university. Paul thought he had seen him before on the trip but couldn't be sure.

The guy stood next to him for a few moments, watching the forest sail by.

"*Spichki est?*" he then asked, pulling out a pack of *Kosmos* cigarettes and offering one to Paul.

Paul nodded, took a cigarette, and pulled out the requested box of Soviet matches, striking one away from him on the side of the box, Soviet style, and lighting both cigarettes.

"*Spasibo,*" the guy said, wordlessly gazing out the window over the shared smokes. He looked as if he might say something but seemed to change his mind, and then headed, presumably, back to his compartment.

Paul would catch glimpses of the guy during the two days of the conference. As expected, the earnest and well-meaning Americans got clobbered during the "free and open" discussions at which the Poles, East Germans, and the rest used their time to disparage U.S. policies and portray the American administration as aggressive imperialists hellbent on dominating the region and crushing its peace-loving peoples. They knew who was running the show and paying the freight here. During breaks, Paul interviewed some of the Americans, finding them shell-shocked from their first day's experience. They had convinced themselves that all would be sweetness and light and that this would be a lovefest of forward-lookers.

The cloud seemed to lift on the second day, though; overnight the Cubans had invited the Americans—including Paul—and some of the other visiting delegations down to their rooms to get drunk and dance to Cuban music. Paul heard more than one of the Cubans and others from various socialist countries explain to the Americans that what they were saying in the sessions was all just bullshit for the benefit of the Soviets. Don't mix us up with the Soviets, one said to a pair of the Americans, we're not the boorish Russians.

On his final day, after the conference had wound down, Paul needed to get away from the now-whining Americans and took a walk around the town.

He sat on a bench in a deserted park thinking about a Moscow story he was working on. One or two people passed him by, including a mother with two small children but none of them paid any attention to him. Then, who should come up but the red-haired guy from the train.

The train guy sat down on the other end of the bench. He opened a newspaper and began to read.

Then, without turning his head, he said, "Your friends got beaten pretty badly in the meetings." He was looking straight ahead, into the newspaper. Despite his very heavy Russian accent, he seemed comfortable speaking English.

This was so unexpected, and so true, that Paul started to laugh.

"Yes," he said, "I think they've read too many Gorbachev speeches."

The guy looked around before putting down his paper, then turned to him and put out his hand.

"I am Oleg Makarov," he said, "underpaid academician."

He watched Paul carefully, gauging his response.

Paul shook his hand.

"Paul Girard," he said, "underpaid Moscow correspondent."

Oleg nodded. He handed Paul a card identifying him as a specialist with a prominent Moscow institute—what Westerners would call a think tank.

"I know," he said, "I've read some of your articles." Then, after a moment, "Will you write a story about this conference?" he asked.

Yes, Paul said, he would. Nothing earthshaking, but the readers at home would go for it, he said. You know, something other than the usual Moscow stuff.

Yes, the usual Moscow stuff, Oleg said, seeming to turn the phrase over in his mind.

"Does it get boring covering Moscow?" he asked.

This was an odd question. Paul was not paranoid, but he wondered whether this guy was a plant, something Paul discussed with his friend and competitor, Gunther Schroeder, who had recently arrived from a posting in Bonn, and a few others. If not, though, for this Soviet to raise the issue showed that he was casting a more perceptive eye on Western journalists' work than most Soviets were, or at least than most Soviets would confess to a Western journalist.

"No," Paul said, measuring his words carefully, "it doesn't get boring, exactly." He thought for a moment, trying to decipher whether this was just an innocent conversation or more.

"Like any beat, though," he said, "it is a constant challenge to get something different."

"*Pravda? Dazhe so znaniem russkogo?*"

"Yes, even though I speak Russian."

Oleg seemed to consider that.

"Ah!" he then exclaimed suddenly in his accented English. "What time do you have?"

Paul told him the time.

"I am sorry, I must go," Oleg said, standing up and retrieving his newspaper.

"I hope to see you again," he said. With that he strode off.

* * *

Paul didn't see Oleg again during the trip and had almost forgotten about him until a week or so later. He was surprised to run into him in Moscow, just after a party at the home of a Soviet friend.

The party had been in one of the legions of high-rise, decrepit apartment buildings that seemed to house most of the Soviets Paul knew, although once through the front door, the apartment had been warm and inviting, with a crowd of people drinking vodka from mismatched cups and glasses, and arguing over politics, poetry, and music. Stones versus Beatles. The great international unifier, even now, in the eighties.

At about eleven, though, Paul decided to head home. He left the apartment and waited in the deserted hall for the creaking elevator to arrive, with its bouquet of stale urine and cabbage smells. He could hear the noise of the party down the hall in one direction, as well as shouting from what sounded like a drunk couple from the other. There was the sound of a glass or bottle shattering on the floor from the drunk couple's direction, then more shouting. Some of the lights in the hallway were out and some flickered, on their way out, so he stood in an eerie semidarkness, but the hallway seemed empty. He was surprised, then, when, just as he got onto the elevator, Oleg Makarov approached him.

Oleg looked at him apologetically as the elevator started its groaning descent, a slight smirk on his face.

"Almost missed it," he said.

Paul didn't know what to say.

"You are riding the Metro?" Oleg asked.

Paul said, yes, he was, and they walked out to the battered parking lot in the moonlight and headed for the nearby subway stop.

Oleg seemed to be waiting for the right moment to say something on his mind.

"I have been reading your reports," he said, "They are very perceptive."

"Thank you," Paul said, "You mentioned that you'd been reading me when we met in Nakhodka."

"Yes."

The seconds seemed to crawl by as they made their way to the subway stop. A dog barked in the distance.

"You are wondering who I am," Oleg said, "whether I am friend or foe."

They walked a few more steps in silence. Oleg seemed to be thinking something over.

They were at the Metro station. Oleg put out his hand.

"Have a good trip home," he said, and turned away, walking down a side street.

* * *

Paul put his Moscow meeting with Oleg out of his mind, but Oleg apparently had not forgotten about Paul.

Their next encounter happened, unexpectedly, about a week later, after a meeting Paul had one night with a contact at one of the big hotels that had sprung up to service the growing numbers of Western business-men crowding into Moscow.

Paul had gone through the usual rigmarole getting into the hotel: the burly guards closely examined his passport and visa to ensure he was who he said he was and entitled to enter the tourist hotel.

He then met for thirty minutes with a visiting executive for a fairly inconsequential interview he would use, or maybe not, in some later story. After the executive left and Paul walked toward the hotel's door himself, one of the gruff gatekeepers who had scrutinized his papers on the way in caught his eye and gestured with his head for Paul to follow him.

Surprised, Paul nodded slightly as the guard said something to his companion, who shrugged and nodded, before heading away from the bar and the main reception area and through a door in a remote corner of the room. Paul followed the guard at a distance and, after a quick look around, went through the door into a service corridor to find the guard waiting.

Paul then followed the guard along a corridor and down a stairway to a storage room of some sort.

Oleg sat on a bench, sipping vodka from a glass. He handed another glass to Paul, filled it, then gave the bottle to the guard, who took it, nodded in thanks, and returned back up the stairway.

"I think I can trust you," Oleg said, once the guard had left, "at least I hope so."

He paused for a moment, watching Paul and turning something over in his head.

"I have something to tell you," he finally said.

"I'm hearing disturbing rumors," he said, "I don't even know if they're even half-true."

Paul nodded. He could hear people walking and talking nearby, and the sounds of dishes clattering, but no one disturbed them.

"You should look into these rumors, though," Oleg said. He paused. "Or someone should."

Oleg reached into his pocket and pulled out a folded sheet of paper. He unfolded it and passed it to Paul.

"Have you ever heard of this man?" he asked.

Paul looked at the paper, it showed a passport or visa photo of a middle-aged man in a suit. The caption identified him as one Lothar Schnabel.

"No," he said, shaking his head.

Oleg took the photocopy back, then, after a moment, handed it back to Paul.

"You may want this," he said before continuing. "Schnabel is a bigtime West German lawyer whose main client is a big international bank in Frankfurt. A shady one."

Paul was impressed with Oleg's mastery of slang and wondered whether his English had come from movies as well as studying.

"Is the bank thinking of opening a branch here?" he asked.

"No. Well, after a fashion," Oleg said. His eyes flitted over Paul's shoulder. Apparently seeing nothing, he continued.

"Some big-shot Moscow officials quietly asked him to come here and made sure he got the right visas. They might want to do some banking in the West in the future."

"I'm not sure I follow you," Paul said.

More kitchen sounds from down the hall.

"Whichever way things go," Oleg said, "these guys figure there's going to be big money to be made in the near future here, money that they would like a piece of. They think, probably rightly, that it would be more convenient if their share were safely in the West without any Soviet—or Russian—fingerprints on it."

Paul noticed the phrasing and wondered whether the idea that the Soviet Union's days were numbered was gaining even more currency than he'd thought. An image flashed through his mind of boats fleeing Cuba in 1959 when the old order there had ended. He turned over what Oleg had said in his mind for a moment.

"They're trying to set up a money-laundering scheme through this German guy, Schnabel," he then said, "just in case."

"Yes," Oleg said.

He mused to himself for a moment.

"Money-laundering, what a term," Oleg said.

"Just in case," he continued after a moment, "they get to make a ton of money fast and need to fly out with—or without—their wives to live the decadent high life in the West. Someplace like London."

Paul thought for a moment.

"Why this bank?" he asked.

"Because it has been, one would say, amenable to such clientele in the past," Oleg said, "at, of course, substantial profit to them."

Paul listened to the noise from the corridor for a moment.

"How do you know all this?" he asked.

Oleg thought for a moment.

"I have my sources," he said, without elaboration.

"OK," Paul said, "Do you have anything I can go on?" In for a penny in for a pound.

Oleg pulled an envelope out of an inner pocket.

"Yes, but please keep this to yourself as much as you can," he said.

Paul pulled the papers out of the envelope. There were copies of correspondence between Soviet officials and Schnabel, apparently referring to tours being set up for Schnabel on his planned sightseeing trip to Moscow and some names and phone numbers of tour guides.

"This is the schedule of meetings he has set up, in code, of course," Oleg said.

The papers, of course, meant nothing.

"Do you have anything hard on this?" Paul asked.

"No, but I know something must exist somewhere," Oleg said.

Paul nodded. If nothing else, he thought, he might find out one way or another whether Oleg was a ringer. He might also find himself on a fast plane out of Moscow—or worse—if he were being set up. Well, as an editor of his had been fond of saying, that was the news biz.

"OK," he said after a moment. He put the papers into his jacket pocket.

With that, Oleg drained his drink and got up. Motioning for Paul to stay where he was, Oleg headed past some storage lockers and down a hall, away from the stairway Paul had used. A few moments later, Paul climbed back up the stairway and through the door into the lobby. He made his way out, past the guards, both of whom ignored him.

As he rode the Metro back to his apartment, he mulled over what Oleg had said. He knew some bankers and financial types here in Moscow but wasn't sure they would be likely to talk, certainly about this, at least to him, on the record. Then, later, as he was nodding off to sleep, he had a thought.

The next day, Paul called around to some of his banking contacts, one or two embassy and U.N. types, with no result. He had to be careful, but it was clear that either they didn't know about such goings-on or didn't want to talk to him about it. By the end of the day, Paul knew he had to go to the Plan B that had occurred to him overnight.

He knew he would be seeing Gunther, who had solid German sources from his time in Bonn, later that evening at a conference. If it were true, they could team up on the story and get it out together quickly.

* * *

That evening Paul had explained to Gunther what Oleg had told him. They held their conversation on the balcony of a conference room in another hotel, where the conference was being held, and spoke in hushed tones to evade listeners.

Bankers, he had told Paul, with whom he had had a certain amount of experience, wouldn't talk to him. They'd protect their asses. He knew, though, a diplomat in the West German Embassy in Moscow, Dieter Klockner. He had dealt with Klockner on financial stories before and Klockner had a wide variety of friends among the diplomats stationed in Moscow. As an added benefit, Gunther was pretty sure Klockner was with the West German intelligence contingent in Moscow. Paul, convinced his own sources were not likely to be of much help, told Gunther to go ahead and see what he could find out.

Gunther met Klockner at the West German Embassy the next day and related what Paul had told him. Klockner listened patiently, asked some fairly detailed questions, and made some notes. This last part was pretty much cosmetic, since, as Gunther suspected as they talked, the room was bugged. Klockner asked Gunther whether he or Paul were planning to follow up, to which Gunther said yes, but only if they could get something more solid. Ah, Klockner said, snapping his notebook shut. He politely thanked Gunther and said he'd let him know if he found anything. He turned the conversation elsewhere, asking a few questions about Paul, but Gunther didn't know much about him other than the sort of thing all the resident journalists, diplomats, and other foreign hangers-on knew about each other.

"So, did anything ever come of it?" Elise asked.

"Well, not for us, actually," Paul said, "Klockner never got back to us, and some other news got in the way, we sort of lost the thread. It wasn't something we could do in a half-assed way.

"Although," he added, "we now know of course that what Oleg told us was true. Russians, the ones we now call the oligarchs, ended up stripping the corpse of the Soviet Union bare and setting themselves up in London and around the world with the help of extensive money-laundering operations like the one Oleg tried to tip us off to."

"Of course," Elise said, "if the information got into Western governments' hands, that would probably have suited Oleg, whether it was through a story you published or through your contacts with an embassy, especially if, as you suspected, your guy was a West German spook."

"Yes," Paul said, "that's what we thought, too, in fact maybe that was Oleg's plan all along—maybe he knew we'd never find anything but that we'd eventually approach someone in a Western embassy so he wouldn't have to. And since Klockner knew so many people, if he found something out, he probably spread it around certain secretive quarters of the dip community in Moscow. Too bad the governments didn't pay any attention to it."

* * *

Paul, Gunther, and Oleg often met after that. In addition, Oleg started helping each of them where he could, although his contacts were more useful to Paul, so the two became closer than Gunther and Oleg did.

Over the ensuing months, Oleg provided a fount of useful information, generally in the form of insights into moves the government was making or reforms in progress. None were earthshaking, but Paul used Oleg's insights to inform his stories and give them a nuance that set his work apart from a lot of the other reporting coming out of the rapidly changing Soviet Union.

Oleg had a special affinity for and familiarity with Asia, which was why he had been at the conference in the Far East, and would, some evenings when the two or three of them were together, wax poetic about Southeast Asia, "where you guys fucked up," he would say pointedly to Paul. He seemed to have a special love for Vientiane, the Laotian capital on the Mekong, having spent some time at the Soviet-built Lane Xang

Hotel there, although he said it had been falling apart since the Pathet Lao had taken over a dozen or so years before. He was even more rhapsodic about Cambodia, detesting the Khmer Rouge for what they had done to what he said was one of the most serene places in the world.

Oleg seemed to have few illusions about either what was happening in the Soviet Union or the rose-tinted view Westerners seemed to be adopting toward his country. Over the span of the next year or so, he seemed increasingly pessimistic about the chances for reform to take hold in the Soviet Union and talked vaguely about leaving.

"This is Russia," Oleg said to Paul one night when the two of them were walking alone, "the Soviet Union is just another variation on the same theme, don't forget that."

They walked a bit further.

"My grandfather was in the Cheka," he said, referring to the first Soviet secret police, "and two of my uncles died in the Gulag.

"Nothing changes here; we open, we close, but it's always Russia. Go back over our history, that's what you will see."

* * *

Eventually, it became time for Paul to rotate out, and he invited Oleg for a farewell dinner with him at a hard-currency restaurant he knew that was connected to a hotel frequented by Westerners.

That, as it turned out, was probably a mistake.

They met that night, each carrying a package. As they sat down, Oleg passed Paul his, actually a shopping bag. Inside, Paul discovered, was a carved wooden building. A prisoner in the Gulag had made it, Oleg explained, a carving of a prisoner's barracks. It was more than that, though.

"Watch this," Oleg said. He slid open a rod along the spine of the roof so the empty inside of the model building was now accessible.

"For cigarettes," he said. Then he pointed to a small stand to mount a box of matches and a small carved wooden dish-like receptacle at one end of the building.

"*Pepel'nitsa*," he said. Ashtray. Paul kept the carving in his office.

Oleg poured himself another drink. Even for a Soviet, Paul thought, Oleg had been drinking on the heavy side, increasingly so in recent weeks.

Paul passed his parcel over to Oleg, shaking his head slightly. Don't open it here, he was saying. It was his Sony shortwave radio that would allow Oleg to pick up Voice of America, the BBC, and other Western radio stations. Oleg seemed to know what it was and placed it under the table without looking inside. He thanked Paul, with a quick smile, but there seemed little joy behind it.

They continued their meal and, while Oleg tried to put up a good front, it seemed only a front.

The room was full, mainly of Western businessmen with newly acquired Russian girlfriends. One of the men got into an argument with his girl two or three tables away. It got loud, quickly, and suddenly, the girl stood up, crying, her eye makeup running down her face. The man screamed an obscenity at her and she ran from the room. The man turned back to his friends, laughing. They looked slightly embarrassed.

Oleg watched, then turned back to Paul. There seemed to be nothing to say.

"Let's take a walk," he said.

Paul paid the dollar-denominated bill discreetly and the two went out into the street and walked in silence for a few blocks. The street was completely empty.

"What you saw tonight is the new Russia," he said.

They kept on walking.

"The hardliners hate Gorbachev," he said. Paul was going to respond, but Oleg seemed to want to keep talking.

"As far as they're concerned, he's Washington's *marionetka*. And they're not alone."

Paul said nothing.

"Your president, your academics, and your businessmen all think we are on the edge of some sort of dawn of democracy here, but it's not going to happen."

They continued to walk. When Paul didn't respond, Oleg resumed.

"Meanwhile, you reporters keep playing along, writing glowing stories and ignoring the serpent's egg in front of you."

Paul started to respond, but Oleg held up his hand.

"I know," he said, "your editors don't care, you've told me that. They want to know who the good guys are, who the bad guys are, and what the score is, and that Gorbachev's team is the good guys and they're winning.

"But someone has to do something," he said. "The new rich here and the hardliners will work with your capitalist friends who are pouring into this country and turn us into a Third World fleshpot with weapons of mass destruction while they make their fortunes, all the while claiming to do so in the name of the spread of your Western democracy."

They walked for a bit more. Paul had not wanted their last night together to be like this. He said, as he had often said before, that he could not convince his editors to take stories puncturing the euphoria in the West over the crumbling of the Soviet empire.

"I know, I know," Oleg said, "you can't do anything."

He paused, thinking about what to say next.

"You need to understand, though," he said, swaying a little from too much vodka, "that that serpent will hatch from that egg and will lash out in a very undemocratic way."

They had reached a corner, and a taxi driver approached, looking hopefully at Paul.

"You should go home to the West," Oleg said, signaling the driver.

Paul didn't know whether this sudden melancholy was a result of the booze or had been in the cards anyway, but he seemed to have no choice but to get in the cab and go home. He would call Oleg before he left, maybe have a proper farewell when no one was shitfaced. He shook Oleg's hand and got into the cab.

He wondered about Oleg's serpent's egg comment.

Paul could not reach Oleg again before he left. Oleg didn't answer repeated calls and, ultimately, Paul had to leave.

* * *

The room went silent for a few moments when Paul finished his story.

"Anyway," he said, ending the quiet, "Gunther and I heard from him occasionally in the following years, but that trailed off. We haven't heard from him for a while. For all I know, or thought I knew until now, he could have been dead."

Elise seemed to take it all in for a moment.

"Where would he be?" she asked.

"No idea," Schroeder said, "maybe Moscow, maybe the Far East, maybe elsewhere."

It took a moment.

"So we should try to find Oleg to verify the document?"

"Right," Schroeder said.

He thought for a moment.

"I don't see any other way," he said, "at least not quickly. This isn't something we can just send some kid from the foreign desk in to dig up."

"And," Paul said, "since we know Oleg, or knew him in the old days, that seems the obvious course to follow."

No one said anything for a moment. Paul took the opportunity to pour each of them a drink. It seemed like the right time for one, although he regretted having to settle for scotch since they didn't have any vodka around, which might have been more appropriate. He thought for a moment and then went upstairs, returning with a laptop that he plugged in and set on the table next to the document. "We need to figure out whether this makes sense or whether someone is trying to hustle us," Paul said.

Gunther nodded.

"There's something not right about all of this," Paul said. He slid the document toward him and flipped through the pages for a moment.

"Why now?" he asked, "Why this staffer for a first-termer nobody's ever heard of?"

He was silent for a moment.

"And who is this guy," Elise asked, "this Archie?"

"Right," Paul said, "Archie Richter, works for this new House member, one from down South."

Paul then turned to the computer and tapped on its keys. He gazed at the screen for a few minutes before turning back.

"OK," he said, "I started to do this before but got sidetracked.

"Nothing remarkable about Archie's boss. She's sort of a run-of-the-mill Republican from that part of the country, believes in Real America, lower taxes, lower regulation, gun rights, all sort of cookie-cutter conservative Republican, nothing to indicate that she'll stand out particularly. She'll probably be there a term or two fighting it out with equally unremarkable Democrats from safe liberal bastions before they all go back home or stay here as consultants, part of the cast of former members who nobody remembers."

"There's nothing to indicate why she would have this kind of a sensitive document, right?" Gunther asked.

Paul looked at the screen and tapped the keys some more.

"I don't think so, but there's no way really to be sure," he said. "I'm looking at local clips from her hometown paper, she's apparently a pretty good speaker and has her finger on the pulse of her district. She'll probably do a good job representing them. There's just no way to tell too much about her. But I don't see anything that would lead me to believe that she would even know what the Russian Far East is, much less have or seek access to our kind of document."

Elise seemed lost in thought.

Paul tapped a few more keys.

"Let me look at her congressional homepage," he said. He looked at the computer for a few more minutes, tapping keys now and then.

"Well, she's on a couple of national security-related committees and some interesting subcommittees, but she's a first-termer. She's sitting at the far end of the bottom row in hearings, gets three questions before everyone packs up to leave, and is probably still figuring out how to find the members-only elevators."

Hang on, he said, tapping some more keys.

"She hasn't sponsored any bills that are relevant here," he said, "I just don't see how she would get her hands on this or anything remotely like it."

More tapping.

"She's not even a veteran," he said.

He looked at the screen.

"She's not the link," he said finally.

"So," Elise said, "we've got to look at Archie."

Paul looked at his watch and then pulled out his phone.

"What are you doing?" Elise asked.

"Texting Archie," he said, "I want to see if I can talk with him tomorrow."

Gunther had been studying the document as Elise and Paul were talking.

"I think we can assume this was actually written by Oleg," he said, looking up.

"Why is that?" Paul asked.

"Hang on," Gunther said.

He thumbed back a few pages and ran a finger down the text until he found what he was looking for.

"Listen to this quote, he said. '*Kogda dveri tyur'my otkroyutsya, vyletit nastoyashchiy drakon.*'"

"What does it mean?" Elise asked, looking at both of them.

"'When the prison doors are opened, the real dragon will fly out,'" Paul said, "or 'a' real dragon, I guess, you can't really tell in Russian."

He turned to Gunther.

"So what?" Elise said.

Gunther looked up from the page.

"It's a quote from Ho Chi Minh," he said. "Oleg is a Southeast Asia guy. No one else would be likely to quote Ho Chi Minh in this when they're talking about the Russian Far East," he added.

Paul remembered seeing it when he'd read the document, but it hadn't registered with him.

"Odd that he would put that in this sort of document," Elise said.

Paul nodded but said nothing, thinking about it now.

"OK," he said, "at any rate, we can't ignore this. We've got to find out whether this whole idea of a move to break the Far East away is actually happening and is something he's found out about. If this is true, it's going to change things for a lot of people, starting with a lot of people in Moscow."

He thought for a moment.

"We definitely need more than this paper," he said, "we'd need to get to wherever Oleg got his information. I mean," he said, "have there been any rumblings on the radar about this?"

He looked at Gunther.

"I don't know," Gunther said, "you may know as much as I do. It's possible that there's been some agitation, but I don't know that it's anything like a serious movement, although we don't have anyone out there. I've tried to follow it, though.

"The fall of the Soviet Union hit that region pretty hard," he said, "and Moscow had to send some goons in to crush demonstrations a while back and I don't think the Far Easterners have much love for Putin or Moscow, while they're pretty sweet on the nearby countries in Asia, like Japan.

"Some of the protesters," he said, "carried signs with, for example, guess what?"

Neither Paul nor Elise responded.

"A tiger, for the Far East, facing off against a bear—Russia, just like our document here," Gunther said.

"Just like our document, '*Tigr i Medved*,' *The Tiger and the Bear*," Paul said, "very clever."

"So," Elise said, "I guess it's possible, but we can't be sure."

"I agree," Paul said.

He looked at Gunther.

"We need to follow it to the other end if we're going to find out if this is legit," Paul said.

Gunther seemed to think the situation over in his head.

"OK," he said, "you're on the foreign desk tab, I'll fix the paperwork in the morning."

"OK," Paul said after a moment, "Let's see if I can meet with this Archibald Richter guy and see where we are after that."

No one said anything for a moment.

Elise looked at the remains of her drink and thought for a moment.

"You guys are forgetting one thing," she said.

"What's that?" Paul asked.

"Guy Lynch," she said, "What about Guy Lynch?" she asked.

"Ah, Guy Lynch," Paul said, "What indeed."

CHAPTER THREE

GUY LYNCH

Former network and cable TV news pretty boy Guy Lynch.

Lantern jaw and piercing blue eyes.

Midnight black hair with a dashing touch of silver at the temples.

Authoritative baritone voice.

A lightweight, all agreed.

Laid off from his high-profile, if cushy, cable Washington correspondent and Sunday morning talk-show host job, he had been brought in by the paper's new owners to add a little glam to the staff and maybe raise the bottom line in the process.

He was known mainly for toadying up to officials in the flashy national security precincts of the government, especially the CIA, in return for whatever they wanted to peddle or plant dressed up as exclusives and scoops. He habitually referred to the intelligence agency as simply "CIA," the way its employees did, rather than "*the* CIA," as did normal human beings, to show he was among the initiated—although Gunther pointed out privately that it made him sound like a Russian. He was also what used to be called a masher and the paper's interns, the female ones anyway, usually learned quickly to give him a wide berth, especially if they were working late.

In return for the glam he lent the newsroom and his proclaimed access to the inner sancta of the shadowy covert ops world, he was to be brought in on all major national security stories. Which he was unless there was a way to humanly avoid doing so.

Gunther had had a testy, at best, relationship with Lynch since he had arrived. This was not least because Guy's preference—outside of his dubious intelligence scoops—for quick, easy-to-understand features, preferably with children, airplane crashes, earthquakes, plucky members of sympathetic downtrodden groups who beat the odds, or stranded pets, had cost the paper some of its best stringers—freelancers around the world who filled in where once well-paid correspondents or well-staffed bureaus had existed. One after another, the stringers had deserted the paper for greener and less embarrassing pastures.

He did not look forward to approaching Guy on this story and tried, unsuccessfully, to figure out a way to avoid it as he drove into town in the morning from his home on a leafy, 1960s suburban street in Bethesda not far from the National Institutes of Health.

He was distracted as he made his way down Reno Road. Although he wasn't sure, he thought he might have seen the same green Toyota Camry behind him as he had come down Wisconsin Avenue to cross the District Line into Washington and then again later on as he turned toward Connecticut Avenue. Nerves, he thought. Every retired grandma in Bethesda and Chevy Chase seemed to own a Camry; there were a million of them.

When he arrived at the paper's downtown offices, he quickly passed through security—everyplace had become like Fort Knox since 9/11— and then to his small office off the twenty-first century, global command center-like newsroom.

Usually, his first order of business as foreign editor when he came in in the morning was to talk with whichever one of his deputies had kept an eye on world events overnight to find out if anything had happened since the evening before. Given the time of day, this handover conversation was usually dominated by events in Asia and Africa, maybe some early news from Europe. Gunther signaled the editor who had drawn the short straw the night before to hold off—he had something to do. The editor nodded wearily and turned back to his screen. He had been up all night, including through one of the computer system's periodic glitches that had taken the kid from IT half an hour to fix because it had taken him longer than usual to pinpoint the problem. The editor was anxious to get home and get to sleep.

Gunther closed the door to his office and sat down at his desk with a cup of coffee. He checked his watch. An hour until the eight-thirty morning news meeting. Flipping on his computer, he sighed and typed out the two-paragraph message for Guy Lynch he had composed in his head on his commute about Oleg's apparent report, and why it was important to follow up. He paused for a moment before adding another paragraph explaining that the report had come to him through Paul Girard, who would be working with the paper on the story. That ought to ruin Lynch's day, Gunther thought with satisfaction, as he pushed the send button.

* * *

It had happened some years back.

A colleague of Elise's and the colleague's husband had come over for dinner with Paul and Elise one night, not an unusual occurrence, given Elise's considerable talents as a cook.

After the meal, the four sat around the table, chatting when the colleague, a Pentagon program director named Patricia, had glanced inquiringly at her husband during a pause in the conversation. The husband glanced back and, after a moment shrugged, then nodded.

Paul had been about to get up and offer another drink to anyone who wanted one but, sensing a change in the air, he stayed at the table.

After a moment of silence, Patricia began her story.

It seemed, she said, that an official, an attorney, in one of the related bureaus down the hall at Defense, was about to be fired, supposedly for incompetence.

The problem, Patricia continued, was that she was being fired because she had not only refused the advances of her boss but had ratted him out to his wife. Not only would this, if it got out, save the attorney's job but it would probably cost the boss his very high security clearance, not to mention his own job. There was more that the attorney had shared with Patricia, the sort of tawdry details of such episodes—propositions followed by professions of love, all rejected, so then followed by injured feelings followed by threats of exposure. The latter, of course, were now being carried out.

"Does your friend have a name?" Elise asked.

"Call her Sue," Patricia said. She glanced at Paul.

"I see," Paul said, realizing why he was hearing this tale and wondering whether this was worth a story or a distasteful personnel matter that should be left to work itself out. He hoped it was the latter. That hope disappeared moments later.

"Who is the boss?" he asked.

Then Patricia told him. It turned out to be a well-known senior official who had held on for several administrations. He was good at playing the kinds of games in Washington that Washington plays and was the sort who appeared frequently on cable television as a sage expert on arcane defense matters. The kind of shows, in fact, where the then-newly hired Guy Lynch had previously often been the host, and, in fact, on some of Guy Lynch's shows.

Sue, on the other hand, was a nobody by comparison, even if by normal lights she had an interesting and important job. "She also, however," Patricia said, "had had drug issues in the past that had caused a few bumps on the road to her own clearance. When it became clear now that she wasn't going to play ball with her boss, he had threatened to dig up the drug issues to ruin her career if she didn't keep her mouth shut."

Incensed, Sue had then confronted the wife.

"She didn't happen to tape those conversations, did she?" Paul asked.

Pause.

"Yes," Patricia said, "she did happen to tape the conversations."

"Illegally, I suspect," Paul said.

"I suspect," Patricia said.

"I see," Paul said.

The next day, Paul met Sue—that was, in fact, her name—in a chili joint in Alexandria, Virginia, across the Potomac River from Washington, to hear her version of the story.

Her version was pretty much as Patricia had recounted it, although she added some odious details about her boss's behavior that Patricia hadn't offered. Plus, Sue was a wreck. She obviously was getting little sleep, petrified at the thought of being out of a job and unable to find another if she'd been fired for incompetence by a famous Washington figure.

Paul asked what the boss's wife had said when Sue contacted her.

Sue took a sip of the Mexican beer she had ordered and looked at it for a moment as if hoping to divine the answer from the bottle.

"The wife," Sue then said, looking up, "had dismissed the whole thing and accused me of trying to entice her husband and ruin their marriage."

The phrase "druggie slut" had been one that she had chosen to use not once but three times in her angry outburst before she slammed down the phone. It seemed, Sue said, that the wife had been rehearsing the tirade and waiting for Sue to call.

"And you taped this conversation," Paul said.

Sue suddenly looked sober as a judge.

"I sure as shit did," she said, "and I don't care who the fuck knows it." Which turned out to be unfortunate phrasing.

Paul paid the bill and they both left for their separate cars but neither had noticed another Pentagon official who, coincidentally, had slid into the next booth while they were talking. The chili joint enjoyed excellent acoustics, and this official had heard everything and heard it well enough to give a complete report to his best friend, who was, as it happened, Sue's philandering boss.

When the boss heard the story and, blessing of blessings, that the person she had confided in was Paul, he pulled up some recent television programs and, after watching one from two months back, picked up the phone to call Guy Lynch, now in his new job at the paper.

Most of Guy's conversations with the official had been initiated by Guy, so he was a little surprised to get this call, but the official made sure his tone indicated that he saw Guy as a trusted member of the club—he'd actually been meaning to call Guy a month or so ago after one of his shows, but, you know, things got in the way. Absolutely, Guy said, he knew how things got in the way.

Anyway, the official, who knew how to deal with reporters, was calling today about something Guy might be interested in. Great, sure, Guy said. He had always known he was one of the press corps' elite, the cream of the crop, trusted by Washington insiders. Other Washington insiders.

The official started out by telling Guy about the contents of a report that would not be released for three more days, on condition that the paper hold any story until the release of the report itself. This was actually no big deal, he had been planning to hand the story to another paper anyway because he knew the best way to get some ink on a humdrum report was to give it in advance to a tame reporter who would give it big play if he or she knew it was a scoop.

That was the first part of the trap. Then came the clincher. There is an important meeting set for next week with some U.N. and NATO officials that's not being announced, he said, lowering his voice, as if he weren't presumably in his private, quite secure office. "I wonder if you would like a background briefing on it, maybe for an advancer attributed to, I don't know, senior Pentagon officials, something like that."

"We're not telling anyone else," the official said, reeling Guy in, "but we think you have the chops to write a nuanced story on it."

The official wondered whether he was laying it on a bit thick.

Apparently not. Guy jumped at the bait. This would be big. "Of course," he said, but managed to pause just a moment first so he could, he hoped, sound blasé about the whole thing. Just another day at the office for a big-time journalist accustomed to being tipped off to important secret meetings with U.S. allies and U.N. officials.

"Oh, and, by the way," the official said off-handedly, at the end of the conversation, "there's something a little bit unsavory going on here that we're hoping to handle quietly, in deference to the parties' privacy."

Sure, or something like that, Guy said, his mind working at how he could work the background briefing story so it would work most to his advantage.

The official then gave Guy a highly doctored version of what was going on with his subordinate. Although he didn't use the phrase druggie slut, as his wife had, the meaning was clear.

"It's all very sad, and please keep this and where you heard about it completely to yourself; this is very sensitive. We're going to try to get this girl some help," he added, the epitome of concern.

"Of course," said Guy Lynch, Member of the Insiders Club.

"She's even talked with one of your reporters," the official said, "so I'm a little worried."

"Really, who's that?" Guy asked.

The official told him.

"I see," Guy said. He hadn't liked Paul from the start with his snotty, disrespectful attitude. He suspected Paul and some of his ink-stained old-school pals ridiculed Guy behind his back as a lightweight. He was right.

"Anyway," the official said, before hanging up, "I hope we can have more of these conversations."

"Me too," Guy said.

Guy floated in the air for a moment or two after the conversation before leaving his spacious corner office. He went down to the newsroom to buttonhole and, in Paul's less regal cubbyhole, told him about the two big scoops he had landed.

"That's great," Paul said, and then he told Guy about the story he had discovered.

After he had done so, Guy seemed to mull it over for a bit before telling Paul how this really sounded like an internal personnel matter, not worth the paper's attention.

Paul was dumbfounded but Guy was adamant and Paul, who didn't have a spacious corner office, knew he was outgunned.

He called Sue and told her he wouldn't be able to do the story. He then did something that he wouldn't have done under ordinary circumstances, he gave her the name and phone number of a competing reporter, who he hoped would jump at the story. She sounded doubtful when she hung up.

Paul didn't know whether she called that reporter or what steps she took, but over the next couple of days, Sue was summarily fired, and Patricia, Paul and Elise's friend, was reprimanded at work, barely escaping dismissal herself.

After hearing this by phone in the evening from a tearful Patricia, Paul and Elise had a long talk and the next day, Paul resigned on the spot.

And that was how Paul had become a former employee of the paper and bête noire of Guy Lynch.

* * *

Guy strode into Gunther's office off the newsroom with his brilliant, TV-ready smile, and a cloud of some sort of expensive scent.

Gunther passed the sheaf of documents across his desk, knowing full well that Lynch could not read Russian.

Guy ignored the papers and asked Gunther some questions about the report and where it had come from. Gunther answered the questions vaguely, referring to unnamable sources and alluding to a familiarity with such documents from his time in Moscow. Guy nodded, although it was clear he was in over his head.

"Very intriguing," Lynch finally said.

He seemed lost in thought for a moment.

"You know," he said, as he looked back up, "I could call one of my sources at CIA on this."

Schroeder had known this would be Guy's reaction and had thought his response through carefully. Guy couldn't possibly have the kind of sources who would know about this, and neither Gunther nor Paul wanted Guy to muddy the waters. On the other hand, it might be that Guy's contacts would be helpful later and there was no point in alienating him.

"Maybe that would be a bit premature," he said, but cordially.

Guy gazed back for a moment, trying to figure out if he was being hustled.

"Premature?" he asked, "Why?"

"Because," Gunther continued, "I think we ought to do a little of our own legwork first."

Guy looked as if he were about to say something, then stopped, reconsidering.

"At least for the moment," Gunther added. An afterthought.

Guy seemed to turn this over in his mind.

"Maybe I can help later on," he said, still unsure if he were being led into a trap.

"Just what I was thinking," Gunther said, smiling a little, "let Paul and I see what we can find out. Can you give us some time before you contact your intelligence community contacts?" "Intelligence community" was how Washington and faux insiders like Guy referred to its alphabet soup of secret services, regrettably taking all of the romance and derring-do out of espionage in favor of anodyne bureaucratese.

Guy jumped a bit at the mention of Paul, but, after thinking for a moment, said, sure, take some time. At least Gunther seemed to recognize that he was an intelligence community insider. Then, there seemingly being nothing left to say, he got up to head back to his fancy office.

* * *

Once on the newsroom floor, heading to the stairs, though, Lynch remembered that he didn't trust Gunther or that prick Paul Girard. As he made his way up to his office, he became more and more certain he was being played. By the time he sat down at his desk the size of a football field he had jettisoned any intention of letting them run with this story that had Pulitzer written all over it. He looked at the wall facing him, loaded with awards and certificates and pictures of him in action—interviewing a foreign prime minister here, in a helicopter there, talking to a GI at a desert military base, that sort of thing. Plus, one with a comely movie actress at the United Nations where she had been named special ambassador for some do-gooder program—Guy couldn't remember what it was—to help the poor in benighted parts of the world. After a moment, he made a call to Andrew Caputo, one of his CIA "sources."

Lynch saw Caputo—"Andy"—as a breezy, Ivy League-ish, member of the agency's PR team, one of a breed of Washington bureaucrats serving as spokesmen, or -women, or -persons, depending on personal and employer taste, in agencies and congressional offices. They managed both the influential and serious reporters and the swarms of lazy and neophyte journalists who did no homework before picking up the phone, provincial reporters, bloggers, assorted kooks, and others who could claim some sort of press status in the Internet Age. The CIA press office, of course, got more than its share of the latter categories.

Given his celebrity, erstwhile though it may have been, Lynch rated one of the office's more experienced handlers. This press office cadre specialized in subtly ensuring that prominent reporters, even when writing about the agency's flaws, quietly burnished the CIA's carefully cultivated image as a cunning, omnipotent, omniscient but shadowy global force for good.

Caputo was good at that job. While he projected the image of a somewhat unremarkable, well-dressed young Washington functionary who might have been at the Agriculture Department or a Senate committee office but happened to be working for an intelligence agency, he had actually worked in several sensitive units overseas and in Langley within the agency and expected to go back to that work when he rotated out of the press office.

When Lynch called him wishing to discuss some "hot news," Caputo read the tone in his voice and shifted into high gear. He invited him out to CIA headquarters—would Lynch like to come out this afternoon? Fine, said Lynch, always anxious to spend time with members of the "IC," as he knew real spook world insiders referred to the intelligence community. Other real spook world insiders, that is.

What followed was as carefully scripted as any of Lynch's previous television reports, although Lynch had no idea that was the case.

He left the office and drove his car, a gleaming red Porsche 911 convertible, through Georgetown and across the Key Bridge. As he made his way up the George Washington Parkway, he stewed, increasingly agitated at what looked more and more like an effort by Gunther and his pal Paul to fuck him over. He felt better when he went through the CIA's front gate, cleared by the nine-foot-tall, armed uniformed guard at the main security checkpoint, which had been alerted to his pending arrival. He then parked in the VIP area near the main entrance of the Original Headquarters Building—the entrance with the seal and the stars for fallen spies, much loved by the movie industry.

Lynch left his iPhone in the car and then walked through the gate to be cleared in by a waiting Caputo. Once through the building's security gate, Caputo escorted Lynch along a few halls to a conference room. On their way, they passed the scale model of Osama bin Laden's headquarters that had been used in planning the 2011 raid. Caputo had recently started ensuring that gullible visiting reporters saw the model when they came. He expected it would help set the mood and was quite satisfied with the subsequent increase in journalists' pliability.

As Caputo worked the combination lock on the door of the conference room, he asked Lynch if he had his cell phone on him, this was a SCIF, after all. SCIF stood for "sensitive compartmented information facility," government-speak for a secure room for classified discussions. Despite the grand title, the room looked pretty much like a regular conference room, but, since the CIA was in the intelligence game and the building itself was hardened, there was no shortage of thusly designated rooms.

The phone question was all a matter of stoking the drama in Lynch's mind anyway, the second such step, after passing the bin Laden model. Caputo knew Lynch knew cell phones were banned in the building completely but asking him reinforced the cachet of the moment. The third step followed moments later.

As they walked in, Caputo seemed alarmed to see what appeared to be drone footage playing on a screen at the end of the room showing a car being approached by troops. A radio conversation among team leaders was audible. As Guy watched the blurry black-and-white footage, the perspective changed to surrounding streets and he could hear one of the voices identify "two, no three, individuals" on a corner, adding "Goddammit, they're fuckin' armed, they're fuckin' armed." Another voice said "Roger, they're fuckin' armed. Take 'em out" before the screen erupted in explosion.

Caputo quickly picked up a phone on the wall, dialed a couple of numbers, and murmured into it. Moments later the screen went blank. Caputo apologized to Lynch and asked him to not use anything he'd seen on this current operation tape. "Sorry," he said, "you shouldn't have seen that."

Lynch knowingly nodded and agreed.

As it happened, the footage was old, unclassified tape but, after much debate with himself, Caputo had arranged for it to be playing when they came into the room. He was a little concerned that Lynch might have already seen it, but that was not the case. He now watched, satisfied, seeing that he had reeled Lynch in, the bubble-headed former TV reporter convinced he had seen forbidden fruit but was trusted to keep his mouth shut because he had an insider's sophisticated appreciation of the fine points of operating in the rarified world of the IC. Caputo made a mental note to use the trick again with other reporters—at least the dumber ones.

After the two had sat down at the room's conference table, Lynch filled Caputo in on what Gunther had told him, at least as well as he could because, as Gunther had surmised, he wasn't quite sure what it meant. Caputo listened carefully, making an occasional note on a legal pad he had brought—unnecessary since he had a small digital recorder on the table in front of him.

When Lynch had finished, Caputo put on a thoughtful look for a moment.

"Well, this may be interesting," he said. "Of course, if there is such a separatist group and they had actually been in touch with us, I couldn't go into it with you,"

"Of course not," Guy said. Two men of the world, well aware of the bounds of propriety and the need to protect *sources and methods*.

Caputo seemed to study his notes for a moment.

"I wonder," he said, "whether you might be able to hold onto this for a while, maybe we can move the ball forward on it a bit."

Caputo detested corporate-speak phrases such as "move the ball forward," but they always worked with people like Lynch.

Lynch, basking in the recognition that he was an important person part of the club, concurred and agreed to stay in touch as things developed. As the ball got moved forward.

On the way out, he and Lynch stopped at the gift shop and Lynch bought himself some CIA cufflinks.

"Hope they're not bugged, haha," he said to Caputo as they made their way to the exit.

"Me too," Caputo said, sharing the amusement, as Lynch passed through the gate and surrendered his visitor's badge before leaving the building.

As soon as he was gone, Caputo turned and went back to his office. Sitting down at his desk, he picked up the phone and called an old friend in the agency section following Russian developments—known as "Russia House" internally—and quickly set up a meeting in a SCIF. A real one this time, not the bullshit one in which he'd met Guy Lynch.

CHAPTER FOUR

PRIVATE MEETINGS

Paul had an appointment with Archie Richter the next day. First, he had a meeting with an old friend, another congressional staffer, that he had set up quickly overnight.

The Rayburn House Office Building, where he would meet both his old contact and Archie, was a twenty-minute walk from home through Capitol Hill. Known locally as the Hill, it was an almost-normal modern, gentrifying urban neighborhood. Almost.

As he made his way past nineteenth-century townhouses on tree-lined streets, he could see the signs of the Hill neighborhood waking up. A door opened for another early riser to rush to work or a newspaper to be picked up. Half a dozen dog owners made their way to or from a nearby square for morning walks.

Sitting quietly, its engine idling, he passed a drab Ford Crown Victoria pointing in the wrong direction in a no-parking spot, nosing up to the crosswalk. Paul could not see the driver but knew that he or she would be giving him a quick scan as he walked by. There was another such vehicle pointed in the opposite direction at the other end of the block. Capitol Police units there because, as Paul, unlike many of his neighbors, knew, one of the townhouses belonged to the House speaker. Important in his own right, plus third in line in the presidential succession.

A few blocks later, shortly before he reached Rayburn, the security became more obvious, with uniformed cops and marked cars suddenly visible.

An almost-normal neighborhood.

As he entered the Rayburn Building, he went through the same security rigmarole Americans suffered every time they got on a plane and put his briefcase through the same sort of scanner gracing every airport departure area since 9/11. In the briefcase was a Word document he'd received from the staffer the night before.

Leaving the crowded entrance area, he made his way down the corridor, stopping at the main Rayburn cafeteria for two cups of coffee to go, and continued on to a cubbyhole office with an unmarked door, far from the visitors' entrances and from the committee hearing rooms where the public and the TV cameras hung out.

He had sent the staffer a text the night before and she had, since they were old friends, pulled some files up on her office-issued laptop, written out a few paragraphs in a Word document, and sent it to Paul before going to bed. The document, which she knew Paul would have read before coming over, was pretty clear. Nevertheless, as they had known each other a long time, she had squeezed him into an otherwise crowded morning.

They met for forty-five minutes in the tiny office, although some of that was catching up. Having read the document, Paul wanted to talk to her, pick up the sort of shadings that might not come through in a written document, plus any details that might have slipped her mind or that she hadn't wanted to put in writing.

After they had talked, the staffer asked him what he was working on, but he gave a vague answer. She looked at him for a moment then down at her copy of the report she'd sent him. "OK," she said, "I hope this has been helpful."

"It has," Paul said. He thanked her for her time and went back down to the cafeteria. He got another cup of coffee and took a table against the wall at some remove from any of the few staffers and others there at that hour—pretty much too late for prework breakfast now, too early for lunch.

Right on the dot, at ten, Archie came up to the table and sat down, a quick good morning as he looked at his watch.

"I hope we can get this story moving," he said, adding, "This is really something we'd like to get out into the public."

"Yes, we do too," Paul said. He took a moment to pretend to scan the memo from the staffer again. He didn't want to be rushed through this meeting.

"The issue, for us, that is to say, the paper," he then said, returning the staffer's paper back to his briefcase, "is verifying the, uh, document you passed me."

Archie twisted around to ensure no one was in earshot.

"It's pretty explosive," Paul added.

"Well, you've got that right, brother," Archie said after a moment, now relaxing a bit. A little good ol' boy charm now peeking out, Paul thought, the kind that must work with constituents from back home.

"How would you do this?" Archie asked, suddenly businesslike, "Trace this report, I mean."

Paul appeared to consider the question for a moment.

"Well," he then said, "ordinarily we'd try to find someone in the Russian government or outside it to vouch for this document."

Archie quickly cracked a country-boy smile.

"You're not going to get any Rooskies to help you out there." He chuckled at the absurdity of the thought.

"Yeah, right," Paul said, grinning a little himself, acknowledging the little joke.

"Well, in that case," he said, back to the business at hand "we'd need to find someone who knows about the provenance of this document."

Archie nodded and sipped his coffee, also serious again now. "I guess that's so," he said.

"I mean, someone must trust it," Paul said.

"Uh huh, absolutely," Archie said. He looked like he was thinking. Or like he was trying to look like he was thinking.

Paul let a few seconds tick by.

"And you can't tell us where you got it, I gather," he said.

Archie's eye twinkled.

"Believe me, they won't talk to you," Archie said. He seemed particularly amused at the prospect of introducing his source to journalists.

Paul let a couple of beats go by.

"You know, Archie," he said, "this is pretty hot stuff."

"It sure is," Archie said, still amused.

"How, if I may ask," Paul said, "did you get hold of it?"

"Well," Archie said, looking as if he'd been waiting to answer that question for his whole life, "that's a damn good question."

He took a sip of his coffee.

"You see," he said, apparently thoughtfully, "we have a lot of veterans and active-duty guys in our district, it's that kind of place."

He looked around at the cafeteria. Obviously not, unlike his district, that kind of place.

"I was at a shindig at the local American Legion," he said, "and I met a fella who's still, uh, you know, working sort of on the edge of that world, not retired or a veteran, but connected now to it, if you get my drift."

Another pause to make sure Paul got his drift. Paul nodded encouragingly.

"When he learned I was working up here," Archie said, gesturing to the expanse of the cafeteria up here, "he put me in touch with someone, who introduced me to someone else. Like that."

Archie stopped talking, watching to see what Paul's response would be. It sounded to Paul as if this were a rehearsed presentation.

"So," Paul said, "sort of a friend of a friend."

"Of a friend of a friend," Archie said.

"Why did he give it to you?" Paul asked.

Archie looked like he had been expecting the question.

"It's pretty important stuff," he said, "he wanted to get it out."

"I see," Paul said.

Archie put on his thinking look again.

"I hope you're not going to try to find this guy," he said.

"No?" Paul said.

"You won't be able to find him, believe me," Archie said, "plus it would really cause problems."

"Like what?" Paul asked.

"Oh, you know," Archie said, "we don't want too many people to know what we're looking into."

"No, of course not," Paul said after a moment.

He let that hang in the air for a moment or two too long.

"I really hope you can verify this story, though," Archie said, breaking the silence, "it's important that it get out."

Paul nodded. More silence that became uncomfortable.

"Maybe we could find the guy who wrote it," Archie said suddenly.

Paul raised his eyebrows. An idea he hadn't thought of. Plus, he noticed Archie had started using "we." Nice touch, he thought.

"Oleg something?" he asked. He looked at Archie inquisitively—who can remember these Russian names?

Archie looked back and just for a moment, the mask seemed to slip, but just for a moment. "Makarov," he said coolly.

"Right," Paul said. He looked relieved to be reminded of a detail he'd forgotten, "Oleg Makarov."

"Have you done any digging into this guy?" he asked Archie after apparently considering this idea.

Archie looked at him, puzzled.

"I'm only asking," Paul said, "because I wouldn't want to duplicate your efforts."

"Oh, right," Archie said after a moment, "I see. I guess I did some internet searches, a few checks that we can do with law enforcement to see if he's in their files, but nothing really came out of it all. Not surprising, him being Russian, and all."

"You know, Mr. Girard ..." he continued.

"Please call me Paul."

"OK, uh, right, Paul, I really don't know how I'd go about finding him," Archie paused, "I'm really pretty new to all this here. I've only been on this stuff for a few months."

"Really?" Paul asked quickly, "What about before?"

"Oh, you know," Archie said breezily, "this and that. Before that, I was sort of general help at the local NRA." Paul, of course, had learned that the night before, and it was logical—Archie's boss had won her office largely on the back of National Rifle Association support. That made sense because her main qualifications for the job had consisted of an unwavering belief in gun rights and the elimination of taxes. She didn't have her now-defeated incumbent opponent's detailed knowledge of policy, in fact, she barely knew how Congress worked. On the other hand, she hadn't been photographed *in flagrante* in the gents' room of a Washington gay bar as he had been either, which pretty much did the trick when the pictures leaked out a week before what had until then been a tight election. No one, though, could figure out how he'd been caught, having successfully hidden his secret life for many years.

Paul seemed to take in what Archie had said.

"OK," Paul said, "let me see what I can find out."

"Is it just you on this story?" Archie asked, sipping his coffee.

"I'm it," Paul said.

"And Gunther Schroeder," he then added, "someone I worked in Moscow with years ago."

"Right," Archie said. He seemed to think that over for a moment. Then something else seemed to occur to him.

"I'd heard that TV guy had gone over to your team," he said.

Paul looked at Archie for a moment.

"You mean Guy Lynch?" he asked.

"Yeah, that's the one," Archie said.

"He's in management at the paper," he said, "I don't have much in the way of dealings with him, although he's aware of the story. I'll be keeping him up to speed."

"Great," Archie said after letting that sink in. He looked at his watch, ready to wrap up the meeting.

"Well, OK," he said, "Let me know what you discover."

Paul looked at him with a puzzled expression.

"Why?" he asked—the point, he added, was to verify the document for the paper, not find the author for members of Congress.

Archie seemed stopped for just a moment.

"Oh, just hoping we can get the story out," he said, a warm smile on his face.

"Us too," Paul said.

* * *

"He made quite an impression when he was with the gun folks," Paul said half an hour later.

He was back home on a video call with Gunther. Elise had pulled her desk chair over to his desk so she could participate.

"How do you know that?" Gunther asked.

Paul told them about the document from the staffer and his meeting with her earlier. She was, he explained, an old contact, an attorney who worked for one of the few activist Democrats from the South in Congress. She had been around for years, having battled her way into a position of power that was rare for a black woman on the Hill and had the scars and contacts to prove it. She had sent Paul a brief description of what she knew about Archie.

Paul had Googled Archie the night before, just before going to bed, and found few references to him older than a year or two. That wasn't unusual, even in the internet age, most people were pretty anonymous, and unless they were in the public for one reason or another, there weren't likely to be many references to them.

"I found his name popping up here and there in relation to the NRA or the local Republican Party, or his boss's campaign in the months leading up to her election, but that was it. Pretty much what you'd expect. Not much to go on or figure out what his story is."

"My friend, though," he said, "told me Archie made something of a name for himself at home.

"Archie came out of nowhere," Paul continued, "recommended to the gun people by one of his professors, something like that, as a bright guy and hard worker committed to the conservative cause, and they hired him during the slow season before campaigns really got going."

"Do we know anything about the professor," Gunther asked.

"No," Paul answered, "no one really cared that much to look. What was important was what Archie was doing, not where he went to school.

"The guy apparently never slept," he said.

"He would do anything—lick envelopes, nag people for money, drive big shots around, pick up dry-cleaning—but it turned out he was really bright and quickly grasped complicated issues."

"Perfect for a new, untested member of the House," Elise said.

"Exactly. When she ran and won, he was a natural choice to go onto her staff. My friend said the local party bigwigs had some people they wanted to put on her staff, and they did, but Archie was the only non-carpetbagger among them, which his boss liked. He started doing low-level stuff in her office but rose quickly as the staff turned over, which it did because she really wasn't very good at being a House member and her staff moved on to better jobs."

"Why does your friend know all this?" Elise asked.

"Well," Paul said, "her issue, for her member, that is, is gun control, that was why she and one of her colleagues noticed him at all. When

Archie moved onto the Hill, they were as impressed as the Republicans were with him, and, with all the school shootings, they were certain that if gun control became a major issue, an ambitious and capable staffer like Archie, who had a background in the issues, was someone they needed to keep an eye on.

"As you know," he continued, "gun control hasn't really taken up any congressional time lately, so he hasn't popped up in that way. My friend had been watching him, though, which I knew from other work, so I asked her about him. She gave me what she had, but since gun control moved out of the spotlight, she's focused on other things."

"How did he end up on national security issues?" Gunther asked.

"He drifted into it after gun control faded, but it's all sort of ad hoc," he said, "I don't think he has a clearance or anything like that. His office is not that active on those issues."

"I see," Elise said, thinking. "Are you going to try to find whoever leaked the document?"

"No," Paul said, "I think our best bet is still to try to find Oleg. Archie's right. His source won't talk to us. Besides, in all likelihood, his source didn't obtain the document. He or she is just someone on the distribution list, probably far from whoever actually got it. Archie's source would probably not be in a position to tell us whether the document is legit or how it was obtained—even if they were so inclined, which they wouldn't be—and would certainly not be interested in referring us to someone who could."

"Maybe that's the whole point of this," Elise said, "maybe someone's trying to use us to verify this document."

"Maybe," Paul said after a moment. "Or something like that."

CHAPTER FIVE

RUSSIA HOUSE

Across the river, at the CIA, a small working group from Russia House was in a SCIF discussing Caputo's meeting with Guy.

Other than the extra sound- and bug-proofing, the SCIF was somewhat like any other small conference room in an international organization. It had a table, swivel chairs, screens and a TV camera for video links. A row of digital clocks showed the time in multiple time zones in 24-hour format, including, for this meeting, Moscow and Vladivostok in Russia's Far East. It also, though, had a sign that could be lit to indicate the security clearance required for whatever meeting was being held there. Today it showed a very high clearance level.

Each of the three at the table had a copy of the transcript of Guy's conversation with Caputo and a classified National Security Agency memo reporting on any intercepted emails, texts, or phone conversations possibly relating to Oleg Makarov or Russian Far Eastern separatism. It was pretty slim pickings.

Next to Caputo, the only one there not from Russia House, sat Andrew Stamos, a burly white-haired man in shirtsleeves and a loosened tie. He looked like the ex-college footballer he was and had walked with a limp ever since an unfortunate incident with a mouthy Russian *spetsnaz* officer in a Vienna alley one night many years back. The incident, away from touristy Stephansplatz had been off a quiet street not too far from the Rochusgasse U-Bahn Station and had turned out to be much more unfortunate for the Russian than for Stamos. Terminally unfortunate.

Also present was a quiet, grandmotherly woman named Evelyn Kilgore, who had made a religion out of studying the Soviet, then Russian, Far East. Like Stamos, she thought the Obama administration's "reset" with Russia was, in a word, bullshit. She thought Vladimir Putin was playing the West for suckers. Many of her Russia House colleagues agreed with her on both counts.

They talked for two hours, turning the situation over, metaphorically, and examining it from every angle. At various points, one or another of them would use a keyboard to call up screen images or audio tapes. Satellite shots of Vladivostok or somewhere nearby. Tapes of cell phone conversations in various languages with maps showing the locations of the participants and translation subtitles on the screen when needed. Videos with sound and English subtitles of Russian officials' ostensibly private conversations and meetings. They watched two officials sitting on a bench in an otherwise deserted park. The video was from an insect's perspective. Not a naturally occurring insect, one should understand, but close enough for government work, as they say.

Stamos rubbed his hand across his face.

The conversation in the SCIF was interestingly similar to the discussion that Elise, Gunther, and Paul had recently had in Paul and Elise's home office.

"I'm not sure what we should be doing with this," Stamos said, thumbing through the transcript pages, "I mean it could be complete crap."

"But it's potentially critical," Caputo said.

"Critical?" Stamos snorted, "it's potentially fucking earth-shaking but I promise you Moscow's not going to let it happen if there's anything to it.

"This is a big chunk of Russia with a lot of resources and a gateway to Asia and Asian trade for them, and they're not going to let it go—they're not going to make the mistake Moscow made when they started letting the Soviet republics go.

"Plus," he said, "they wouldn't want to send a signal to other groups who might be nursing an urge to pull out of Mother Russia.

"Groups," he continued after glancing around the table, "we might even help along—on the QT, of course."

The other two chuckled knowingly but said nothing.

Stamos thumbed through the pages.

"On top of all of that," he said, "if there's a serious, credible move to split the Far East from Russia, that changes the whole picture on Russia in the Pacific, by which I mean Russia won't be in the fucking Pacific.

"I'm not sure," he said, "that Russia necessarily has plans at this point to be a major power in Asia. They may be more likely to leave that to their buddies in Beijing. But if Russia aspires to return to superpower greatness, and I think they do," he looked over at the grandmotherly Kilgore, who nodded, "they certainly can't let the Far East go."

"On the other hand," he said, "they're moving a lot of weapons into the Pacific region, I'm looking at places like Vietnam, Indonesia, and the Philippines. Those are all places where they could try to balance China's expansion, expansion those countries are not completely happy about—especially the ones who are pissed about China's apparent plans to take over the South China Sea.

"All of that could go out the window if the Far East breaks away—or even if it doesn't," he said. "If this region is riven by a separatist movement and Moscow has to send in troops to quash it, it's going to effectively pull the Kremlin out of the game in the Pacific, at least for the moment.

"Although," he added after a moment, "I'm not sure what the longer-term implications would be. It could strengthen their hand in the region if they were successful."

"And this would be just at a time that we're focusing on that part of the world," Caputo said. The Obama administration had made its "pivot" to the Pacific region a central tenet of its foreign policy.

"Not only that," Kilgore said, "but, if successful, this would be bad news for Vladimir Putin, the new czar of the new Russia and his dreamed-of reborn Soviet Union."

Kilgore had long experience with Moscow. She was old-school, trained by the first generation of postwar Kremlin watchers, and had served under diplomatic cover at the U.S. Embassy in Moscow with distinction, having played critical roles in major intelligence coups—the kind that involve dead drops, clandestine meetings, long surveillance from vulnerable positions and dangerous exfiltrations requiring balls and timing, not sitting on her ass in front of a computer screen. Now, in her final years with the agency, she was a well-respected analyst with a collection of contacts around the world and friends on the seventh floor, where the director's office was located. She had known all about Russian President Vladimir Vladimirovich Putin, the former KGB officer in Dresden, when East Germany was still East Germany, and Putin was working out of No. 4 Angelikastrasse. She thought he was a third-rate intelligence officer but a dangerous leader to have in the Kremlin.

"If he has to deal with a Far East separatist movement on top of everything else, he can kiss the notion of a new Soviet Union good-bye," she said.

"Do we have any reporting on this?" Stamos asked after a moment, looking down at the papers in front of him.

"No," she said, "but that doesn't mean anything."

"OK," Stamos said, looking at his watch, "let's chase this down and see what we can find."

"But let's keep this to ourselves," he said after a moment, "no one else needs to know about this at this point."

* * *

It was quickly clear to Paul, beginning his search for Oleg over the next few days, that the Russian had taken steps to hide himself from Moscow or anyone else who might start looking for him.

Paul spent a few hours, as he assumed Archie had, scouring the internet to no avail. He then spent a few days reaching out to contacts in all the usual places—academics, officials, former officials, business executives, and the like in the United States, Europe, and Asia. Discreetly, of course; he didn't want to tip his hand, and, besides, one never knew who was listening these days.

And, in fact, despite the steps he'd taken, Paul's calls and emails attracted some attention of course. Word started to get about that he was nosing around about something to do with Russia and the Far East. The NSA picked up some of the calls and emails because they were to foreigners the agency was allowed to target, as did the agency's foreign counterparts, including the Brits and other members of the Five Eyes Western intelligence alliance, as well as a number of other countries' electronic intelligence agencies. That included, of course, Russia's *Spetssvyaz*, or Special Communications and Information Service. Each agency passed the information along to sister organizations for any appropriate action.

CHAPTER SIX

PACK THE SUNTAN LOTION

Paul continued to have little luck with his old sources, which was not surprising, since a lot of water had passed under the bridge since he had last dealt with Oleg. Nevertheless, he held out hope that one of his old contacts might have an idea where Oleg might be or, failing that, some knowledge of events in the Russian Far East.

After hours spent emailing and calling an assortment of Russian specialists, officials, academics, and old colleagues, he came up dry.

Almost.

Like many members of the Washington press corps—the real one, not the one in the movies and on TV—Andrew Warwick toiled away in the vineyards of the trade, or specialized, press away from the glamor of cable networks and the big national papers. Working for an expensive and profitable energy industry news site that had started as a weekly newsletter in the seventies, he reported on issues of interest to a small, expert audience that was willing to pay big money for that reporting on otherwise obscure subcommittee hearings, federal contract offers, agency decisions, foreign deals, and industry developments.

Warwick had no patience with the popinjays of the new media landscape. He had worked hard to establish his reputation in the industry and among his colleagues by knowing his subject and making extensive contacts at trade shows, congressional hearings, think tanks, company gatherings, and union offices. Other reporters covering the beat knew that if they got an interview with an oil executive, a meeting with a key bureaucrat in the Federal Energy Regulatory Commission or another of the many federal agencies handling energy policy, or time with a visiting oil minister from West Africa, odds were at the very least fifty-fifty Warwick would have gotten there first.

Paul had met Warwick after he had left the paper while working on a freelance assignment for a political risk firm, a project covering unrest in one of those West African countries. Their paths had crossed because Warwick was working on a profile of the country's energy officials. One of those officials, Paul knew, had been secreting U.N. development funds in a bank account held under the name of an innocuous-sounding holding company the official controlled through attorneys in Zurich—which rang a bell with Paul, having tried to chase down the money-laundering scheme in Moscow. Somehow Warwick had found out that Paul was working on the political risk project and tracked him down.

Paul had been limited in what he could say, but had a drink with Warwick, gently nudging him away from too glowing a picture of the official. Paul was vague, elliptical, but clear in his meaning. Warwick got the message.

He was surprised when he saw Warwick's article to see that the piece, while skirting what might have gotten Warwick and his publishers into legal trouble, made it clear that the official was laundering U.N. money he had filched.

Paul had met Warwick for another drink later and congratulated him on the story, only to learn that Warwick had been able to trace the money to the Zurich attorneys. A dirty money pal in the Treasury Department's counterterrorism and financial intelligence—aka "guns, drugs and thugs"—unit told him, off the record, that Treasury, with Interpol and U.N. help, had confirmed the money was being hidden by the West African official. Warwick, it turned out, had reported on banking before he started covering energy issues, so he had been able to do more with the information Paul had given him than most energy reporters would have been able to. The two had stayed in loose touch since.

Now, as a result of his queries, one of his old contacts had steered Paul toward Warwick, who was working on some major Russia project.

Paul had left Warwick a voicemail saying that he was trying to dig up a source for a piece on Russian energy exploration in its eastern reaches, which sounded logical enough not to raise any suspicions on Warwick's part—hopefully—but interesting enough that he would call back if he had any advice.

Paul had not necessarily expected much but was rewarded an hour or so later with a text from Warwick proposing a drink that night after he had cleared his deadline.

A few hours later, they met at a bar off K Street, deserted except for a few lawyers and lobbyists in bespoke suits absorbed in their own conversations. There were no other reporters there; the drink prices did a good job of discouraging such riffraff.

Paul went through his cover story that he was working on a project for a client looking at Asian markets for natural gas from Russia's Far East.

Warwick watched Paul as he listened to Paul's account.

"This is a little far afield for you, isn't it?" he asked.

"Yes," Paul said. The ice cubes clicked as they melted in the twenty-dollar scotches. "Well," he continued, "you know, the political situation." An afterthought, it seemed. Trailing off at the end.

Warwick smiled at that. He was clearly not convinced. "What kind of sources are you looking for?" he asked after a moment.

"You know," Paul said, "officials, émigrés, defectors, foreign specialists, the usual, whoever you might know."

Warwick's eyes followed the waitress as she walked by. She looked like an overworked mother who was anxious to end her shift and get home.

"How deep do you need to go?" Warwick asked. The waitress disappeared behind the bar, oblivious to the two of them talking.

"I mean," he continued, "are we talking about tame ex-Soviet academicians who now are teaching eager young minds at Princeton and Georgetown, or are we talking about the oligarchs and the tough ex-KGB hard men they've attached themselves to?"

"Probably the former," Paul said, then he stopped and looked at his drink for a moment. Oleg had apparently stumbled onto something pretty explosive, and he seemed to have disappeared from sight. Maybe Paul would have to go beyond the think tankers and policy wonks of the world that Oleg had always occupied.

"Maybe more the latter," Paul said, swirling the ice in his drink.

Warwick took a sip of his drink and seemed to think for a moment.

"OK," he then said, "I hope you know what you're doing."

"You'll share anything I might be able to use if you can?" he added.

"Of course," Paul said.

Warwick had no idea that Paul was digging into a potentially earth-shaking story about Far Eastern separatists. He had in mind anything Paul might find out about oil leases, shifts in ministry positions, that sort of thing—catnip to Warwick and his readers but of little interest outside that circle. Paul had no qualms about promising to share that sort of information, which he was unlikely to find anyway.

"This may be your lucky day," Warwick said. He had recently stumbled upon some interesting Russian sources for an article he was doing on oligarchs' energy investments.

"What kind of sources?" Paul asked. He was still thinking about his epiphany about shady sources and needed to make sure that he was headed in a direction that might actually lead to Oleg Makarov.

"A really interesting bunch," Warwick said, "some Russians here in the country who had fled Russia in recent years but were in various academic and ministry positions before the fall. Quite talkative once they got to trust you. And they have friends."

He looked around to make sure no one was close enough to overhear them before proceeding to tell Paul about some of these émigrés and their background. Paul pulled out a notebook and started taking notes. One name rang a bell, but Paul said nothing, letting Warwick continue.

When Warwick paused, Paul looked at his notebook page, studying what he had written. The lobbyists had left, and the waitress was now sitting at the bar reading her email off her phone while she waited to see if these two would order another round. They looked like good tippers. The lawyers in the fancy suits had stiffed her. No surprise.

Paul asked about two or three of the names Warwick had mentioned, including the one that had seemed familiar. How can I reach them, Paul asked, and Warwick told him, consulting his own phone. Paul wrote some of the details down.

They talked a little while longer before waving for the check. Paul paid, leaving a big tip, and the two left. After shaking hands, as Paul walked toward his car, he pulled his Blackberry out of his pocket and called Elise at home.

"Pack some suntan lotion," he said when she answered, then he told her where they were headed.

CHAPTER SEVEN

GOING OUT FOR A CALL
AND A SMOKE

As Paul and Warwick talked over drinks, ex-network pretty boy Guy Lynch parked his Porsche—*Porschuh*, if you don't mind—in front of a quiet bar on Capitol Hill, the engine ticking from its workout.

Lynch had had growing misgivings about the Oleg Makarov story since his meeting with Schroeder. He didn't like Schroeder but wondered where this story was going. He had sat at his desk that afternoon, turning the situation over and over in his mind, wondering whether it was possible for him to take control of, and credit for, the story. A satisfactory solution did not reveal itself no matter how much he sat and stared at his computer screen. Finally, he decided to cut out early and go for a drive. He left his office and went down to the company garage and fired up the 911, peeling out of his assigned parking space and onto the street, heading for Virginia.

In fairness, it must be said that that car was probably the most authentic thing about Lynch. He had loved to drive since his teen years in the Midwest, having graduated from a battered red Chevy Impala convertible with a two-speed Powerglide transmission to a souped-up VW Bug and then a British racing green Triumph TR4. He had loved sports cars since the TR and loved driving them, tearing up the roads among the farms in college, and ultimately, with his television salary went through a series of cars—a Datsun Z and a Corvette before finally settling on the first of a few Porsche 911s. Why fuck around? This one was a red convertible with a black interior. What he thought of as the Nineties Drug Lord version.

On this evening, he had done what he enjoyed doing most in his car. He put the top down and crossed the bridge to the George Washington Parkway, speeding north toward the Beltway. Staying on that highway, he cut across the river and then turned north on the twisting roads through Great Falls and Potomac before looping back on the Maryland side of the river and heading back downtown.

He never played the radio when he did this; he lost himself in the driving, the feel of the wind, the sound of the engine, engaging all four of his limbs as he worked the transmission up and down the scale, maneuvering through the curves at just the right speed and then down the straightaways. It felt as if he were teasing the exact right notes in a complicated composition out of a musical instrument he had mastered. There was nothing better in the world to forget the stresses of his job. Maybe nothing better in the world, period.

Even though the traffic had been light, the ride had taken a couple of hours. Having now pulled the car into a space on Pennsylvania Avenue and raised the top, he got out and locked the doors. He gave the car one last look, his eye lingering over the blacked-out rims and "Porsche" lettering in black on the engine compartment in the rear. Nothing had changed since high school; the car never failed to banish the pressures of work.

He went into Mr. Henry's, one of the last of the old-school Capitol Hill bars, a vestige of the neighborhood's bygone days when it was populated by blue-collar workers, young staffers who could walk to work at congressional offices or the Library of Congress, reporters starting out, and the like. He was known in the bar and, despite being busy with a number of customers, the bartender waved at him as he entered. One or two of those at the bar looked around as he came in but otherwise, like the odd current or former member of Congress who dropped by, or other Washington big shots, he got no special treatment despite his modest, if fading, celebrity. Everyone was an equal on the Hill.

He settled in for a relaxing meal and a beer or two.

* * *

The next morning, Paul and Elise packed up for a two-day jaunt to Ocean City, the beach resort on the Maryland shore. It was a little unusual this late in the year, a few weeks into the autumn with something of a nip in the air, but that just meant the traffic would be light.

They headed out of Washington, along Route 50, past Annapolis, stopping for crabs at a place they knew down a narrow, formerly rural, lane on Mill Creek. They crossed the Chesapeake Bay Bridge to the Eastern Shore where, after a couple of hours, they checked into an old, romantic hotel in the picturesque town of Berlin, not far from Ocean City.

Elise had brought her laptop along to work on, so she did not accompany Paul when he left, but they agreed to meet for a drink and dinner when he returned.

Paul crossed the final bridge into Ocean City and quickly made his way up the main highway toward the Delaware border, through a mind-numbing succession of cheap motels and strip malls until he found the address Warwick had given him. There, on the end, next to a T-shirt store, he found the pizza parlor he was looking for.

It was a long room, with old movie posters along one wall and a line of tables with cheap plastic chairs. On the other side was a counter and the pizza ovens, manned by a teenage boy with a surly look on his face.

The place was empty, and the only other staff was a girl of about twenty behind the counter.

Paul thought that the two were probably the last of the summer break college students hired by the Russian immigrant owner for the season. The girl smiled politely and told him, in heavily accented English, that her name was Nataliya and asked how she could help him today.

There was a sign on the wall welcoming visitors from "Gino" in jolly lettering. Paul assumed Gino was the owner, né Yevgeny Yuryevich Skosyrev, previously senior specialist in Southeast Asian offshore petroleum reserves in a Soviet Academy of Sciences institute and previously frequent visitor to Vietnam, Cambodia, Laos, and other then-fraternal commie outposts of the then-socialist empire in that part of the world. Current source of Andrew Warwick, Washington energy reporter, and one-time source of Paul Girard, Moscow newspaper correspondent.

"I'm looking for Gino," Paul said to the girl, smiling. She looked at the boy working the ovens.

"*Gde Yevgeniy Yur'yevich?*" she asked.

"*On v ofise, otdyhayet,*" the boy said, his eyes flitting to another customer who had just come in, a kid with scraggly sideburns that failed to hide his acne and too many tattoos.

After a pause, the girl turned back to Paul, smiling again.

"He is working on books in back, would you like me to get him?"

"Yes, thank you," Paul said. He looked around. The boy had said that "Gino" had been taking a nap in the back office, so he gave it a few minutes. Presently a slightly rumpled man, white hair a bit askew came out and stepped behind the counter. His well-worn jeans and shirt and calloused hands bespoke someone working hard to get by. He stopped for a moment when he saw Paul, then smiled broadly and gestured for Paul to join him in one of the booths in the back. He held up two fingers to the boy, who disappeared before returning with a bottle of vodka and two glasses before retreating.

It took some time for the two to catch up, Yevgeny stayed in touch with old contacts in the region but had established himself here in Ocean City and pretty much did his best to avoid any attention from Russia or Russians other than the other émigrés who frequented his pizza parlor and whose kids provided some of his summer help.

Eventually, Paul got around to the matter at hand. He was vague about the details other than he was trying to see if he could locate Makarov. Yevgeny had been a trusted source and had known Makarov in Moscow; he probably had suspected Makarov was feeding information to Paul, although he never said as much.

"Can you tell me why you want to find him?" Yevgeny asked.

"Only that it is for a story."

"Ah," Yevgeny said, "like the old days." He took a sip of vodka and looked around the room.

"You wouldn't bullshit an old friend, would you?" he asked.

"I might," Paul said, "but I'm not bullshitting you now."

"Is this going to get me into trouble?"

"I sure hope not."

Yevgeny looked at him for a moment, then shrugged.

"This sounds like exactly the kind of thing that will get me into trouble," he said.

He looked out at the pizza joint for a moment, lost, Paul assumed, in the old days when he led a different life.

"I have no idea where he is," he said, coming back to the present.

"Let me give this some thought, though," he then said, taking one of Paul's business cards and putting it in his shirt pocket, "I might get an idea later on."

* * *

An hour later, Paul sat with Elise in a bar near their hotel in Berlin. She had finished her work for the day and was anxious to hear how Paul's afternoon had gone.

They were almost alone in the bar, although some kids were drinking further down the bar. Paul told her about the meeting with Yevgeny, and that he hoped to hear back from him in the coming days.

"How forthcoming were you with him?" she asked.

"Well, I didn't tell him much," Paul said, "but I told him we're looking for Oleg—I mean he knew Oleg and that's the whole point of this, so I had to tell him that," he said.

She nodded and then signaled the bartender for another drink.

Paul could hear kids behind him and looked around quickly to see that they were talking among themselves, one with his back to Paul. Elise's drink arrived.

"Well, as long as you don't tell him Guy Lynch is trying to spike the story, as you know he is, or will be," she said.

"No," Paul said, "I don't think we need to mention that. Besides, I think we'll be able to head Guy off if we do our job," he said.

That seemed to exhaust the subject for the moment and their conversation turned elsewhere before they headed to a table for dinner.

Naturally, Paul hadn't recognized the scraggly kid who had been the customer from the pizza place among the group of kids near him at the bar, as his back was to Paul. He might not have even recognized him if he'd been turned around, although he might have been put off if he'd noticed how hard the kid was trying to eavesdrop on his conversation with Elise.

When Paul and Elise had left, the kid separated himself from his friends, so he could go out, have a cigarette, and call his girlfriend, he told them.

Once outside, he did light a cigarette and make a call, but not to a girlfriend. Using a brand-new cell phone he had purchased on the way to the hotel from a convenience store, he called a number that was answered near Centreville, about 70 miles away, on Maryland's Eastern Shore.

He spoke in a roundabout way, not using any words that might trip any alarms to listeners, automated or otherwise. He did refer directly to "Guy Lynch," but he couldn't figure out a way to mask that reference and, in the event, no one other than the recipient of his call took note. He then went in, had another drink with his friends, and left.

On the way home, he stopped by the bay, removed the battery and SIM card from the phone, and flung all of them as far out into the water as he could.

CHAPTER EIGHT

VERONICA CREVIER

Paul's queries received immediate, high-level attention in Moscow, where intelligence specialists, including a cadre of specialists on U.S. affairs from several intelligence units, pored over them in an ultra-secure conference room.

The room was the equivalent of the SCIF at CIA headquarters in Langley, although, of course, the décor had a somewhat less Western character. After mulling over the possible import of these communications, vague though they were, the specialists had prepared a message to be encrypted and forwarded to one of their colleagues.

Then, on receiving it, the colleague had read the message, taken the actions dictated, and waited for the results. When they came in, the colleague drafted a reply to Moscow, looked at his watch, and decided to take a walk. It was predawn in Moscow, so he had some time and thought it would be a pleasant evening to get some air and look at the stars. He enjoyed walking in the nearby countryside. It was one of the benefits of being stationed in the embassy's dacha away from Washington, near Centreville, on Maryland's Eastern Shore.

* * *

Meanwhile, in Langley, Caputo, Stamos, and Kilgore were not making much progress. A seemingly routine cable had gone out to agency stations and liaison services in the region inquiring about any vibrations in the air about any nascent Russian Far East separatist movement, based on reporting from a source of unknown and maybe doubtful veracity, or Oleg Makarov, among other, innocuous-sounding subjects.

Aside from the Western intercepts of Paul's calls and emails, there wasn't much to deal with. The gist of the intercepts ultimately made their way through the allies' and U.S. intelligence structures to the NSA and, ultimately, the CIA, where Kilgore, Stamos, and Caputo tried to determine—"assess" was actually the preferred verb among the intelligence cognoscenti—the worth of the new information.

They looked at the information on Paul's various emails and phone calls and considered what to do. Stamos and Kilgore thought this new information might justify stepping up attention to the issue, maybe bringing in more troops. Caputo, however, who knew the ways of journalism better than the other two, counseled caution. They already knew that Paul was digging, he said, all that has happened is that he is reaching out to people he knows for more information. The fact that he was doing so, Caputo said, didn't increase or decrease the likelihood that the alleged document from Makarov meant anything or required action.

Stamos nodded and, shooting a glance at Kilgore, said they would keep an eye on Paul's progress, but carefully; there was a limit to what could be done with regard to an American journalist without risking the wrath of the snowflakes and crybabies on Capitol Hill.

* * *

Meanwhile, things didn't seem to be going that swimmingly for Paul. It seemed that Oleg had gone truly underground, as they used to say, or off the grid, as they sometimes say now. None of his contacts had any idea where Oleg might be.

Using an alias email, Paul had written to Oleg's former institute in Moscow asking to contact him, with no result. Meanwhile, none of the congressional staffers, U.N. contacts, researchers, lobbyists, and more, the usual suspects for reporters digging for facts, Paul reached out to were of any help.

He mentioned this in a phone conversation with Gunther after he'd returned from Ocean City.

Paul could hear newsroom sounds through the phone; apparently Gunther was at his desk out on the floor, rather than in his office. He started to say something, then swore at someone who was trying to get his attention. Give me a minute, he said to Paul, I'll call you right back.

A minute later, Paul's Blackberry buzzed as Gunther called back.

"I have a thought," Gunther said. Paul heard the sound of him closing a door, then quiet; he was back in his office.

"What was the name of that woman in the U.S. Embassy in Moscow who did all that human rights stuff with the groups, you know, the Estonians, the Lithuanians, like that?"

Paul kicked himself for not thinking of her before.

"Rachel Horvath," he said, "Standoffish, but she was sort of a low-grade pain in the ass to the Sovs. She pretty much stayed just inside the line."

"She's here in Washington," Gunther said, "working for one of the big think tanks, probably the same kind of work, hold on."

After a moment, Gunther came back on the line. "I've actually talked to her a few times," he said, "I'll let her know you're looking for her." He then gave Paul her phone number and direct email address.

It sounded like someone had come into Gunther's office to nag him about something. He wished Paul good luck and hung up.

* * *

Paul had not known Rachel Horvath well in Moscow, she had had little use for reporters. She seemed to feel, with some justification, that she was doing some variation of God's work, setting up links with some of the groups Moscow was ignoring—or worse—be they intellectuals, artists, Jews, disgruntled Tatars, or Latvians. She seemed to have enough on her hands dealing with the Soviets on one hand and American anticommunist activists on the other, not to mention congressional staffers and various flavors of do-gooders that she didn't want to waste any time with reporters, whose coverage could attract undue Soviet government attention to her activities. Any time she wanted to say anything to the press, she did it through the press office. On such rare occasions, the press office would handle the reporters, possibly making her available for a brief, no-nonsense interview, with the information on "deep background," meaning it could not be attributed in any way—seemingly drawn from the reporter's own knowledge. Her name had never appeared in print, so far as anyone knew.

Then, surprisingly, Paul had run into her one day, seemingly by accident, on a slow day, when he had taken the afternoon off to stroll through Red Square, past the imposing walls of the Kremlin.

It was overcast that day, not the sort of afternoon for postcard photos of the bright sun shining on the onion domes of St. Basil's Cathedral. Nevertheless, the plaza was crowded, and the faithful of another sort were lined up at Lenin's mausoleum.

As Paul had walked across the plaza toward Lenin's tomb, a police officer had stopped him and gestured to his open bush jacket and motioned him to button it up. This was not a theme park, so show some respect seemed to be the message—either that or fuck you, American.

Chastened, Paul had stood at the tomb in a crowd of Russians, from elderly war veterans to giggly young girls with white bows in their hair, as three stone-faced guards in formation approached the entrance to the tomb, stiffly goose-stepping, with two equally stone-faced guards at either side of the entrance itself, facing each other.

Then, in a smooth, elegant ballet, two of the new guards and the guards at the entrance changed places, with what could only be described as clockwork precision. Then the two relieved guards goose-stepped away with the remaining member of the relief troika.

Paul never tired of watching the impressive ceremony and, as it ended, he turned to see Rachel Horvath behind him, also watching.

She had been standing there for a few moments, not realizing he had been in front of her. They exchanged cursory greetings and Paul left her, making his way back to the Metro.

As time went on after that, they would talk now and then when they ran into each other, establishing a cordial, if distant, relationship.

He was surprised, therefore, when she showed up, unannounced at his farewell dinner, as he was leaving his Moscow assignment. It was a dinner at a hotel restaurant, and she came up to him, seemingly by accident, as if she were there for something else and had noticed the crowd of reporters and their friends. She congratulated him on completing his assignment and said she had enjoyed reading his stories. She then turned and left the group gathered around Paul.

That was it. He had been in touch with her once or twice in the years after he left Moscow on stories. She had been little help, but had been friendly enough. Using the address Gunther had given him, he wrote an email, asking if they might meet.

* * *

A couple of days later, Paul waited in a clearing in the National Arbore-tum, a spacious park out New York Avenue, toward the Prince George's County suburbs, waiting for Rachel Horvath. She had responded right away to his email, probably because of Gunther's call, suggesting they meet here, away from the office.

He sat, as arranged, on a weathered bench, shaded by the spreading branches of a lacebark pine. Then, a few minutes late, she made her way from the muddy path that led up from the road.

It was a cloudy day in the middle of the week; there were few other visitors to the park.

Paul realized that she must now be close to 80, but she showed few signs of age as she strode over to the bench. She wore the requisite Wash-ington pantsuit, comfortable shoes, and a light quilted jacket. She looked around and, seeing no one, pulled a pack of cigarettes out and lit one, after offering one to Paul, who thanked her, but no.

After brief pleasantries about what each had been doing in recent years, she glanced at her watch and asked how she could help him.

Paul told her he was trying to find an old Soviet colleague who seemed to have dropped off the map.

She looked at him quizzically. "Why do you think I can help you," she asked, taking a drag of her cigarette.

"There's a connection to the Soviet—Russian—Far East," he said, "you had a lot of tentacles in out-of-the-way places," he said.

"Ah," she said, nodding. "You've checked wherever he's worked, all the usual places, your friend's employer, that sort of thing," she asked after a moment.

Paul nodded.

She thought for a moment.

"Is this person likely to be in trouble with the new Moscow rulers?" she asked dismissively. Her attitude toward Russian authorities appar-ently had not changed.

Paul thought for a moment.

"I don't know," he said, "possibly."

She hadn't asked him who he was looking for.

"Do you know if he—or she—is even still in Russia?" she asked.

No, Paul said, he didn't.

"Listen," she said, looking at her watch again, "this is the twenty-first century. If you want to find your old eighth-grade girlfriend, you can go to the internet and find out where she is, who she married, how many kids she has, and whether she was sentenced to life for killing one of them, all over a single cup of coffee. If you can't find him or her, then he or she is trying not to be found."

She stopped talking for a moment, studied the tip of her cigarette, and watched a bird land and then fly off. The silence was broken as a family of tourists passed through the clearing, parents and three young kids, all in baseball caps, with the children wearing shirts saying they were with the FBI. One, a son, about eight, turned around and stuck his tongue out at Rachel and Paul as the family made their way back down the path.

She looked at the path down which the tourists had vanished, then back at Paul.

"I don't think I can help you," she said.

Then, after a moment, "If you really can't find him, it may be that he's changed his name," she said.

"Why would he do that?" Paul asked. After all, his name was on the report.

"I have no idea," she replied.

She looked at her cigarette, realized it was about spent, and stubbed it out on a rock. She looked for a trash can, then gave him a tight smile before standing up to leave.

"Nice seeing you again, Paul," she said, "Good luck."

She carried the cigarette stub with her as she left.

* * *

Back home, thirty minutes later, Paul pondered his situation.

He knew that the end of the Cold War meant many of the people he was reaching out to had, like Paul himself, shifted their attention away from the now-former Soviet Union.

The 9/11 attacks had supplanted communist nukes as the most pressing existential threat in the minds of policymakers, the media, and all of their camp followers, so many drifted away from watching Moscow to probing the currents of terrorism. Others were now following economic developments in sub-Saharan Africa, China's bellicose actions in the South China Sea, or some other newly pressing crisis that would yield better jobs, more income from clients, or attention from editors, think tanks, and agency officials. The world is a target-rich environment for the policymaking and -watching class. Even the few who still followed Russia had drifted away from Oleg and his world. Oleg, one said, could be running a bar in Brighton Beach, for all he knew.

The Far East document, though, was not, Paul knew, written by someone who had retired to Brooklyn to measure out shots of vodka and his remaining days.

* * *

Not being able to find Oleg struck Paul as odd, as he told Elise that night over dinner. Oleg had apparently been willing to put his own name on an explosive document, and that document had slipped away from whatever closed channels Russians used for such documents. It had found its way into the hands of an obscure, junior U.S. congressional staffer.

"Maybe you should try a new tack," Elise said. She had heard some of the phone calls Paul had made to sources from the other side of the office where she had been working.

"I guess," he said. He was surprised at his inability to glean anything from his queries; he was even surprised he could not even find some sort of forwarding address or contact information from Moscow.

They turned it over more after dinner, reaching no conclusion. Eventually, Paul decided to put the matter aside for the night and went to bed. Something was nagging at him, but he couldn't figure out what it was. Something someone had said to him, but he just couldn't put his finger on it.

* * *

Back at the paper, the next afternoon, Guy Lynch had been beginning to wonder about the story. He hadn't spoken to Gunther since their meeting, and he couldn't get Caputo at the CIA to return his calls. He was also beginning to wonder again whether he should get more involved in this story and how to do so. He had concluded he should not kill it—it could be big and could help him get back where he belonged, which is to say the higher-profile, and higher-paying, television journalism world.

He looked at his watch. Maybe it was time to cut out for a drive.

He went downstairs and fired up the Porsche, thrilled again, as he always was when he gunned the engine and was rewarded with the iconic sound.

He took his favorite ride again, over to Virginia, up along the river, and across into Maryland, feeling his cares evaporate as he reveled in the feel of the car gripping the twisting roads near Great Falls and the cool, fresh breeze of the early evening.

He ended the drive, as he habitually did, again at Mr. Henry's.

Sitting on a bench seat and waiting for his hamburger, he noticed a young woman who had sat down at the next table after him, quietly talking on a cell phone.

She was about thirty or so, with dark hair to her shoulders. She had a little makeup on but nothing flashy, and plain, if manicured, nails. She wore a sort of work shirt-blue jeans combination that went well with the quiet jewelry she wore—a bracelet and watch, some sort of stone on a chain around her neck, like American Indian jewelry from out West. And, most importantly, no wedding ring.

She had taken some things out of her purse to retrieve her phone, and Guy noticed a key ring with a car key emblazoned with the Porsche emblem. When she got off the phone, he apologized for interrupting her but asked her if she drove a Porsche.

She looked at him for a moment and he braced himself to see if she would recognize him from his TV days, but no flash of recognition came, she just said yes, why do you ask—guardedly. She was attractive and probably spent more time than she wanted to fending off unwanted advances.

He fished out his own key to show her and, after a moment, she smiled, and that's how the conversation started. She was some sort of researcher in some obscure area who had come to Washington to work at the Georgetown University Library and was renting a basement apartment near the university. She had no idea who he was, which was surprisingly refreshing, and, even more refreshing, she loved to drive her sports car around on weekends, a second-hand Porsche Boxster, as it turned out. Sadly, she said, she didn't know the area or where she might find an enjoyable drive. He, as it happened, knew lots of places.

They talked late into the night and as she finished her final drink, she looked at her watch, gave him a thoughtful look, and said she had to go. She smiled as she got up and took out a small notebook and pen and wrote her number and name, Veronica Crevier, on it.

"Just don't ever call me Ronnie," she said before turning and leaving.

CHAPTER NINE

TEXAS

Paul, at home the next morning, was scanning another set of emails from contacts who, to their regret, could not help him with his search when his Blackberry buzzed. The number, with an unfamiliar 406 area code, was not one he recognized. When Paul clicked his phone one, he heard Yevgeny's thick Russian accent. He could hear the sounds of a cash register and someone ordering a pizza in the background. Another person was complaining loudly about the oven being too full. Yevgeny had, he said, a lead for Paul, although he was not optimistic.

"This guy may be some help, and he owes me a big favor," he said. Paul heard the pizza joint sounds growing fainter through the phone, replaced by traffic noises, and the sounds of shoes hitting the ground as if Yevgeny were walking away from his restaurant and toward a busy street as he talked.

"His name is Arkady Zoshchenko." Yevgeny then gave Paul an email address, which Paul wrote down on a scrap of paper.

"To be honest," Yevgeny continued, "this guy is your best bet, although he's sort of a *mudak*"—asshole.

"What kind of a *mudak*?" Paul asked. There were, after all, different flavors.

"The kind who did well after the Soviet Union ended. Really well."

"OK," Paul said, getting the picture, "I'll deal with him."

"He's in Texas, a big shot there. Houston."

"Got it."

"And very flashy."

"OK."

"And he hates reporters."

"Great," Paul said, "I can't wait."

He said goodbye and hung up.

Paul looked up the 406 area code on Google and found it covered Montana. Either Yevgeny had hopped a quick flight to Bozeman to make the call or he was using a burner.

Paul didn't bother to write the Montana phone number down. He knew Yevgeny would have already pulled the SIM card out and disposed of it and the phone. Paul erased the number from his phone's log.

Moscow rules.

* * *

"You know what," the guy, whose name was Bob something, said to Paul over a beer the next evening, "I just get tired of us getting kicked around by the rest of the world."

In a bar amid a suburban-looking strip of shopping centers, tire shops, and fast-food joints, Paul nodded understandingly. He'd looked the bar up on the internet and taken a cab from his Houston hotel. Bob was one of a half a dozen customers tonight. He was about forty, wearing a ball cap, a golf shirt, and jeans. He had been watching the three TVs tuned to sports events and one to Fox News behind the bar and halfheartedly flirting with the barmaid. The barmaid, maybe a few years younger, seemed to take it all in stride. It felt like a well-worn familiar game, particularly since they both wore wedding rings, and particularly since each asked about the other's spouse at one point.

Bob looked at Paul again. They both drank draft beers. The jukebox, or its twenty-first-century equivalent, played a medley of rock and country oldies—a little Bob Seger, a little Johnny Cash or Buck Owens now and then.

"Where'd you say you're from—Paul, right?"

"Right, Paul," Paul said. He took a sip of his beer. "I'm from D.C."

"Huh," Bob said, looking Paul over. Paul wore pretty much what he always wore when he was working if he didn't need to wear a tie—dark blue jeans, a quiet sport shirt, and a pair of Australian Chelsea boots he liked. They stuck out a little bit sometimes but drew no attention here in Texas, where boots were common.

"So," Bob continued, "what do you think about that?"

About America getting kicked around by the rest of the world, he meant.

"I hear that some," Paul said. He had gone out of his way to arrive in Houston a day before his meeting with Arkady Zoshchenko, the *mudak* who hated reporters, hoping to sniff the air a bit outside Washington, hear what people were saying beyond the Beltway.

"Yeah," Bob continued, "I just think we need some kind of new leadership."

"I don't know," he then said, glancing up at one of the sports shows above the bar.

Someone had put Merle Haggard on, singing *Workin' Man's Blues*.

"Maybe you like the president," Bob said, looking questioningly at Paul.

"He's got good and bad points," Paul said noncommittally. He was here to listen, not to talk.

Bob seemed to be holding back, listening to the music.

Haggard sang in the background about it being tough just getting by with nine kids and a wife.

"I mean," Bob said, "I guess it's great we have a," he stopped for a moment and looked at Paul, "an African American president," he glanced again at Paul, who nodded neutrally.

"But I just think we're not the country we were before," Bob said resignedly.

He looked down at Paul's wrist. Paul wore a battered Rolex of a style that had been common in the military during the Vietnam War.

"I guess you were probably in the military, you know what I mean," Bob said.

Paul shrugged.

They both listened for a moment to Merle Haggard.

Paul had always liked this song and tapped his foot in time with it.

Bob looked down and, noticing, soldiered on.

"I mean," he said, "I think we're just kind of apologizing for ourselves too much, I want to be proud to be an American again."

"Aren't you proud to be an American now?" Paul asked. He spoke carefully, not wishing to make it a challenge.

"Sure, of course, but it's hard," Bob said after a moment, "and I just don't trust Hillary or the Democrats to be tough."

"What about the Republicans?"

Bob looked at him.

"Are you a Republican?" he said.

Paul smiled. "I pretty much stay out of it, I'm retired," he lied.

"Well," Bob said, "I can't say I'm really impressed with them either." He looked sad as he said this.

He studied his beer for a moment. Haggard had finished.

"To be honest, they're a lot the same if you ask me, the Democrat and Republican parties. We need someone new," he said, "someone to really shake things up a bit, maybe."

He paused for a moment.

"Listen," he said after a sip of beer, "I'm doing OK, don't get me wrong, but I could be doing better."

He seemed to be collecting his thoughts, grateful for a stranger to unload a bit on.

"My father supported all of us on a factory salary," he said, "It wasn't easy, but he did it and we had a pretty good life, a nice life. Those days are over, and I don't see anyone telling me how they're going to bring them back."

He stopped talking, looking at his beer again.

"I don't think you're alone," Paul said, glancing up at the TVs, then back at his beer.

Bob thought for a moment before speaking again.

"It's not just me who feels this way," he said.

His eyes flitted around the bar briefly.

"And there's a lot of hotheads around," he then said. He glanced at Paul's watch again.

"You know," he said, "some of these guys have some pretty crazy ideas, and they have, you know, guns and training, like that. You wouldn't want to set them off."

"No," Paul said, "of course not."

"And, let me tell you," Bob said, "I don't think it would take a whole lot to do that."

Just as he said this there was the sound of an old-fashioned phone ringing and Bob pulled a flip phone out of his pocket. "Hi, honey," he said, holding a finger up to Paul, asking him to wait. Paul turned away. Someone had put on *Courtesy of the Red, White and Blue*, by Toby Keith. Paul listened to the song and concentrated on his beer as Bob talked with his wife. It looked like the conversation was going to go on for a while.

Paul signaled for the barmaid and paid his check, buying a drink for Bob.

He walked out of the bar to the street and flagged down a cab. He had the driver drop him a few blocks from his hotel so he could stretch his legs and think.

It was a warm night—what do you expect, this was Houston—and traffic was heavy as he walked by a series of anonymous hotels and office buildings. Mexican music blared out of a pickup stopped at an intersection and a pretty girl with olive skin and long, jet-black hair in the passenger seat flashed a dazzling smile at him as the light turned and the truck pulled away.

He stopped for a drink in the hotel bar before he went up to his room. There were about a dozen oil company workers there, executive types, most with wives, apparently back from a stint in Saudi Arabia. They all drank expensive cocktails and complained about the inconvenience of flying these days, even if it was business class, and something about the housing in the compound they lived in, then something having to do with one of the several golf courses and the hired Saudi help that took care of them. One of the wives lamented that she had to cover up more—even in the compound, *our* compound, if you could believe it, goddamn it—after one of the Saudi groundskeepers bitched about her skimpy Western attire. The others made sympathetic noises. Life was apparently pretty rough in the compound.

Paul listened for a while, finished his drink, then went up to his room and called Elise.

"How was the voice of the people," she asked.

"Not like the voices we hear in Washington," he answered.

They talked for a while, then he turned off the bedside light and lay down.

He slept uneasily.

CHAPTER TEN

SOVSEM CHUT'-CHUT'

Zoshchenko, *mudak* that he was, was, of course, late.

Fifteen minutes so far.

It was the next evening. Paul waited at a table in a pricey Houston restaurant. He glanced at his watch. He wore an expensive navy Italian suit, a white shirt, and an elegant subdued red paisley silk tie.

Zoshchenko had picked the place and emailed its particulars to Paul after Paul had asked to meet. Its clientele, according to the travel guide Paul had perused, was mainly high-level executives from the oil industry, which seemed to be true. A dozen or so long-legged young women were scattered among tonight's selection of executives, an archipelago of overdone make-up, clingy dresses, and stilettos. The young women would no doubt be introduced as nieces or something similar in the unlikely event that an introduction suddenly became necessary.

As Paul watched the entrance from his seat at a corner table, a middle-aged man with a shaved head and Slavic features entered and looked around before Paul caught his eye.

Arkady Zoshchenko was a decade or so younger than Paul and had well-fed the look of someone who had made the most of the gangster world Russia had become after the fall of the Soviet Union. Once an underpaid Soviet bureaucrat, he had seized the opportunities presented by the post-Soviet chaos to become a valued contact for American energy companies looking to exploit opportunities in the former Soviet Union or to otherwise make contacts among Russia's new ruling class.

He looked the part, just as Paul had expected.

His dove gray suit was exquisitely tailored with a sheen to it just short of sharkskin. His white shirt bore his monogram on his right cuff, just above a gold watch on an alligator strap that Paul figured had set him back fifteen or twenty grand. Wedding ring with diamonds in it, but no doubt now and then showed up here with a niece of his own. Probably a gold chain or two under the shirt, Paul figured. Class all the way.

Zoshchenko, approaching, cast an appraising glance over Paul, absorbing what he saw, before sitting down with no apology or other comment about his tardiness.

He ordered an expensive single-malt scotch on the rocks. A double. The waiter nodded and left for the drink.

"Yevgeny says you're OK," Zoshchenko said, turning to Paul. As his drink arrived, he took not one, but two cell phones out and placed them next to the drink. He was a very important man.

"What can I do for you?" he said, all businesslike. His eyes flicked to the phones as he talked. A man who at any minute might have more important business to deal with, one should understand.

Paul was, he said, trying to find an old Soviet friend and that Yevgeny had said Zoshchenko might be able to help.

Zoshchenko seemed to consider that for a moment. His drink arrived and he took a long pull.

"Could be," he said, dabbing his lips with a cocktail napkin, "that's not really my line of work." As he talked, Paul heard a rustle of fabric nearby and watched as Zoshchenko's eyes flitted to watch a statuesque brunette in a short black dress and stratospheric heels glide past. She smiled at Zoshchenko. Maybe she knew him.

His attention returned to Paul.

"Who is your friend?" he asked.

Paul told him.

"Oleg Makarov," Zoshchenko repeated the name, swirling his now half-empty drink around, the ice clattering against the heavy glass. "Who is he?"

"Just an old friend," Paul said.

Zoshchenko looked at him without speaking. This was obviously some bullshit, Paul heard him think. Paul hoped Zoshchenko really owed Yevgeny a favor.

For a moment Paul saw something threatening in Zoshchenko's eyes, but then it disappeared like the handle of a dagger revealed only momentarily.

"Can you tell me a little bit about him?" he asked, the dagger sheathed for the moment.

Paul told him where Oleg had worked in the old days and the basics of what he had done there.

Zoshchenko considered what Paul had told him, then took a sip of his drink.

"Yevgeny thinks I'm connected all over the world," he then said airily, "but really I'm just a businessman, I can't pick up a phone," he gestured helplessly at the two instruments on the table in front of him, "and find someone like some sort of movie spy." His eyes twinkled at the madness of the thought.

"Well," Paul said, suddenly unsure that this little meeting was going to be worth the trip, "you do know a lot of your fellow Russians around the world who might know something."

"Yes, I suppose I do," Zoshchenko said, distractedly. He looked around for a moment, seeming to think he had wasted his time.

"These guys don't really like to talk to reporters," Zoshchenko said, turning back to Paul and poking at the bowl of almonds on the table between them with a thick, manicured forefinger, "if you'll forgive my saying so."

"Of course," Paul said, forgiving his saying so.

"They're not so sophisticated, like us," he said, "you know, they are a little *nekul'turnyy*," uncultured, he said, smirking.

His eyes flitted to something behind Paul's back. Another temptress walking by, Paul assumed.

"I don't know how I could help you, though," Zoshchenko said.

Zoshchenko studied his glass, deciding whether to stick Paul for another twenty-five-dollar scotch. He apparently made up his mind, because he flagged the waiter down and ordered another one. When it arrived, Zoshchenko swirled it around in the glass a bit again before tasting it and nodding, satisfied. At least he was getting a couple of free drinks out of this meeting.

Something nagged again at the back of Paul's mind. Then, again noticing the monogram on Zoschenko's cuff, he remembered his conversation with Rachel Horvath in the park in Washington.

"It could be he changed his name," he said.

Zoshchenko looked up from his scotch.

"Yes?" he said, rubbing his chin. He looked at Paul; he had the look of someone trying to decide which among a group of live chickens to strangle for dinner.

"Why would he do that?" he asked.

"Oh, you know," Paul said, "sometimes people need to leave the past behind." He smiled conspiratorially at Zoshchenko.

Zoshchenko considered this new idea. He didn't smile.

"OK," he said abruptly, "Maybe I help you, you don't seem like the reporter assholes I know. Besides," he said, "Yevgeny likes you and I owe him."

Paul tried not to seem like the reporter assholes Zoshchenko knew.

"Tell me the name again," Zoshchenko said. Paul told him.

"OK," he said, "no promises, but I look around for you, maybe send you tip." He took a sip of his drink.

"Maybe help you *sovsem chut'-chut'*. You understand Russian, *da*? Is Russian. Means just a little bit," he said, "Why not?"

That seemed like the best Paul could hope for. He took out one of his business cards and slid it over. It bore Paul's name, a Washington phone number, and an email address, all in a simple, raised Copperplate Gothic font. Zoshchenko glanced down, then ignored it, shaking his head slightly.

After a moment, Paul took the card back, and on the back wrote an email address on a Swiss-based encrypted server and passed it back.

Zoshchenko looked at what Paul had written and nodded before slipping the card into his coat pocket.

"Tell Yevgeny we're even," he said as he got up to leave. He didn't offer to pay the check.

CHAPTER ELEVEN

DINNERS IN NICE RESTAURANTS

By the time Paul had returned from Texas, he was not optimistic about his prospects.

No one had been of much help so far. For the most part, his contacts had had no information or weren't around or weren't returning his calls or emails. He had reached an old stringer contact who had worked for the paper years before in Seoul and now lived in Tokyo, maintaining contacts in Northeast Asia. Stringers were a mixed lot though. This one had mostly done soft features or check-the-box pieces on North Korean escapees and that country's nuclear program, turning out to be no help. Now, he had wasted a couple of days, not to mention airfare and money for a hotel stay and overpriced drinks, for a conversation with Zoshchenko, who struck Paul as a slippery snake who couldn't be trusted.

He grew increasingly uneasy. He wasn't sure, but he thought he was seeing the same car or the same driver over and over. He didn't know if he was actually seeing anything or being paranoid. One or two Hispanic nannies seemed to linger in front of his house for unreasonably long times as they took their toddler charges to the nearby dog park, and there seemed to be something of an uptick in young kids making their way along the street in the evenings. One night, coming home from the dry cleaners he noted a car pull up across the street from his house. He stopped and watched; no one got in or out for fifteen minutes. Not wishing to draw any attention to himself, he walked back the way he had come, circling back from the other direction. The car was still there.

The events of the next few days didn't allay his nervousness but did yield progress.

Sitting at his desk, mulling over what to do next, Paul saw on his screen that he had received an email from Zoshchenko using his Swiss email account. Opening the encrypted message, he discovered it simply contained a name, "René Micheletti," the word "Rome," and the admonition "Don't use my name." There was no identification of who René Micheletti was. It wasn't clear what to do with the name.

Paul heard Elise come in behind him and sit at her desk on the other side of the room. She heard him tapping his fingers on the desk in frustration. She came up behind him and looked over his shoulder.

She said nothing for a moment.

"I know that name," she then said softly. She went back to her desk.

He heard her clicking on her keyboard, then silence for a few moments.

"Can't find him on Google," she said.

More clicking.

Then, "Huh." Whatever she meant by that.

More clicking. Then silence. Then he heard her pick up her phone and talk quietly into it for a few moments. He turned so he could see her.

"No," she said after listening for a few moments, "René. With an accent on the e."

"I don't know either," she continued, "but it sounds familiar, doesn't it?"

Pause.

"Oh, right, of course," she said, "how could I forget?" She shot a look over her shoulder at Paul as she continued listening.

"Yes, it's for something Paul's working on," she said into the phone. Another pause. "Come on, this isn't sensitive if his name came out in court papers and the press."

Pause.

"Well, OK," she said, "a blog, that's the press these days, even if no one reads it."

Longer pause.

"No shit."

Pause.

"I see. No shit."

Pause.

"Well, I could, if I put some things off."

Longer pause.

"OK, that sounds good, let's make it seven."

Pause.

"No, on us." Then, "On Paul, and don't skimp on the wine or the dessert."

She clicked the phone off and turned to Paul.

"Man, you picked a humdinger," she said.

"What do you mean?" he asked.

"You'll find out, but it's going to cost you."

"What's that supposed to mean?"

"You're buying dinner tonight for Frank and me."

Frank Lang was a Commerce Department investigator Elise had worked with for years and always spoken highly of. Paul detested him.

Frank Lang was a runty-looking guy who had somehow become an investigator in Elise's shop. He used the power and authority of the badge to compensate, Paul thought, for years of being pushed around, and lorded that power and authority over any target he deemed appropriate. Plus, he was a loudmouth and a blowhard.

Paul looked at Elise for a moment. "OK," he said. He couldn't figure out how Elise had become friends with this asshole.

"And it's going to be an expensive one, so don't bitch," she said. "It will be worth it," she added.

"OK."

"And the wife."

"Alright already." Christ. The wife too. She was as bad as Frank, in her own way. This was going to be a long night.

* * *

That night, Paul and Elise met Frank Lang and his wife, Catherine, a shy woman of no discernible personality at a restaurant in Arlington, Virginia. If Paul remembered correctly, she ran some sort of secondhand store that catered to other comfortable bourgeois wives looking to either unload some no longer used clothing or add a little retro charm to their wardrobes.

It was the middle of the week, and they had the place almost completely to themselves. Nevertheless, they were seated at a corner table, away from the few other customers. Frank wore a golf shirt and khakis and Catherine wore a quiet navy pantsuit. They looked like any other middle-aged couple in the solidly middle-class area of the suburb.

As they sat down, Frank, Paul could see, was already easing into his James Bond persona, realizing he held all the cards this evening. He was going on to Elise about some case he was working on, throwing in a lot of jargon. Catherine was silently studying her untouched wine spritzer.

Paul and Elise ordered drinks and perused the menu while Frank prattled on.

After they ordered—eventually—the four made small talk. Frank pretty much ran the conversation with plenty of name-dropping and references to how important he was. Paul tried to stay quiet, fighting the urge to stalk out and take the Metro home. After the drinks had arrived and the waiter had been dispatched with their orders, Frank waited for a moment before he spoke again. Paul didn't know whether he paused to ensure they wouldn't be overheard or for dramatic effect. It turned out, though, that he was glad he hadn't left.

"You really picked a winner with your pal René," Frank said, his mien abruptly changing. He seemed suddenly serious, no bullshit about him. Paul had never seen his professional persona and was struck by the metamorphosis, like a turtle suddenly emerging from his shell. Frank waited to see if Paul responded, which he didn't.

"We know this guy," Frank then said. His eyes flitted between Paul and Elise. Catherine sat quietly, now sipping her drink, as Frank continued.

"He's sort of the king of high-end fake IDs, at least in Europe," Frank said. "If you want to lose yourself, this is the guy to go to." He took a pull on his drink, a gin and tonic, adding, "If you know where to find him and can pay the tariff."

"He's hard to find?" Paul asked.

"Yes, he's the real deal and he doesn't need to advertise.

"Micheletti," he continued, still all business, "is in a pretty rarified world. The people who come to him are people who need to disappear fast because they're on the run from people who are looking for them, and those people looking for them are not some cheap private dick with a storefront office next to Nancy's Nails. Micheletti's clients are on the run from drug cartels, or trafficking gangs, or people who stole something big, or are holding someone for ransom, or are moving guns or warheads, or killed somebody important, and they'll do it again."

Another sip of the drink. He seemed submerged in his story, which he recounted without emotion. Like an intelligence report in a department meeting, Paul thought.

"Or they're on the run from people that work for agencies like the one I work for," he said. Anyone else might have smiled at this point. Frank, in his new persona, didn't. He looked at Paul to make sure he was paying attention. He was.

"Just to give you an idea," Frank said, "there was this big-time spook—by which I mean an intelligence guy—from one of your poorer developing countries I don't want to name, who, along with his boss, had fallen out of favor with the country's top dog. He and his boss knew that falling out of favor with the top dog meant their estimated life expectancy had taken a dive. A big one. He and the boss headed out of Dodge, but his boss ended up shot in the head three days later in his Dubai hotel room. The boss had brought a new friend home for the evening, and they plugged her too—just bad luck on her part. It was very messy. Fortunately, our guy had had the foresight to grab some walking-around money before he hit the road. He quietly booked unofficial passage on a cargo ship bound for Europe and ultimately made his way to Rome and Micheletti, who was known in his circles. Micheletti was able to set him up and he now lives safely under a new name in Europe, although he keeps a gun or two under his pillow just in case."

He looked at Elise before continuing.

"We know him," he nodded at Elise, "because his name came up in a matter we were working on."

He paused to see if there was any reaction.

"I see," Paul said. He looked at Elise, who said nothing. She was listening to the story.

"The case," Frank continued when he got no further feedback from Paul, "involved some Russians living in London who decided to finance their retirement by selling," he stopped, choosing his words, before continuing, "a piece of equipment to some Middle Easterners with aims contrary to what one would call the interests of the United States."

"Frank, I—" Elise started to interrupt.

"No," he cut in, after a moment, "as you said, it's been in the press already—on a blog, whatever. Besides, I'll skip over the juiciest details."

"OK," Elise said. She looked wary.

The waiter came with their appetizers.

"Besides," Frank said, scanning the wine list and asking the waiter for one of the better bottles, one James Bond would pick, "we're screwing Paul out of a lot of money tonight and he should get good information out of the deal."

"OK," Elise said, contemplating her food.

"So, anyway," Frank resumed, "what happened was these guys decided that some colleagues back home in Moscow who had helped them, were demanding too big a cut." He studied his drink for a moment.

"You know," he said thoughtfully, "if they hadn't been so fucking greedy, they would have made it."

He seemed lost in thought at the implications of what he had just said.

"So, René Micheletti?" Paul said, hoping to return to the matter at hand.

Frank looked at Paul sharply.

"Right," he said, coming back to the present.

"These guys," he resumed, "were stupid enough to think they'd pull one over on their Moscow pals, but not stupid enough to think they had a prayer of getting away with it once the Moscow pals found out about it if they didn't take measures. They were some pretty heavy hitters, these Moscow guys."

"So they needed new identities," Paul said.

"Correct," Frank said, "and they needed good ones.

"Somehow," he said, "they found out about René Micheletti."

"And they led you to him?" Paul asked.

"No," Frank said, actually smiling this time, "that's the funny part, he led us to them, in a backassward kind of way. We, or one of our sister agencies, in," he stopped to look at Elise, who shook her head, "well, in Europe somewhere, had tapped his comms and then tipped us off that Micheletti was dealing with them."

"The Europeans knew you were looking for the London Russians?" Paul asked.

"Yes," Frank said, "I had a liaison relationship with the cooperating service." He was obviously happy to show what a big shot he was and use spy talk terms like "liaison relationship" and "cooperating service." Guy would have felt the same way, although Frank wasn't a dolt like Guy. At least not the same kind of dolt.

"So that's how your outfit knew about Micheletti?" Paul asked.

"No," he said, "that is how Elise and I came to personally know and deal with Micheletti."

"I see," Paul said, "but how does that help us?"

There was a pause in the conversation while the waiter arrived with the main dishes, then retreated.

"Well, this is where it gets kind of, what you call, classified," he said as they all began to eat. He looked at Elise. She looked back at him for a minute and then shrugged.

"Might as well," she said, "it's not going to do any harm now."

Frank let a few seconds tick by, for effect, Paul figured, then resumed his narrative.

"The problem," he said, "was that the Moscow heavies knew that these dumbasses would make a run for it, and the heavies eventually figured out that the dumbasses had gone to Micheletti. By that point, though, Micheletti had already handed the dumbasses new IDs, so the heavies were now after Micheletti to get him to rat out their new identities, which put him in an uncomfortable spot, naturally.

"We found this out through, uh, technical means," Frank said, glancing at Paul for emphasis, "which gave us an opportunity.

"We reached out to let the heavies know, obliquely, that they would have some real problems if they went after Micheletti. Then we had a little talk with Micheletti and earned his undying gratitude because he knew what would have happened if the Moscow heavies had gotten to him."

"Undying might be a little strong," Elise said.

Frank looked at her for a moment.

"Well, he's still apparently around," he said.

Frank paused the story as one of the other couples in the restaurant came over to admire the French prints on the wall. They had apparently spent some time in Paris and had an animated discussion about whether they had seen similar prints on their visit. Frank, Katherine, Paul, and

Elise concentrated on their meals silently while they waited for them to leave.

When they had left, Frank contemplated his drink for a moment before resuming his story.

"Micheletti told us how to find the dumbasses, though, so we came out ahead," he said as if there had been no interruption.

No one spoke for a few seconds.

"What happened to the dumbasses?" Paul asked finally.

The waiter came by, cleared the dinner dishes, and dropped a dessert menu in the center of the table.

"The heavies actually somehow got to them before we did," Frank responded when the waiter was safely gone.

"We heard they beat the shit out of them and buried them outside of Rome," Frank said, "while they were still breathing," he added as he studied the menu. Mister Cool.

"Scared the shit out of Micheletti, though," he said after a moment, "but he knows we saved his ass."

He signaled the waiter.

The waiter came over and took dessert orders. Frank ordered an Armagnac. Jesus, Paul thought.

"Anyway," Frank continued once the waiter left, "I assume you're looking for someone who has disappeared."

Paul nodded.

"OK," Frank said, without pressing the point, "if someone sent you to Micheletti, he probably helped with some papers."

"Do you know how we could find him?" Paul asked.

"Yes."

The waiter came over with desserts and Frank's Armagnac. Anyone else want anything, Frank asked generously. When no one did, the waiter handed a leather folder with the bill to him. Frank shook his head and pointed with his chin toward Paul. The waiter nodded and left the folder at Paul's place as he left.

"OK, he won't want to talk to a stranger on the phone," Frank said. He pulled a Commerce Department business card out of his pocket, wrote something on the back with a cheap U.S. government ballpoint, and passed it to Paul.

"I hope you don't mind going to Rome," he said.

Paul took the card. It wasn't like most Commerce business cards. It said Office of Export Enforcement prominently, and instead of the standard engraved U.S. seal in the corner there was a larger gold Commerce special agent badge. On the back, Frank had written and signed a note to Micheletti asking him to help Paul.

"I can go tomorrow," Paul said, he looked at his watch, checking the date, and then turned to Elise. "I'll call you from there and let you know when I'm coming back," he said.

Elise and Frank exchanged looks.

"I think I'd better come with you," she said.

Paul looked at her.

"Yes," Frank said, "I think that's a good idea."

"Why?" Paul said.

"I think you'll find things go more smoothly that way," Frank said. Then he pulled a pocket notebook from his jacket and wrote something on a sheet, which he passed to Paul. It was an encrypted email address like the one Paul used.

"Try him here when you get to Rome," Frank said. "He'll be expecting you in a couple of days."

"By the way," Paul said, "what happened to the equipment the Russians were selling?"

Frank looked at Elise, who nodded her head slightly.

"Never got delivered," Frank said. He stopped for a moment and then continued.

"Must have fallen off the truck," he said.

His moment of glory over, he retreated into his shell.

Paul looked at Elise, then reached for the check to pay it.

* * *

Frankly, things weren't going so well for Guy in the taking over the Russia story department. He'd tried to figure out how to worm his way in, but Gunther Schroeder was a tough customer and Guy knew he'd better be fully loaded to take him on. Gunther didn't give a shit about Guy's big-time TV history. Guy decided to call Veronica.

Disappointingly, she didn't recognize his voice when she answered the phone, but at least she didn't ask, "Guy who?" He said he was thinking about taking off early and going on a ride out through Maryland and wondered whether she would like to join him for dinner and an enjoyable drive. She seemed to think about it a minute too long but agreed. She surprised him pleasantly by asking him to meet her at her basement apartment off MacArthur Boulevard and she would follow him. He was disappointed that she didn't want to ride with him, but after a moment said he hoped she could keep up with him. There was a pause before she answered, yes, she hoped so too. He couldn't tell if she was offended or not.

He was pleasantly surprised when he got to her address. If there was any doubt that she was serious about driving, that disappeared immediately. She leaned against her car, which was a pristine gunmetal grey and without a speck or a scratch on its polished surface. She had also, he noticed, ditched her neo-hippie look from before in favor of a longish khaki skirt and linen blouse. She kissed him on the cheek, which he interpreted to imply possible future intimacy if he played his cards right, before getting into her car and starting it up. She motioned for him to lead, and he headed back to MacArthur toward the Maryland line.

He took it easy as he headed out of the city and toward Great Falls but began to step on the gas a bit as the traffic eased off and as the road became curvier. He noticed, though, in his rear-view mirror that she kept up with him and, as they moved further afield, she drove like a pro—two hands on the wheel at ten and two o'clock, shifting up and down at the right points, hugging the inside on turns, easing off on the straight stretches. He guessed that, like him, she might not have the radio on but might be just enjoying the drive and the melody of the German car engine.

Eventually, as he had planned, they ended up on a somewhat rural road near an Italian restaurant he knew. He pulled into the restaurant, parked, and got out of the car, listening to the engine ticking as she pulled up next to him, killed her own engine, and got out. She had a slight smile on her face as she gazed at the restaurant.

She brushed some hair out of her face.

"Looks like a good place to bring chicks," she said, walking toward the door.

He was a little taken aback by that, but followed her, reaching out at the last moment to open the door for her.

The place was almost empty, as he'd hoped it would be, so they were able to order drinks as soon as they sat down. Veronica left for a moment but came back shortly. Guy wasn't sure, but he thought she might have put new makeup on. A pleasant scent he hadn't noticed before wafted toward him as she sat down.

"It is," he said.

"Excuse me?"

"A good place to bring chicks," he said. He'd meant it as a joke but wasn't sure it worked. She didn't look like she was laughing, but she smiled when her drink arrived, so he figured he was on, or still on, solid ice. Maybe.

"How is your research going?" he asked when they were settled. Better change the subject, he thought. All he remembered was that she was doing some sort of research. He couldn't remember what it was even about.

"Oh, fine," she said, "I've reached an obstacle. You don't know anything about links between the abolitionist movement, temperance, and the suffragists, do you?"

Uh, no, actually, he didn't. He felt the ice under his feet growing thinner.

"I didn't think so," she said. She watched him, amused.

"What about your work?" she asked after a long moment of silence.

It started slowly. At first, he tried to buffalo her with the usual generalities about the news business and working in the Capital of the Western World, but she seemed sincerely interested in his work. When he mentioned that he had been in TV, she raised her eyebrows in interest but seemed more interested in the actual business of news and reporting. Which was unusual. In his experience, his broadcast work usually drew more interest than the nuts and bolts of reporting, but it was enjoyable to talk about it, and it was in his interest to spur her interest.

She continued to probe about the news business. An old friend from college, it seemed, worked for a newspaper in Oregon or Idaho or somewhere, so it was interesting for her to hear about it from the inside, she said. She didn't get much of a chance to talk with the old friend. Guy made some sort of throwaway comment about how real journalism really lived on in the traditional local newspapers and their authentic old-school reporting, although, honestly, he thought he would rather slit his throat than cover school board meetings for some bumpkin rag.

At some point, he somehow drifted to the Oleg Makarov story. He felt, of course, that he could not discuss the meat of the story with her, and she didn't press. He did, however, talk in roundabout terms about an important story some members of what he described as "my team" were working on. She seemed impressed by it, although, she said, it was a little outside her experience.

They finished their meals, and she looked at her watch and said she had to get back in, could he show her the way home.

The two sports cars meandered their way back into the city, more carefully now that they had had a couple of drinks and Guy pulled up in front of her place.

She got out of her car and came up to his side of his car just as he was optimistically reaching to open his own door. She placed a restraining hand on his shoulder.

"This has been fun," she said, "why don't we have a real date this weekend?"

With that, she gave him a kiss and went into her apartment.

Guy watched through the window as he saw a light go on inside, then switch off. After a moment, he shifted into first and headed home.

CHAPTER TWELVE

IVO JEZEK

Rome

Elise seemed preoccupied with something as she and Paul made their way down Via Santa Melania through a quiet residential neighborhood toward Via Marmorata.

It was evening, two days later and they had arrived in Rome earlier that day, then taken a taxi to their hotel off this quiet street. Once through the double gates, a pleasant courtyard and elegantly subdued reception area revealed themselves. Their room had been spacious and comfortable enough for a refreshing nap and showers to help alleviate jetlag before a quick dinner nearby.

Now, as they walked, Elise seemed lost in thought. They turned down a side street after a few blocks on Via Marmorata. They found the quiet restaurant Micheletti had specified, a neighborhood place on a square, apparently not popular—at least tonight—with tourists.

They were not sure what to expect; Paul had emailed Micheletti on his encrypted email address and simply received instructions to meet at this restaurant. There was, however, no doubt when he walked in the door.

Micheletti was in his forties, deeply tanned, and had black hair with a little silver showing. He had a soldier's build—fit, but not health-club fit—and wore a dark blue suit and a black open-necked shirt that might have been silk.

After scanning the room quickly, he came over to their table and sat down with Paul and Elise wordlessly. He said something to the waiter and, after consulting his watch, murmured to him in quick Italian.

He looked at Paul and Elise. Then back at Elise. Paul thought he was surprised to see two people there, but maybe there was something more. He couldn't put his finger on it.

"So," he said to Paul as the waiter brought what looked like grappa, "you are a friend of my friend in Washington?"

As the waiter left, Micheletti looked at Paul expectantly. It took Paul a moment to realize what he was asking for. He looked at Elise. She fished Frank's business card out of her purse and slid it across the table, keeping it covered with her hand until it was in front of Micheletti. Like a bribe.

Micheletti placed his own hand over the card and then looked at it briefly before turning it over to read the note from Frank.

He looked at Elise for a moment before his eyes flicked over to Paul.

"You are not the police," he said. He glanced for a moment at the card which sat face-up on the table, its badge emblem showing.

"No," Paul said.

"I don't need the trouble," Micheletti said. He peered again at Elise for a moment. His eyes were slightly hooded.

"Tell me your name," he said to her. She told him. He looked at her again for another thirty seconds, glanced at Frank's card, still on the table, then back at Elise.

"With Frank Lang, I think," he said finally, "before."

Elise said nothing.

Micheletti looked at her for another moment, uncertainly, as if trying to puzzle this situation out, then looked back at Paul.

"You I don't know," he said. He looked at the card again. "You are also with Lang?"

"He's with me," Elise said.

Micheletti looked back at her, then back at Paul.

"And you are doing what?" he asked. Directing the question to Paul. Testily. He looked like a man who had realized he had walked into the wrong hotel room.

"I'm helping a friend," Paul said.

"What kind of friend?"

"A journalist."

"*Un giornalista.*"

"Yes."

Micheletti put his hands on the table as if to leave but Elise motioned him to stay where he was. Her gesture was barely visible but had the desired effect.

"Let's not forget," she said so quietly that Micheletti couldn't help but hear her, "what good friends Frank and I were to you a few years ago."

She and Micheletti stared at each other for a moment, neither blinking.

"Yes, OK," he said after he seemed to have enough of the staring contest, "but this is it."

Elise didn't say anything.

Micheletti pulled out a slim leather notebook and a Montblanc pen. "Who are you looking for?"

"A Russian," Paul said, "from Soviet days."

Micheletti turned to Paul and knitted his brows.

"I deal with a lot of Russians," he said, "I don't want to fuck around with them—staying on their good side is good for business, getting on their bad side is not." He glanced at Elise.

Paul nodded. Micheletti seemed to be hoping for more of a reaction from Paul or Elise. When none came, he opened the notebook and uncapped the pen.

"Name?" he asked, then quickly, "I mean his original name." Not a crack of a smile at what could have been a little joke under other circumstances.

"Oleg Makarov," Paul said. He spelled it out using English letters.

"Patronymic?" Micheletti asked.

Paul thought Micheletti was showing off a bit here, it seemed unlikely that Micheletti had so many clients named Oleg Makarov that he needed a middle name to figure out which one Paul was asking about.

"Borisovich," Paul said.

"Oleg Borisovich Makarov," Micheletti repeated, writing in his notebook. "Doesn't ring a bell. Oligarch?"

"No," Paul said, "far from it." He stopped, realizing that he really didn't know what Oleg had been doing. He might have won a piece of the post-Soviet jackpot. Probably not, though.

"He was an academic."

"Ah, OK," Micheletti said, snapping his notebook shut and recapping the pen before putting them both in an inside pocket.

"Let me check my records, I may be able to help, but I'm not optimistic."

"Why is that?" Elise asked suspiciously. Micheletti looked at her, then shrugged.

"I don't deal with *marmaglia*, the rabble, here, do you understand?"

Elise nodded. Micheletti was all business now, Paul realized he was showing the persona customers were allowed to see.

"My clients need a solid product that will survive real scrutiny," he continued. "You know," he said, "like Bourne's bank box." It took Paul and Elise a moment to realize this time he actually was making a joke; the reference was to a spy movie. He seemed to be trying to ease the tension in the conversation.

"I am not well-known to the general public," Micheletti said, "so this sort of person would not likely come to me.

"At the same time, though," he continued, "if you two have been referred to me, someone thinks your Oleg Borisovich Makarov is doing business with me."

Elise seemed to turn this over in her mind.

"How would someone like Oleg even know about you?" she asked. "I'm not sure he would have been traveling in the right circles."

"Maybe, maybe not," Micheletti said, "Some of the Russian *bogema*—bohemians you would say, the artistic types—maybe are on the edge, close to black-market trading, drugs, that sort of thing, he could have found me that way."

"I see," Paul said. He looked at Elise. He wasn't sure he would have thought of Oleg as hanging out with the *bogema* crowd, but who could say?

"I'll check for you," Micheletti said. He glanced at his watch again.

It seemed there was nothing left to say. Micheletti finished his drink and said he would call or email Paul as soon as he knew something. He left the check with Paul and Elise. It occurred to Paul that were he a customer he might not be comfortable with Micheletti keeping records, but, then again, he wasn't a customer.

After Micheletti left, Paul and Elise walked more or less toward their hotel. The only sound was of their own footsteps, as they saw no other pedestrians. Elise looked lost in thought.

After forty-five minutes or so, Paul received an encrypted email from Micheletti. "Czech passport in the name of 'Ivo Jezek,'" it said.

A photo was attached to the email. Paul opened it, unsure of who he was looking at, before realizing it was a photo of an altered, older Oleg. He certainly didn't look like the Oleg that Paul remembered.

"Thanks for the drink, our business is done," the email said. Paul showed his Blackberry to Elise, who smiled and nodded.

They walked up the Via Santa Melania toward their hotel.

"I guess I put the fear of Uncle Sam into him," she said distractedly. Paul looked over as she spoke. She seemed preoccupied with something.

They walked up the hill, through the elegant residential neighborhood. The curbs were lined with well-maintained European cars, the lawns and bushes were neatly trimmed, and rooms that were visible from the street looked comfortably furnished, with expensive furniture and bookshelves full of neatly arranged books. Paintings and framed art posters were visible now and then.

They entered the hotel through its gates and, as they made their way along the stone courtyard, Paul gestured toward a door leading to a lounge where they could have a nightcap.

Elise hesitated for a moment.

"Why don't you go ahead and order, I'll just be a moment," she said. She gave Paul a reassuring smile.

He nodded and went into the lounge. There were a few tables, but the room was empty other than a bartender looking at a magazine. Paul ordered two drinks. He brought them over to the table and waited for Elise.

Elise joined him ten minutes later. She sat down but studied the table before speaking and looking at Paul.

"We need to take a little side trip tomorrow," she said.

"Really," Paul asked, "where?"

"A museum," she said.

Paul tried to probe further but Elise was not in a talkative mood. They finished their drinks and retired to their room.

The next morning, over breakfast, Elise told Paul they needed to go to the Galleria Borghese. This was pleasant news for Paul; he enjoyed the museum with its collection of Caravaggios, Titians, and Berninis, and had managed to see Bernini's *Apollo and Daphne* on each of several visits to Rome over the years.

After breakfast, they took a cab in the rain to the gallery. Elise continued to seem to be preoccupied on the ride over. Paul tried to engage her in conversation a few times to no avail. He commented on the rain, pointed out tourists on their way to the Colosseum and a restaurant they had visited in the past. Nothing; she nodded silently, seemingly in a world of her own as she watched the traffic going by.

Entering the museum, she went to an information desk and spoke to one of the attendants, showing her passport. After a brief conversation with Elise, the attendant checked something on the computer screen in front of her and then gestured for Paul and Elise to follow her.

Ignoring the long lines, they made their way through the museum to a room crowded with tourists gazing at the Bernini statue. As Paul and Elise watched, the crowd thinned out as it moved to an adjacent room. An Italian man, clearly not a tourist, remained.

Tall and thin, he was immaculately dressed in a dark suit, white shirt, silk tie, and flawlessly polished expensive dress shoes. He had a head of thick, well-trimmed hair without a strand out of place. As he approached Paul and Elise he had a faintly military bearing.

He looked at Elise, then Paul, then Elise again, raising his eyebrows slightly.

"Paul," Elise said, "this is Colonel Adriano Serino. He's with—" she stopped for a moment when Colonel Serino glanced at her, "the Italian government. We worked on a case together some years back."

"Adriano," she said, turning to the colonel, "this is my husband, Paul."

Serino bowed stiffly as he shook Paul's hand with a frosty smile.

"Pleased to meet you," he said with only a slight Italian accent, as if he had spent a lot of time in America or with Americans. His eyes lingered on Paul for a moment before he turned to Elise.

"You can trust Paul," Elise said after a minute. Serino looked dubious, then turned back to Elise.

"OK," he said. He motioned them to follow him.

They passed through several exhibition rooms, then found themselves in a corridor away from the crowds of tourists. Paul and Elise followed Serino down the corridor. As they approached a door with an electronic lock, Serino pulled a card key out of his jacket pocket and opened the door to let them pass.

Passing through, Paul and Elise found themselves in a small room with a table and four chairs. A window looked out on the garden outside. A bottle of mineral water and glasses were on the table, as well as three demitasses of coffee, still hot.

Serino closed the door behind them and motioned Paul and Elise to the seats. He sat and took a sip of one of the espressos before speaking.

"You have a name," he said. A statement, not a question.

"Yes," Elise said. She fished a slip of paper out of her purse and handed it to him.

Paul poured water for himself and Elise and looked at Serino, who was ignoring him.

Serino looked at the paper Elise had given him for a moment and then put it in his pocket.

He started to say something in Italian, momentarily forgetting the circumstances before returning to English. "This is a little unorthodox," he said, looking at Paul.

Elise paused for a moment, then looked at Serino.

"It's only a name, Adriano," she said—a little petulantly, Paul thought—"we're not asking for much. For old times' sake."

Serino seemed to think it over for a moment. He and Elise watched each other.

"OK," he said finally. "For old times' sake."

He looked out the window. The rain had stopped and the sun had come out, leaving the gardens verdant. Just the kind of place for a relaxing walk, Paul thought.

"You're out?" Serino asked. Elise nodded.

"And you, Paul," he started to ask, turning toward Paul, "are you—"

"He's on vacation with me," Elise said, cutting him off.

Serino seemed to take that in. Then he gave a satisfied nod and stood.

"OK, I'll see what I can do," he said, "for old times' sake."

Paul and Elise followed him out into the corridor and then the main entrance.

In the street, an official-looking car waited at the curb, blinkers flashing and engine running.

Serino looked at Elise again.

"Nice seeing you again," he said. He turned to Paul. "Very nice to have met you," he said, mustering—Paul thought—as little enthusiasm as was humanly possible. Without further conversation, he got into the waiting car, which pulled into the traffic immediately and disappeared.

After a moment, Paul looked for a cab.

"You didn't give him both names?" he asked, as a passing Fiat cab ignored them.

"No, just the new alias," Elise said. She hooked her arm in his, suddenly relaxed. She was clearly relieved that the meeting with Serino was over.

"Adriano is a good guy," she said, "but if we give him both names, he'll quickly figure out that they're the same person, which we don't want."

Paul nodded.

"We don't want a bunch of spooks muddying the water for us," she said, as a cab swerved to pick them up.

* * *

The cables that had been sent out from Langley to allied intelligence services had gone to all the places that any follower of the news or spy novels would expect, Italy among them.

Serino thought about Elise's request as he rode back to his office. The request had been, as he had said, a little irregular, something maybe he should report up the chain. No, he then thought, she had been helpful in the past. Why stir up trouble?

He was a little concerned about the husband, but he trusted Elise. She seemed to think he could keep his mouth shut, so, he thought, he should probably not worry about him. Besides, he realized, what did he care? Whatever this was Elise's business, not his.

He looked at the note Elise had passed him and what was written on it. "Ivo Jezek, Czech." The name meant nothing to him.

As his car pulled to the curb, he put the note back in his pocket.

He entered the building showing his pass and went through the main security checkpoint. He then went to his office in an even more secure area of the building. Once seated at his desk with another cup of coffee, he turned on one of his secure computers and read through the mountain of overnight messages. The CIA had sent queries on a number of targets.

He scanned through them quickly, noticing that one asked about a Russian name, Oleg Borisovich Makarov, which he had heard mentioned in a briefing a day or so earlier but otherwise, it meant nothing to him.

He was making his way through the rest of the messages when he remembered the Czech name Elise had wanted him to check.

He looked at his watch. He was late for a meeting, and he thought maybe he could put it off. On second thought, why not just get it over with.

He went into another system and punched in Ivo Jezek's name. Within ten seconds he was rewarded with a ping.

CHAPTER THIRTEEN

HEADING EAST

Oleg Makarov, now officially Ivo Jezek, looked at his plate, examined his tacos, and took a sip of beer. He had never eaten Mexican food before. The restaurant was empty and the pretty waitress, sharing a plate of some sort of rice dish with the bartender, was starting to look at Oleg oddly. Time to dig in, he told himself. He didn't need to attract undue attention.

It had all started after Oleg had gone to that goddamned party and met that guy who wouldn't shut up.

He didn't want to think about it.

It was immediately clear afterward what he had to do, though, starting with disappearing, and doing so under a new name. As Micheletti himself had surmised, Oleg had reached out to an unorthodox contact and ultimately gotten Micheletti's name and an email address.

Going to Micheletti had seemed to be a better idea than taking his chances in the booming passport market wrought by the flood of refugees, migrants, and terrorists crisscrossing Europe these days. The last thing he wanted was to get arrested because of some shitty cut-rate document or to end up with a knife in his gut in an alley from a thug preying on the desperate stateless. Besides, his needs were more ambitious than those of the throngs of war refugees just trying to get away.

Once he'd been in touch with Micheletti, Oleg arranged for what he told his colleagues in Moscow was a research trip to Italy, telling them he would also be taking some time off. On his first night in Rome, he stayed in a hotel under his own name, which felt like a risk but really wasn't much of one when you thought about it. As per Micheletti's instructions, he had registered for several nights, even though he only planned to be there for one night. He left the hotel early the next morning, careful not to be noticed by the desk clerk, with the small amount of luggage he had brought from Moscow. Following further emailed instructions, he found a cab a few blocks away and went to a coffee bar away from the center of the city to meet Micheletti.

Oleg seemingly arrived first in the almost-empty bar. He scanned the few other customers before taking his espresso—he was trying to fit in—to a table where he could watch the door. The other customers were absorbed in their own worlds and the barman watched a sports commentator jabber incomprehensibly in Italian on a television set high on the wall.

After about ten minutes a man whom Oleg had hardly noticed and who had been quietly sitting in the corner put down his newspaper and approached Oleg's table. He showed Oleg a printout of the email Oleg had sent and introduced himself as Micheletti as he sat down. Asking for identification under the circumstances seemed pointless.

He wore what one supposed was an Italian supplier of high-end false IDs' version of business casual; black jeans, a dark sport shirt, and a very lightweight brown leather jacket that looked like lambskin. As Micheletti put the folded paper down, Oleg saw the holstered Beretta nestled under the jacket.

Micheletti smiled faintly and asked Oleg how his trip was so far, then asked him to describe what he was looking for. He had an idea of what Oleg wanted but needed to get final details and a fuller picture of his new client. While the two talked, he cast a practiced eye over Oleg as he spoke, taking out his notebook and pen and making some notes. He looked carefully at Oleg's face and eyes as the Russian spoke. He asked Oleg to go to the counter and ask for another coffee. Just be yourself, he had said, act natural. As Oleg did so, Micheletti watched him walk and observed his posture and how he moved and gestured.

When Oleg returned, Micheletti took out his phone and, turning away, quickly made a call in barely audible, indecipherable Italian. He looked at the notes he'd made as he spoke. His tone sounded as if he were negotiating something. Then he turned to a back page of the notebook, said a few more words in quick Italian, and ended the call. As he turned back, Oleg could see the notebook was now open to a calendar page. Micheletti looked down at the open notebook and told Oleg to meet him at another café in ten days. As he wrote down the address on a blank page of his notebook, he looked at Oleg again and then seemed to have a thought. He asked Oleg if he had brought the photos Micheletti had asked for.

Oleg gave Micheletti passport photos he had had taken the day before. In the photos, he stared stiffly into the camera, dressed in a jacket and tie, as Micheletti had asked.

Micheletti looked at Oleg, then back at the photos. They were unremarkable depictions of a very Russian, shaggy, academic-looking Oleg. Micheletti looked at him carefully and thought for a moment.

"I tell you what," he said, passing the pictures back to Oleg, "why don't you get a haircut?" He wrote the name and address of a barbershop on the notebook page. He looked Oleg over again, studied his face, then glanced at his clothes.

"Get some new clothes, too," he said, "Nothing fancy, but not what you would usually wear." He wrote the name and address of a clothing store nearby on the notebook page before tearing it out and passing it to Oleg.

Oleg felt as if he were out of his depth, suddenly. He looked doubtfully at the addresses Micheletti had written on the notebook page, then back up at Micheletti.

Micheletti looked at Oleg.

"This isn't a game," he said quietly, "you've come to me because you need to disappear, right?"

Oleg nodded, saying nothing.

"I have an idea who you are dealing with—or trying to avoid dealing with—and we can't fuck around, OK?"

When Oleg didn't say anything, Micheletti continued.

"I've done this many times and if you do exactly what I say, there won't be any trouble for you," he said. "Or me," he added.

"If you don't, we may both regret it," he said.

Oleg felt beads of sweat starting to form on his forehead. Embarrassed, he wiped them away with a napkin. It was damp as he put it back on the table.

"Listen," Micheletti told Oleg after a moment, "this is what you're paying me, and paying me well for. We're going to create a new man, a man no one is looking for, so you can get out of here safely. Let's create that new man. OK?"

Oleg nodded, tentatively.

"OK," Micheletti said, putting his notebook and pen back in his pocket.

Meeting over.

"Meet me here in two days, same time," Micheletti said, glancing at his watch.

Oleg nodded, calmer now but still a little shaky.

Micheletti looked at him for a moment.

"You'll be fine," he said, "Create an image in your mind, someone other than yourself, and shop for him. Before you know it, you will be that man—at least enough to pass for him."

Oleg nodded again, trying to look confident.

"Great," Micheletti said, "I'll see you here then, same time."

"You'll need this, too," he said. He handed Oleg another piece of paper with an address on it, an apartment Micheletti knew of nearby where Oleg could stay without registering at another hotel.

* * *

Oleg took a cab to Micheletti's barber shop and had his bushy hair cut into a less conspicuous style and had his beard trimmed way down, almost to stubble. Then, at the clothing store Micheletti had recommended, he picked out some jeans and a few shirts that he judged would make him look less Russian. On a splurge, he bought a pair of hard-guy black folding Italian sunglasses. It would be sunny where he was going.

Satisfied with his purchases, he carried his things into the apartment Micheletti had referred him to. He put on some of his new clothes and, more than satisfied with his new appearance, took himself out for dinner a few blocks away. No one gave him a second glance on the street or in the restaurant, which he took as a good sign.

At the appointed time, armed with new photos, the new Oleg met Micheletti again.

Micheletti's eye lingered on Oleg's new appearance and nodded approvingly when he saw the photos.

There was no turning back now, Oleg thought.

The two parted and Oleg walked for a few blocks, breathing in the foreign air of Rome. He realized he really was becoming someone else. As the cars and motorbikes whizzed by and he passed the outdoor tables of chattering Italians, he was aware that they were not seeing Oleg Makarov, Russian academician, but the figure he would become. Oleg Makarov was about to cease to exist.

Oleg kept a low profile while Micheletti worked on his papers, staying mostly in the apartment, but venturing out occasionally to get some air or eat a meal in some anonymous café.

He was growing more apprehensive by the day. He knew that at any point, someone in Moscow might wake up and smell a rat—a missing rat, in fact—and he'd be in trouble. He rode metros or buses and walked and stayed away from tourist areas. He paid for everything in cash and did nothing that required him to show an ID. In the evenings he mainly watched television or went out to one or another of the nearby local bars for a couple of drinks, usually vodka, to help him sleep. He sat in a corner if he could and kept his eye on who came in or left.

* * *

Oleg was in large part an easy client for Micheletti. He was only trying to disappear and not on anyone's radar, so far as Micheletti knew. At least not yet.

After he had collected the new passport photos from Oleg, Micheletti, using a false name, had sent them to an accommodation address in the Czech Republic. Four days later, having received a coded email from the owner of the accommodation address, he made his way to the airport with only a small carry-on bag for a flight to Prague, using a deceptive passport that wouldn't set off any alarms, one of several he kept for his own use. On the plane, he hung his sharp leather jacket on the hook in front of him. He had not brought his Beretta, of course, but he figured he probably wouldn't need it; he had done business with this Czech group before. Then he stowed his bag below the seat in front of him. Seemingly, there was nothing particularly remarkable about the bag, whose contents were limited to a change of underwear and socks, a second shirt, a paperback, and some toiletries. And, at the bottom, under the underwear, a thick envelope full of a wad of worn, small-denomination euro notes. Micheletti had pulled the notes from a stash in his safe that he kept around for transactions he didn't want flashing up on anyone's screen.

When the plane had reached cruising altitude, he pulled the paperback out of the bag before smiling at the middle-aged woman in the adjacent seat. Expressionless, the woman glanced at him before returning to her own reading.

In Prague, he took a cab to an elegant hotel at the Old Town Square near the Týn Cathedral. He left his bag in his room, putting the envelope of euros in his room safe, and wandered out to the square, losing himself in the throng of sneakered and cargo pants-clad tourists. He walked down to the river, past the same assortment of pretentious shops and expensive cars every rich city seemed to boast now. He glanced at a window now and then as if shopping for an expensive bauble of some sort, noticing no one paying any particular attention to him. When he got down to the river, he crossed the street and made his way back to his hotel, still checking a window now and then.

He had time to kill, and he had planned to wander around the city a little more, but he had noticed a brochure on the hotel desk and, after querying the exceedingly polite and solicitous desk clerk, he made a reservation and attended a string ensemble performance in the Týn Cathedral, particularly enjoying Smetana's *Moldaur*, one of his favorite pieces. He was in front of a backpacker couple on the way out and he overheard the girl thank her boyfriend or husband for taking her. The boyfriend or husband sounded unimpressed with the concert, but Micheletti thought, with amusement, that this was one of the benefits of living in cultured Europe and the kid would eventually grow to appreciate that. If he played his cards right, Micheletti thought, the kid might get to appreciate it later that night.

As he walked from the cathedral, he saw no repeating faces, no one avoiding his glance.

Making his way through the crowd, Micheletti found an empty outside table at a restaurant overlooking the now almost-dark square, sat down, and ordered a beer. He sipped it slowly, watching the crowds milling around. Europop played in the background. At the next table, a young couple spoke earnestly to each other in rapid German. She had red hair to her shoulders. He had a nearly shaved head and a sparse beard. Absorbed in their own world, they never noticed him. Nor, Micheletti was careful to ascertain, did anyone else.

Watching the swirling crowd, he lingered over his beer for a little while longer. He then checked his watch, paid his bill, and went back up to his room. Once there, he retrieved the envelope from his safe and put it into the inside pocket of his leather jacket.

He quickly took the elevator down to the ground floor and left the hotel by the front entrance before making several turns off the square onto now nearly empty side streets.

One street was almost deserted, except for a few parked cars. It curved off to the left gently between storefronts with the odd lit sign here and there, a blue-lit cathedral tower visible rising majestically beyond. As he stopped next to an empty Mercedes sedan, apparently to admire the view of the tower, he looked around to ensure he was alone. Then, after a moment, another tourist appeared a block or so ahead, where the street curved. The tourist made his way toward Micheletti, looking periodically at a *Rick Steves* guide, then looking up and around.

Micheletti glanced around again, then walked forward toward the approaching bewildered tourist. Suddenly, the tourist looked again at his tour book and snapped it shut as if he had found what he was looking for. He walked forward seemingly with new confidence. As the two passed, Micheletti reached into his pocket and pulled out his packet, which he exchanged for one the tourist had had in his own pocket. The exchange happened so quickly it would have been invisible to the untrained eye, although there were no eyes, trained or untrained, around.

After returning to his hotel by a roundabout route, with no surveillance visible, Micheletti went straight up to his room, opened the packet, and checked its contents. Then he resealed it and put it in the bottom of his bag and turned in for the night with his book. In the morning, he showered, put on his clean clothes, and had an enjoyable breakfast in the dining room overlooking the square. He had one more errand before he left Prague. He walked a few blocks to a modern shopping mall a world away from the Disneyland version of Prague around the hotel for a quick purchase and then returned to the hotel. Once there, he retrieved his bag and went to the airport in the comfortable Skoda sedan the hotel had arranged for his morning flight back to Rome.

* * *

Micheletti arrived at the third meeting with Oleg with his main purchase from Prague, provided by the seemingly confused nighttime tourist near the cathedral: a genuine Czech passport, which had originally been issued to a real Ivo Jezek but now with Oleg's photo in it. The actual Ivo Jezek was a junkie habitue of Prague's seedier quarters, well away from the world of string quartets and upscale boutiques, more in need of fast cash than international travel papers.

Having this document was obviously a better idea for Oleg than a doctored stolen passport that would eventually show up on Interpol and other international law enforcement lists.

Micheletti had also procured a matching airline ticket to Singapore and a debit card for a new account in an Italian bank through other contacts, into which Oleg made a large deposit through Micheletti in preparation for the trip he was about to make. Micheletti rounded things out with a Czech identity card and some pocket litter—a receipt for a pricey duck meal at an elegant Prague restaurant, a spent museum admission ticket, and some other scraps of paper that a globetrotting Ivo Jezek might be expected to have, all courtesy of Micheletti's Czech contacts, along with a slightly worn man's wallet of a type readily available in Prague. Plus, just to make sure, a toothbrush, toothpaste, and some other toiletries Micheletti had purchased from a pharmacy in the Prague mall. That's what you get when you go to a class operation instead of some shlock shyster you met through some other poor bastard in a refugee camp.

He passed the plastic shopping bag across to Oleg under the table and returned to his coffee.

"Remember," he said quietly, "no one wants you to be hiding anything."

Oleg nodded.

"When you use these, remember, the border guard isn't looking at the passport, he's looking at your face."

Oleg nodded again.

"Relax, think about a pleasant time with your wife or children or a nice night you had with a woman. Don't give the guard a reason to wonder."

With that, Micheletti took a final sip of his coffee and left. He didn't shake Oleg's hand, but he did leave money for the check—client relations are important in small business.

* * *

After finishing his own coffee and paying the bill, Oleg took his new identity back to the apartment where he was staying. Holding the new passport and other documents in his hand after he had unpacked the shopping bag was jolting. Oleg took the euro bills he'd had folded in his trousers pocket and put them in his Czech wallet. He thumbed through the pages of the passport, realizing his life had just changed, possibly irreversibly. He switched the Czech toothpaste and toiletries for the ones he had brought from Moscow and threw out the old ones.

Now, he realized, he had to surface, in the flesh, as Ivo Jezek. Suddenly he was aware of how big a step this was. He not only might have begun to attract the attention of Russian authorities since he'd left, but he was carrying a fake Czech passport and a lot of other things a Czech would carry, and he didn't even speak Czech or know his way around Prague or any other Czech city. He'd have a lot of opportunity, he realized, to fuck it up.

* * *

The next day, Oleg woke up and, armed with his new documents, took a taxi to the airport. He hadn't slept much the night before and was nervous.

He concentrated on what he was doing to avoid panicking.

As it happened, none of the security officers seemed to take any particular notice of him. Check-in was likewise uneventful for the newly minted Ivo Jezek, and he made it into the international departures area with no alarms going off.

He waited quietly in the boarding area until, finally, his flight was called. Boarding the plane, he made it to his aisle seat without incident.

The flight was long, overnight, with a layover in Frankfurt, which also passed uneventfully until, after a lifetime, he boarded his onward flight. An eternity later, he landed in Singapore, exhausted, but knowing the next step would be even more stressful.

Initially, Oleg felt relieved by Singapore's cleanliness on his taxi ride to his hotel, but the sterility of the place quickly put him off.

After leaving his luggage in his new room, he strolled along nearby Orchard Road, with its malls, bars, and restaurants. As he walked past glitzy shops, he felt as if he were suddenly in some sort of nightmare version of American suburbia—at least as it seemed from the TV shows from the West he had seen—transplanted to Asia. As he walked, he considered how he had reached this place. There was certainly no turning back; if Moscow authorities weren't looking for him yet, they would be soon. He couldn't just disappear unnoticed, he knew. He wondered whether he should start keeping more of an eye out.

He stopped in front of a shop window to watch the reflection of people behind him to see if anyone was following him. He'd learned from Western spy novels that this was what spies did to spot surveillance. He supposed that any Russian agents tailing him had also read those spy novels, so they probably had figured out how to counter it, though. Moreover, this sort of thing might, in fact, attract attention from agents just looking for suspicious characters. He turned away from the window.

Resuming his walk, he almost froze when he heard someone speaking Russian behind him. However, slowing to let the Russian speaker pass, he saw that it was a guy with two toddlers talking with his wife. Oleg stopped and watched them disappear into a store. The toddlers screamed at the tops of their lungs—in Russian—and it was all the man and his wife could do to keep them under control. Not a likely FSB surveillance team, he thought, but the episode did nothing to calm him. Oleg looked around and decided no one else seemed to be following him. He decided he was being melodramatic and took a taxi back to his hotel. After trying, unsuccessfully to relax a bit, he went out in the dusk and had a meal of some sort of noodles nearby. He walked around a bit again before returning and collapsing into bed. He concentrated on enjoying the soft bed and pleasantly arctic air conditioning. He would likely be missing it soon, he thought.

After sleeping fitfully again, Oleg awoke early and headed back to the airport. He made sure to enjoy his hot shower and hotel breakfast before leaving in preparation for the privations he expected during the next twenty-four hours. Despite Micheletti's apparent competence, he was glad he had planned the next stage in a way to keep him close to the edge of, if not off, the grid.

Oleg, which is to say Ivo, was headed to Bangkok. Instead of taking a direct flight, though, when he arrived at the airport, he bought a ticket on a budget airline flight that would take him part of the way, to Kuala Lumpur, up the Malay Peninsula, in Malaysia, a step he thought would throw off any watchers.

He waited for the flight in the gate area, reading a copy of *The Economist* he had picked up on the way. As he read the magazine and sipped some coffee, he began to relax more than he had since going into hiding in Rome while Micheletti worked out his new identity. Things seemed to be working out pretty well. He looked around. No one in Singapore seemed to notice him, and he thought that perhaps he might get away with all of this.

Later, after his flight, when he'd landed in Kuala Lumpur and had retrieved his luggage, he began to relax even more; everything seemed to be going according to plan. He waited around for a while in the main terminal until his fellow passengers seemed to have left the airport. He then waited ten minutes more and, noticing no one paying attention to him and no one who looked familiar, he took a taxi downtown to the crowded long-distance bus station.

He had not planned his next step in detail, but it seemed he had various options available to him to get to Bangkok, all of which involved a probably unpleasant, overnight bus trip up the peninsula into Thailand and, finally, to the capital city. He was weighing his options when he overheard a conversation between two businessmen speaking English. They obviously spent a lot of time in the region and were headed north. Eavesdropping on their conversation, a new and unexpected possibility revealed itself.

A few hours later, Oleg boarded a comfortable minibus headed overnight to Hat Yai, just over the border in Thailand's Songkhla province. He had purchased a ticket for cash—conveniently, without any burdensome paperwork involving identity documents—from a kid one of the businessmen had pointed out to the other when he was talking.

This was not a common way for European tourists to enter Thailand, partly because of the inconvenience—why would they?—and partly because of the shadowy and dangerous Islamic insurgency in that part of the country that had somewhat dampened the tourist appeal of Thailand's southernmost provinces. The other passengers were not your typical fun-loving Southeast Asia travelers—they included the businessmen Oleg had seen at the bus station, traders of some sort, as well as one or two aid workers, and a churchy-looking man with thick eyeglasses who might have been involved in some good deed-ish manner of work. Or moving arms to the rebels.

The trip was pleasant. The minibus had comfortable seats, and Oleg had armed himself with bottles of water and snacks before he left. He presumed that he would not stand out in this crowd, a presumption confirmed when the sleepy border guards passed him through to the Thai side, barely looking at his Czech passport.

It was early morning when the bus deposited Oleg and his fellow passengers at the Thai bus terminal in Hat Yai. Oleg gave passing thought to spending the night there, what with, he assumed, the insurgency loosening up the accommodation situation and all. In the end, though, he decided to keep going. In the bus station, he changed his Singaporean and Malaysian money into Thai baht and, despite the hour, bought an ice-cold and very welcome beer before boarding another bus. None of his fellow passengers joined him for this leg of his trip—a promising sign, Oleg thought.

Many hours later, Oleg was exhausted when he checked into his small hotel in Bangkok on Convent Road. The long bus ride from the southern border had felt as if it were through two separate countries rather than one, as tourists seeking sun, sand, and sex in Thailand's beach provinces increasingly populated the bus as it left the insurgency behind. Nevertheless, Oleg tried to keep a watchful eye out for anyone who might be looking for him among the sunburned tourists in their silly shorts and flip-flops who joined him on his all-day trip.

Finally, the bus deposited Oleg at the Southern Bangkok Bus Terminal. Oleg did not speak Thai, but he had printed the name and address of the small hotel he had found online in Thai. The Thai taxi driver at the station got him there half an hour later.

The hotel was modest but clean and Oleg checked into the pleasant room, peeled off his clothes, grimy from the endless twenty-four-hour-plus air and land journey from Singapore, and took another luxurious hot shower. He drank some coffee in the hotel lobby and then, suddenly beat, went up to his room to take a nap. He awoke in the early evening, and asked the desk clerk, in English, whether there was a nearby restaurant he could recommend. The desk clerk, anxious to help this Czech professor who was obviously new to Asia, suggested he try a strip of restaurants a block or so away.

As it happened, the first restaurant he found was a Mexican restaurant. Since Mexican food was as exotic to him as Thai food, he went in and had his first taste of tacos. Not too bad, he decided after his first taste. The beer was good too.

After the meal, he stopped at a nearby bar for a couple of drinks, watching the buzzing motorbikes and tuk-tuks pass by in the sweltering night on the busy street.

He drained his drink and went back to his hotel.

One more border to cross.

* * *

Oleg deserved credit for the measures he had taken to elude any pursuers, but these days it's a little harder than just slapping on a fake mustache and watching out for shady men in trench coats.

Faster than you could say "the jig is up," Ivo Jezek's flight plans from Rome to Singapore to Kuala Lumpur zipped across the airlines' supposedly secure networks and triggered exactly the chain of events Oleg had hoped to avoid.

Back in Rome, once he had gotten his initial ping on Ivo Jezek's name, a name that he assumed was false, Serino used one of his agency's search tools and discovered that an Ivo Jezek had in recent days flown from Rome to Singapore. Once he had that, Serino was able to quickly trace Jezek's progress to his hotel in Singapore and then his flight to Kuala Lumpur. Jezek seemed to disappear there, but immigration databases showed him crossing into Thailand by land at Hat Yai in the middle of the night on a scheduled minibus, the last record Serino could find.

As Oleg had hoped, his roundabout route to Bangkok had, at least for the moment, thrown Serino off the trail. He couldn't yet tell whether Jezek had stayed in Hat Yai or gone on to somewhere else, but that route was certainly suspicious. Serino knew that part of the world and could broadly visualize the trip Jezek had taken. It was clear this guy was on the run from something or someone or doing something else suspicious.

Rome to Singapore made sense; both were major international hubs. The subsequent trip raised all kinds of red flags, though. There was no legitimate reason for anyone to take the route he had used. It seemed that this Jezek, who was probably involved in smuggling or something similar if Elise was interested in him, needed to reach the border region and talk with someone in Singapore or Kuala Lumpur first. Otherwise, he could have more easily flown to Bangkok and then down to Hat Yai. Maybe from Singapore to Hat Yai, Serino didn't know. Jezek could, of course, be trying to dodge watchers, though, Serino thought, but if so, not those with access to the systems he was tapping into. Or, he realized, Ivo might be just covering his bases, having taken initial steps to avoid detection by using a false name, and he was just making sure he was clean. Something, though, was fishy.

He looked at the screen to see if anything jumped out at him. Nothing.

No matter, he'd fill Elise in and be done with it. It was none of his affair and he had other, more important work to do.

Serino called Elise and, using veiled language, let her know that her guy seemed to have headed from Singapore to the Thai border and that he would probably have more information the next day. The next morning, Serino arrived at his office early to query the system again on Ivo Jezek, discovering that Jezek had stayed at a small hotel near Silom Road in Bangkok, but that was the latest information available. He typed the information into an encrypted email, which he sent to Elise and wished her luck, adding that he would be unavailable for a day or two because he would be out of town, although he would check his databases while he was away and let her know if he found anything else out.

Elise, sitting with Paul in the courtyard of their Rome hotel, looked at the message from Serino on her Blackberry and told Paul what it said.

Paul turned the information over in his mind, then looked through the gates to the street outside. There was little traffic; Via Santa Melania was a quiet street.

"He's either staying in Bangkok," Paul said, remembering Oleg's fascination with Southeast Asia, "or going to ground someplace nearby.

"Either way," Paul continued, "our best bet is to go to Bangkok before we hear from your friend again."

"You go ahead," Elise said, "I have a few more people to check with here and I can talk to Serino when he's back."

Then, after a moment, she asked, "Should you look up Sands?"

Paul looked at Elise.

"Sands? Why?"

"We have to start somewhere," she said.

Paul thought for a moment.

"I suppose," he said.

"I'm not sure we want to widen the circle," he added after a moment.

"But he knows people, he might be useful."

Paul gave it more thought.

"OK," he said, "why not?" He looked at his watch and then pulled out his own Blackberry. He fiddled with it for a few moments, tapping out a message.

He started to put his phone away, but it buzzed as he was putting it in his pocket.

Paul looked at the screen for a moment and looked back at Elise.

"He says let him know when I get to Bangkok," Paul said.

CHAPTER FOURTEEN

SANDS

Norman Sands was a long shot, Paul thought.

The afternoon heat was blinding as he got into the taxi outside of Bangkok's Suvarnabhumi Airport.

Driving along the divided highway from Suvarnabhumi, with its well-marked lanes, billboards and swarms of traffic, it almost felt as if he were in a Western city in the same sort of Toyota.

A misleading illusion, he knew from experience.

As he looked out the window, a Thai child in a passing car stared at him and made a face.

Paul turned away and wondered whether Oleg was in Bangkok. Southeast Asia was a big place if you were trying to find someone, especially if that person was trying to hide. He wondered whether he was on a fool's errand.

A couple of hours later, he was settled into his room at the Sheraton on the river. He put the Thai SIM card he'd bought at the airport into one of the cheap cell phones in his bag and called Sands and arranged to meet the next morning not far from the hotel. He called Elise in Rome to let her know he'd arrived and found out she had no news for him. He was tired and a little apprehensive. He took a stroll around the neighborhood and down to the river. Two monks in their orange robes, one older and one younger, passed him. He politely *wai*ed them, putting his hands together in front of his face and bowing his head slightly. The younger monk smiled at him. After a quick dinner nearby, Paul went back to the hotel, had a drink watching the boats on the Chao Phraya River, watched a little CNN, and turned in for the night.

In the morning, he arose early and made his way to a coffee shop near the foreign correspondents' club on Ploenchit Road. It was in a busy commercial area, crowded this day with a mixture of Thais working in nearby offices and foreigners—either residents in comfortable business dress or tourists in an assortment of garish T-shirts and shorts, many carrying backpacks.

He felt himself readjusting to the familiar rhythms of Bangkok. The traffic was choking, but not as much as it had been years ago before the arrival of the SkyTrain elevated rail lines. Smart office girls in skirts and pressed blouses rushed past beggars sitting cross-legged in front of their bowls, their heads bowed and hands clasped in front of them in supplication.

Arriving at the coffee shop as arranged, he found a seat at a corner table. Momentarily, he saw Sands come through the door.

Sands looked the part of a longtime Asia hand; his sandy hair and beard were cut short, and he had a deep tan. He was in good shape, as befitted someone who periodically disappeared for days to return with interviews with guerilla leaders or military officers in remote border regions. He wore khakis and a plain dress shirt. Simple and comfortable.

Paul had shared a jeep with Sands on a press trip out of Rangoon some years before and they had spent several days together in the remote Wa region on the Burma-China border listening to earnest United Nations officials explain how opium production would soon end, replaced by broccoli or something else, Paul couldn't remember what. Which, of course, it hadn't.

He and Sands had gotten to know each other a bit during the three or four days the reporters had spent together up there before returning to Rangoon by an arduous jeep and plane route. Paul had then run into Sands during the three days the Burmese authorities had inexplicably allowed Paul to stay in Rangoon. During that time, he conducted a series of forbidden interviews with opposition figures. The resulting magazine story, as expected, got Paul banned from Burma for the duration of the junta's rule. It was one of Paul's proudest achievements.

Paul and Sands had been in touch occasionally in the ensuing years and Paul would see Sands' pieces periodically online.

Now, after a few minutes of catching up, Paul told Sands he was looking for a Russian friend he suspected was in the region, laying low, possibly using an alias. He wondered whether Sands might be able to point him in the right direction, groups of Russians or places where a Russian might feel comfortable.

Sands thought for a moment before replying. He knew some Russians, he said, oligarch types enjoying the easy life and maybe making money on the side, would Paul's friend be comfortable with them? This, of course, was why Sands was a long shot; it was unlikely that Oleg would be hanging out with the people Sands had written about, although those contacts might lead to others who were more promising, as had been the case earlier when he had met with Yevgeny in his beachside pizza joint.

No, Paul said, he was pretty sure his friend would not be comfortable with the oligarchs.

Well, Sands said, that might make it difficult. Then, he seemed to have an inspiration. He could check around with some others he knew, away from the sleazy oligarchs, a few Russians hanging around Bangkok trying to put together a life.

This sounded potentially useful to Paul, so, yes, he said, that might be helpful. In the back of his mind, though, he was hoping Elise was finding something in the way of a solid lead in Rome. He wasn't sure random Russians would be helpful the way Yevgeny had been.

OK, Sands said, looking at his watch, but he couldn't get to it today, he had to go huddle with some Asia political risk big shots meeting quietly this week at a nearby hotel.

Paul had been about to say something but stopped at that news.

"Really?" he asked, "Do any of them follow the Russian Far East?"

"Sure," Sands said casually, distracted by something outside, "there's an American professor there who follows it, why?"

Friend or no friend, this was not the time to be too forthcoming with Sands, Paul thought.

"There's something else I'm working on," he said vaguely, "I wonder whether I could talk with him."

"Her," Sands said. Then he thought for a moment, looking at his watch again.

"Sure," he said, "can you meet us around two? I'm talking to her about something at one-thirty."

Paul nodded.

"OK," Sands said, "meet us then in the hotel lobby at two or so." He told Paul the name of the political risk conference hotel.

"I hope this turns out to be useful for you," Sands said.

He had no idea, as it happened.

* * *

Paul used the next two hours to wander around the coffee shop's neighborhood, reacquainting himself with Bangkok, or at least this part of it. Construction had boomed, with more and more office buildings and more and more fancy shops. He expected that much of the city, away from tourist areas like this one, was less polished, with commuters from poorer districts relegated to buses while tourists enjoyed the efficient SkyTrain. He stopped at a street stall for a bowl of noodle soup and watched legions of young Thais troop by talking to each other or on cell phones. Checking his pockets, he suddenly realized he had left his Blackberry in his hotel room. No matter, he thought, he had his Thai SIM-equipped phone with him.

Paul eventually made his way to the lobby of the hotel where the political-risk shindig was being held and found Sands talking to an intense-looking, dark-haired woman. She, he discovered, was Doris Pollack, a professor from a New England college Paul had never heard of, but who lived and breathed all things Russian Far East. Sands told her that he and Paul were old colleagues and that she and Paul might have some things to discuss. After a little chitchat, he then excused himself to attend to other business.

It was comfortable in this spacious, air-conditioned lobby in the sort of hotel favored by executives on expense accounts. Traditional Thai music—the kind that made Westerners think of the Mysterious East—played softly in the background as Paul and Doris Pollack faced each other on the elegant, cushioned teak sofas sipping drinks served by equally elegant Thai waitresses in shimmering modern interpretations of Thai dress. The local variation on a theme in corporate hotels from Bombay to Albany, New York, Paul thought.

"Norman says you wanted to talk with me about the Russian Far East," Doris Pollack said.

Paul waited until a nearby waitress had headed toward a distant table. He hesitated; this would be a major step.

"*Vy mozhete mne doveryat'. Ya ponimayu, delo, navernoe, delikatnoye,*" she said with a smile. You can trust me, she had said in easy Russian, I understand that this is probably delicate.

"I know who you are," she added in English, still smiling, "I've read some of your excellent coverage."

"Thank you," Paul said. He thought for a moment, then decided to take the plunge.

"Can you keep what I'm about to ask you completely to yourself?" he asked.

"Sure," she said. Nonplussed. As if she got similar requests from reporters every week. Maybe she did.

"It's pretty hot," Paul said.

"I think I can handle it," Doris said drily. She sipped her drink, waiting for him to reveal whatever the big secret was.

Paul paused for a moment, then proceeded to outline the claims in the Oleg document, without mentioning Oleg's name or that Paul was trying to find an incognito Oleg in Thailand or maybe elsewhere in Southeast Asia.

Doris listened to him without interrupting. When he had stopped, she sat for a moment, as if considering her response. Her flippancy now seemed to have left her.

"We're talking about a Far Eastern split from Russia, or at least the plan for one, in simple terms," she said.

"Yes," Paul said, "but it's more than that." He proceeded to fill in more details, including the suggestions of contacts with outsiders and references to communications with the West and with the CIA.

"Do you have the document?" she asked.

No, not with him—actually he had brought a copy from Washington but it was in his hotel room safe—but it seemed credible to him, he said. Paul thought she might ask what made him think it was credible, but she didn't. Maybe she was, in fact, used to dealing with sensitive information.

She thought again for a few moments.

"Do you know if there's anything behind it?"

"No," Paul said, "it could just be talk. Assuming it exists."

She thought for a moment.

"No," she said, finally.

Paul looked at her, startled.

"No, what?" he asked.

"I really don't think so," she said. "I spend a lot of time on that part of the world and nearby with a lot of sorts of people and this just doesn't ring true to me. I'd say there is no such separatist movement like this."

"That you know of."

"Of course," she said, "but I'm pretty plugged in. I think someone is pulling the wool over someone's eyes."

She took a sip of her drink.

"Trust me," she said, "I think I would have heard about this. At least something, some sort of vibes or rumors."

"Doesn't this count as hearing about this?" Paul asked.

She smiled. "No offense, Paul, but I don't think that if such a movement wanted to reveal itself, or someone wanted to get it out there, they would do so this way."

She didn't know about the information coming from a leak from Archie, the congressional staffer, but still, Paul had to admit, she might have a point.

They talked a little more as they finished their drinks, but she needed to get back to her conference and Paul headed back to his hotel. He took a cab. He didn't feel the need to absorb the exotic sights and sounds of Bangkok at the moment.

Arriving at his hotel room, Paul discovered he had missed a call from Elise on his Blackberry, which was now almost out of power. Using his new Thai phone, he called her. He decided not to tell her about the conversation with Doris Pollock. He wanted to think it over first. She told him that Serino had learned that "their friend" had traveled to Phnom Penh, although he did not know where he was staying. She was about to leave for the airport now. Since he was in Bangkok ... then the connection died.

Paul called her back, and she said sorry, the phone had gone out, but she was about to make a flight reservation to Cambodia and would meet him in Phnom Penh.

Good idea, he said, he'd try to get a room at the Royal, across from the American Embassy. The line sounded a little scratchy. Can you hear me OK, he asked. Sure, fine, she said, I'll see you at the Royal.

She wasn't the only one able to hear the conversation clearly.

* * *

Paul easily caught a flight later that day to Phnom Penh, around an hour away by air. He was, of course, making a trip similar to the one Oleg had made a week or so before when he had left Bangkok for Phnom Penh himself.

On that morning, after discovering the joys of Mexican food the night before, his first morning in Bangkok, Oleg had a breakfast of some sort of chicken and rice soup that was a surprisingly tasty way to start the day, then ventured out to the busy Silom Road. He had errands to run before what he hoped would be the final leg of his journey.

He quickly found an Internet café and, using his new Ivo Jezek debit card, bought a ticket for an afternoon flight to Phnom Penh online. He spent another thirty minutes scanning websites before erasing his search history, signing off, and heading out into the heat.

He wandered around for a few hours. He had now been in Southeast Asia for only a few days but felt he was beginning to adjust to its tempos. Bangkok seemed more relaxed than Singapore had, and he was adjusting to the tones and rhythms of its language. He took a quick trip on the SkyTrain to catch a glimpse of the Chayo Phraya and then, realizing time was marching on, took a taxi to his hotel for his bags, then to Suvarnabhumi Airport in time for his flight.

A couple of hours later he was walking out of the airport in Phnom Penh, flagging down a taxi into the city. He had had no problems either leaving Thailand or entering Cambodia with his false papers. He quickly changed his Thai baht into U.S. dollars before leaving the airport—as had been promised by the tourist information site he had consulted that morning in Bangkok, the dollar was the universal currency now in Cambodia, making things easier than they would have been had he had to deal with Khmer-language Cambodian riel.

That morning, he had quickly searched online for an unobtrusive hotel or guesthouse and stumbled onto one called the Mekong Dreams. The name appealed to him, and the comments on the site suggested it was clean and well-managed. This being off-season, he was able to reserve a "deluxe" room for an extended stay.

The taxi driver had the radio on to a Khmer station, which Oleg enjoyed listening to. The language sounded like Thai to him, but it provided a pleasant backdrop as they drove through the city—bigger than he'd thought—toward his hotel. For his part, after failing in half-hearted efforts to interest Oleg in the services of girls, then boys, as well as weed, the driver kept to himself, absorbed in the radio.

When the taxi arrived, the hotel looked exactly like what Oleg was looking for. The four-story building was modest and a little past its prime, but the desk clerk was efficient and offered to show him to his deluxe room, which was large and comfortable and had a balcony looking out onto the street below. For another twenty-five dollars, he promised to have a cheap cell phone with a Khmer SIM card for Ivo the next day.

That was how he found himself hoping he was safely hidden at the anonymous Mekong Dreams hotel on an anonymous lane during the anonymous off-season in the steamy, off-the-beaten-path capital of Indochinese backwater Cambodia.

CHAPTER FIFTEEN

A NIGHT AT THE BALLET

On the other side of the world, as evening fell in Washington, Guy thought to himself that this was definitely not what he had expected.

He stood in the elegant lobby of the Kennedy Center, whose parapet offered a dramatic view of the Potomac River, all the way from the spires of Georgetown University to the north, down along the river toward Alexandria, Virginia, to the south. His car was in the basement parking lot in a space he judged relatively safe from inconsiderate drivers of the lower orders who might scratch it.

Veronica had called him in the morning, leaving a voice message, saying she had gotten tickets for a ballet that evening, and would he like to meet her, a welcome prospect that had been on his mind for the rest of the day.

Going to a ballet, of course, was the last thing Guy wanted to do, but he was free that evening and he had not heard a peep out of Veronica since he had dropped her off at her apartment, despite her promise of a date, and this seemed like a relatively painless way to try to get back on the road to scoreville.

He had come straight from work and was waiting for her near one of the lobby bars before the show, as she'd requested, keeping an eye out for her.

As he spotted her coming through one of the doors, she looked around and waved when she saw him. As she approached, he could see from her expression she was happy to see him. He was somewhat glad to notice that she was dressed in a skirt and blouse that, while modest, seemed tailored to show off her figure, and that she had apparently done something quite appealing with her hair.

What he was not glad about, was her arm linked with that of a burly blond man as they both walked toward him. Mr. Blond wore a blazer and white shirt with grey flannels. He gave Guy a big smile.

Veronica gave Guy a peck on the cheek when they arrived. Mr. Blond continued his smile, but continued to gaze appraisingly at Guy.

"Guy, this is Peter Thorsen," she said. She seemed oblivious to the silent battle Guy believed he was going to have to wage with this new guy.

Guy and Peter Thorsen shook hands and exchanged pleasantries. Thorsen then looked at his watch and, with a slightly alarmed look on his face, declared that the show was about to begin. He gestured to Veronica, who led the two of them to their seats, a few rows back.

Because she had led the way, when the three of them landed in their seats at the end of a row, Guy, to his dismay, ended up on the end with Peter Thorsen between him and Veronica, with whom he was engaged in an animated conversation that Guy couldn't make out.

Over the next hour, Guy began to wonder whether to abandon his pursuit of Veronica. Not to mention wanting to shoot himself in the head so he wouldn't have to endure the boring-ass ballet.

At the break, the three walked out to the lobby and Guy let Peter go for drinks for the three of them. As he left, Veronica hooked her arm in Guy's and, with a twinkle in her eye, leaned over to whisper in his ear.

"Don't be jealous, he's just an old friend I met in Canada," she said.

Guy tried to appear blasé about the news but from the smile on Veronica's face, concluded that he had not succeeded.

Peter returned, drinks in hand, apparently unaware of both Guy's relief and the events since he had gone to fetch drinks.

They only had a short time left before the show resumed, which Peter seemed interested in filling. He was apparently Canadian, which Guy found interesting, since he had spent some time there, and worked in Toronto as an investment counselor of some sort—commercial real estate or something else that Guy found not at all interesting.

Peter, on the other hand, apparently found Guy's work fascinating and asked several probing questions. Guy gave him the sorts of pre-cooked answers that seemed to satisfy civilians while inflating the glamor and importance of his own role in Washington's journalistic firmament.

The second half of the ballet sped by more quickly to Guy—now seated between Peter and Veronica—and, when it had ended, the three of them walked out into the lobby. Let's have a drink, someone said, just one since it's late, and thirty minutes later they had each parked near a quiet bar in nearby Georgetown.

Over drinks, two rounds, not one, the three talked about the ballet but after a while, Peter turned the conversation away, asking Guy more about his work.

It turned out that Guy, to his surprise, was fairly impressed with Peter's questions, learning that Peter had a cousin in some sort of journalism in Canada, although, since it was local news, Guy wasn't inclined to give a shit. Peter also seemed fairly well-informed on world affairs. Master's in international relations, it turned out, from some school in Canada Guy had never heard of before he had turned his attention to investment. Guy also found out that Peter planned to be in Washington for a couple of weeks or more for some sort of negotiation involving a corporate merger or something. Really boring, not worth a story, he assured Guy unnecessarily.

As the evening wound down, despite Guy's objections, Peter handed the waitress a credit card for the bill. "Next time," he said, waving Guy's protests aside.

"Say," he said, "this is really my first time out of Canada, I wonder if we might meet for a coffee and chat about your work at the paper, I mean if it wouldn't be too much trouble," he said. He handed Guy a business card.

Guy glanced at the card and pocketed it and looked over at Veronica, who nodded, seemingly amused by the idea.

"I think you should do it, Guy," she said. "Peter could use a conversation about something other than his boring work." Guy hesitated, but then, after a moment, she continued, "Why don't you two come to my place Saturday night and make an evening of it."

Well, this changed things, Guy thought, an image of a drawbridge lowering across a castle moat flitting through his mind.

"Splendid," Peter said, then, turning to Guy, "what do you think?"

There seemed little question in his mind.

A moment later, the waiter returned with the check and a pen in a leather folder. Guy and Veronica watched as Peter signed the check.

The three walked out to their cars. Peter had a rental car, but it was parked in the opposite direction from Guy's and Veronica's cars.

Veronica linked her arm in Guy's once again as they got to her car.

She pulled her key out of her purse and clicked it, flashing her car's lights on as the doors unlocked.

"He's a nice guy, you'll like him," she said.

As Guy mumbled some sort of agreement, she kissed him. For real this time.

"Bring your toothbrush," she said, getting into her car.

CHAPTER SIXTEEN

A NICE HOME-COOKED MEAL

Sitting in an anonymous office building, but one easily reached by Metro, Marina had been sipping her almost-cool tea and listening to the voices coming through her headphones as she transcribed the taped conversation onto the screen in front of her. This was easy so far. The words came through clearly enough and there was no background noise.

She looked down and made sure she hadn't splashed any tea onto *The New York Times Magazine* next to her. It was open to the crossword puzzle, which she did every week. In ink. Usually in an hour. Rarely a mistake.

Marina was proud of her position, among the top members of her elite cadre in the rarified world of what could only be described as modern intelligence's professional snoopers. She had unusual talents, and she knew that those talents were being put to good use, to protect the country.

She had shown an aptitude at a young age for languages, one that was quickly spotted by teachers during her early years in school and that had enabled her to race ahead of other students, who were struggling with what was for them an arduous process of learning a foreign language.

It didn't hurt Marina that she had well-educated and -connected parents, who had doted on her. Her mother was a respected professor of comparative politics at a prestigious university and her father was a decorated military officer with a couple of advanced degrees of his own— including one in literature, showing that he had more than just a sharp military mind.

With such a background, and its consequent connections, status, privileges, travel, and opportunities, it was not surprising that Marina had plenty of chances to expand and exploit her emerging prodigious linguistic abilities. As the child—the only child, one might add—of such prominent and public-spirited parents, it was not surprising that when she finished her education, she chose to forgo the lucrative opportunities to make big money by helping globalizing companies extend their grasp. Instead, she chose public service, hoping to help the country defend itself against the new and frightening perils emerging in the first years of the twenty-first century. Her parents were proud and so was she.

The government was grateful and, once it recognized that Marina's extraordinary abilities could be extremely useful in dealing with the foreign threats increasingly menacing the country, it offered her even better training and opportunities than she'd had in academia—not only in language but also political and operational areas. Who knew where such a talented and patriotic young person might ultimately be useful?

With that training and those opportunities, she was able to work, as she was now, at the pinnacle of the security and intelligence establishment, making what she knew was a real and discernible contribution to protecting national security. Much better than helping some global shoe company screw sweatshop workers in poor countries so they could sell overpriced gym shoes to spoiled teenagers in L.A. or London—or Moscow, for that matter—she thought.

Marina was now fluent in half a dozen languages. Naturally, she could translate between Russian and English easily, but she dismissed that as no big thing—that had been her first language. She had taken a liking to Southeast Asian languages in her teenage years and could now handle several. She was fluent in Thai, Lao, and Khmer, even able on a good day to pick out incidental conversations behind the speakers she was listening to. She had picked up a bit of the odd hill tribe language here and there, sometimes useful, she'd found, for following some of the background chatter when she was listening in on drug and arms deals being worked out in dodgy bugged karaoke bars or on purportedly secure phones.

It was another world on the inside, she had discovered, one she could not have imagined before. It was a world of committed professionals, many of whom had excelled, as had she, in parts of their academic work in ways that had attracted the attention of security and intelligence agencies. Many had traveled widely and talked glowingly of time in far-flung places most people had never heard of in the Middle East or Africa or Latin America. She had even eventually taken a few short trips herself, under a false name and using a misleading foreign passport, of course.

At one point, Marina had been taken to an office building in an unmarked car by one of her managers. The building looked ordinary, even mundane, from the outside, but inside the main door was a forbidding security checkpoint staffed by burley soldiers with automatic weapons. Marina and her manager were admitted after their credentials had been thoroughly examined by one of the unsmiling guards. After they had surrendered their phones and passed through what looked like metal detectors, they were escorted down a hall to an electronic door by one of the other guards. The guard pressed numbers in a keypad then looked straight ahead as his retina was scanned. When the door opened, he stepped aside for Marina and her manager to enter the room beyond.

After passing through a small reception area where another armed guard checked their names on a list on his screen, they passed through an ordinary sliding door into a cavernous room with pods of desks, each desk with an analyst watching screens and typing on a keyboard. The wall was dominated by an electronic map of the world topped by digital clocks showing time zones around the world. Lines of different colors shot constantly among world cities. It made what she'd seen in James Bond and similar movies look like kid stuff.

As they walked through the room, watching the analysts and overhearing their conversations, it was clear they were monitoring email communications, chatrooms, and websites around the world.

"Let me show you something," her manager said, guiding her over to one of the pods.

Half a dozen analysts watched the screens and typed. The manager said something to one of the analysts who nodded and beckoned Marina to look at his screen, relinquishing his chair to her. Sitting in his seat, she could see what appeared to be a conversation, presumably in a private chatroom, in English between an American in Idaho and a German neo-Nazi in a town Marina had never heard of about the need to maintain white dominance in the West and the potential for violent action to ensure it. Both chatters seemed to think that violent action was inevitable—and welcome, as far as they were concerned.

"We keep an eye on this sort of thing, if quietly, for obvious reasons," her manager said.

Marina nodded as she surrendered the seat back to the analyst.

Heading back to the car, after passing through the security checkpoints and retrieving her phone, she wasn't sure that this kind of monitoring was what she would choose to spend finite intelligence resources on, but this was, as the saying goes, above her pay grade. Moreover, she was, as she always was, impressed with the vast capabilities deployed to protect the country, unbeknownst to the civilian world, even if she wasn't sure she would agree with the priorities of that deployment.

There had been other field trips, to see other impressive aspects of the world she was now in, but it was a two-way street. Many of the people she met were anxious to meet her. For their parts, the other linguists and specialists were happy to have someone with whom they could speak in their adopted language, compare notes on slang and regional accents, and tell jokes they'd picked up in their eavesdropping—humor was often the most difficult, and telling, aspect of another culture. Even among this polylingual crowd, she was something of a star.

It was Marina's impressive assortment of language skills that had brought her here today, seated at this terminal with expensive noise-canceling headphones on her head.

A few days before, she had been called in from more routine duties and assigned onto this new project by her section chief. He was unusually anxious on this occasion and said he knew nothing about the new project other than that it was something his superiors had specifically requested her for.

She then met with an obviously very senior official in a better suit than she was used to seeing in the intelligence bureaucracy—no one here was 007, after all—who told her that she was needed for a special assignment that needed immediate attention. He said the machines, meaning the whole hardware end of the spying business that was largely as unknown to her as the far side of the moon, had apparently pulled a suddenly important conversation out of the ether with the promise of more to come. The intelligence team dealing with the conversation and what was expected to follow in the coming days or weeks needed someone immediately who could speak both Russian and English and translate for them, and who might be called on suddenly for one or more Southeast Asian languages. Some of the work might not even involve translation, the good suit told her, it wasn't clear at this point.

It had to be, though, he said, someone trusted who could keep his or her mouth shut, even more so than was usual in the intelligence world. Do this well, was the implied message in the look he gave her, and you will be a legend. Blow it and you'll be translating provincial Lao bus timetables on the overnight shift in some windowless basement office until pension time.

She had relinquished her old workstation, along with her tapes of oil executives cutting secret deals with corrupt officials over what they believed were secure lines, gunrunners debating the best routes across borders that existed only on paper, and politicians verifying their bribes were deposited into the correct numbered account—all plucked from the sky through the magic of twenty-first-century technology.

Now she was in this separate, heavily guarded, building, alone with her headphones and computer, listening again to the conversation between Bangkok and Rome.

It seemed simple, it was a short conversation, and she easily typed it up and sent it electronically to the team's electronic inbox before returning to her crossword puzzle.

Her new supervisor came in shortly. We'll need you to stick around for a few days or so, he said, apparently having read the file she had sent. You speak Khmer, so we may need you to follow up, he said.

Of course, Marina said without hesitation. She was excited and flattered to be part of such an obviously important effort and was proud to help the country in any way she could.

She went back to her puzzle.

* * *

Paul had caught an afternoon flight out of Suvarnabhumi and, once he had landed in Phnom Penh, quickly made his way to the Royal, across the street from the American Embassy.

Raffles Hotel Le Royal. A bit of faux imperialist luxury to evoke the old *Indochine* of *colons*, opium dens and Graham Greene, with its liveried staff and elegant forecourt that seemed built for the gleaming white Mercedes parked out front as Paul arrived. A graceful combination of Khmer, Art Deco, and French Colonial styles, the Royal dated to 1929, when its opening was attended by Cambodian King Sisowath Monivong. Like Saigon's Caravelle and Vientiane's Constellation, it had been a war correspondents' haunt. Moreover, Jackie Kennedy visited in 1967, a visit celebrated by the photos on proud display in the hotel. It had hit the skids during the Vietnam War and Khmer Rouge years before being restored to glory in the nineties. It now boasted luxurious rooms, elegant bathtubs, glorious dining facilities, uniformed bellmen, and the Elephant Bar, where guests could live out that part of the fantasy, all with lots of glitz and hardwood.

Elise had arrived later in the afternoon, feeling tired, but after checking in, she took a shower, and then she and Paul took a ride around town.

Phnom Penh had changed since they had been there last. The riverside had become sleazy and touristy and the traffic, once dominated by motorbikes, was now a honking congested mass of tuk-tuks and cars. Skyscrapers rose here and there out of the formerly sleepy city's decaying, graceful, and low-slung aging skyline like towering malignant fungi left by alien invaders. A new mall, where more shoppers wore shoes than sandals, showed that the city was, like much of the region, rushing headlong as quickly as possible toward an Asian vision of the twenty-first century, replete with glitzy stores that catered to the growing legions of *nouveau riche*, or at least *nouveau* not-poor.

Paul and Elise ate dinner at a noisy second-story restaurant overlooking the Mekong and then repaired to a quiet bar away from the hubbub. The sun had set, and the heavy tropical night air was filled with the sounds of traffic along with the smell of burning charcoal. Over Elise's shoulder, Paul saw a string of rats run along the curb. Through the opening to the street, Paul could see a *cyclo* driver dozing under his baseball hat on the other side of the street and a beggar with a stick making her way along the street. She glanced through the opening at Paul and Elise for a moment before continuing her way.

After drinks had arrived, Paul told Elise about the conversation in Bangkok with Doris and the professor's skepticism about the Oleg document.

"Do you think she's right?" Elise asked.

"I don't know," he said. He noticed that the rats and the beggar had vanished. The *cyclo* driver, having awoken, was looking at a newspaper by the light of a streetlight and sipping something out of a bottle. He didn't seem to be in a rush to get anywhere.

"We don't really have any kind of window into what's going on there," he said, "we just have Oleg's paper that we got from Archie Richter."

A pair of Western kids strolled by along the curb, seemingly looking for something, referred to in their open *Lonely Planet* guide. They didn't look at Paul and Elise but concentrated on their travel guide.

"Her thoughts aside," Elise said, "and assuming the document is legit, we don't know if Oleg is just spouting off or if there are others who are involved or know about this supposed movement. And those others could be a bunch of drunks sitting around some bar with dreams of secession."

She looked over Paul's shoulder at a couple of customers at the bar.

"I mean," she said, "is this even a real possibility?

"What about the Chinese?" she said, turning back to him, "What about the Japanese? What about the Koreans—North and South? This would shake up their part of the world pretty dramatically. Would they let this happen? Would they want this to happen?"

Paul said nothing for a moment.

"We don't even know if he really wrote the paper, actually," he said.

"We do know he's traveling here under a false name, though," Elise said, "so something about him is amiss."

"Right," Paul said. He looked out to the street. The kids had gone over to the *cyclo* driver and apparently asked him something, but he waved them away. He then looked over at Paul and Elise.

"Let's get out of here," Paul said.

* * *

Veronica's apartment was the sort of stripped-down place a visiting academic would find herself in. It had a living room that, with a small table, doubled as a dining room, at least for tonight, as well as a cramped kitchen. There were two doors off the living room. One led to a small patio and the other, closed, led, Guy presumed, to a bedroom. Which he hoped he would see before too long.

Guy had arrived wearing a sport jacket and slacks, greeted by Veronica in a blouse and jeans, who gave him a peck on the cheek as she took the bottle of red wine he had brought over to open. Peter had already arrived and rose to greet Guy. He was drinking what looked like some sort of whiskey and motioned to a row of bottles set up on a sideboard, apparently the bartender for the evening.

Guy nodded toward a bottle of Dewars and asked for it with ice. Not his usual, high-priced, hard-to-pronounce choice, but he had other things on his mind.

Peter, however, paused over the bottle, then turned to a shopping bag in a corner and pulled out a bottle of ten-year-old Talisker single malt.

"I got this from a client yesterday, why don't we break it in?" he asked.

This was a pleasant surprise, and Guy gratefully accepted a generous portion, which he sipped neat.

Veronica came out of the kitchen with a glass of white wine and the three sat down to chat before dinner. To Guy's satisfaction, Veronica sat next to him on the loveseat while Peter sat across a low table in a chair.

Guy asked Peter how he liked Washington, to which Peter said that, never having been to the United States before, he was dazzled by all of it. He had found time to walk by the White House, gone to the Tomb of the Unknown Soldier—very moving, he added—seen a couple of the Smithsonian museums, and visited Congress.

He had found Congress a little confusing, he said, but Guy sagely outlined the rudiments of how the House and Senate worked and their relationship to the presidency and the Supreme Court. He even tossed in some references to committee markups and conference reports but allowed as how those could wait for another day. Peter nodded as he listened, grateful for the explanation from such a knowledgeable expert.

A few minutes later, Veronica went into the kitchen and returned, announcing that dinner was ready. She asked both men to help her bring out the dishes: an academic's pasta standby with some sort of sauce, some garlic bread, and Guy's Chianti.

The three talked some more at dinner, Veronica about her research and Peter a little bit about his work, but Peter really seemed interested in Guy's work and how the U.S. system was different from Canada's.

Guy was not only happy to share his insights as a Respected Journalist, but he noticed Veronica admiring his explanations of the arcane machinations of Washington. He steamed on when they'd finished the meal and were enjoying the last of the wine but was careful not to appear pedagogical—nothing turns the chicks off like condescension over drinks, as he'd learned the hard way.

Peter, though seemed to eat it up, apparently dazzled by Guy's casually mentioned high-level contacts and familiarity with obscure congressional procedures—not to mention his inside stories about members of Congress or administration officials who Peter may or may not have heard of.

Feeling he was on a roll, Guy started to switch to what was usually a winner with visiting firemen, tales of covering the Pentagon and national security but, it seemed, it was getting late and, Peter said, looking at his watch, he'd better head home. He liked to run in the morning he said, and he wanted to make sure his wife—that was good news, Guy thought—had packed what he described as essential running gear, "sneakers and aspirin."

He seemed to understand the situation with Guy and Veronica, so after finishing his drink he made to leave, and Guy and Veronica bid him good night.

Then, as Peter left, something nagged at the back of Guy's mind, but as Veronica closed the door, she gave him a look that distracted him from whatever that was.

Until the next morning, when he left early to go home and change his clothes for work.

CHAPTER SEVENTEEN

SOMETIMES IT'S BETTER TO SKIP A PARTY

As restful as the Mekong Dreams hotel was, Oleg, now Ivo, was feeling tense.

The adrenaline rush from his spy novel-like adventure slipping out of Europe and into Asia had worn off, leaving the awareness of the gravity of his situation in its wake. He knew he'd better figure out what to do, and fast.

If only he hadn't gone to that fucking Moscow party, he wouldn't be in this mess.

It had been a quiet Saturday night, and he had felt at loose ends. Some academic he had met at a recent seminar in Saint Petersburg, he couldn't even remember the name now, had been in town to meet with some government big shots and had called to ask him to come along to the gathering.

Oleg had known it was a mistake right away. The room was full of oligarchs and their hangers-on and a profusion of too-young girlfriends. Oleg had stuck around to avoid offending his new friend but had retreated to what he'd thought was a safe corner, away from much of the crowd.

As he sat there, nursing a warm vodka, trying to come up with a plan to get out without offending his friend, a pudgy white-haired man, his tie loosened and with some sort of stain, had tipsily come up to him. Mistaking Oleg for someone else, the drunk guy—Vladimir Alexandrovich something or other from the Foreign Affairs Ministry, in case the guy who Oleg wasn't didn't remember him—had started blathering on about some sort of assignment involving classified information interpretation of some kind. Apparently, it was an assignment he and the guy who looked like Oleg were working on, or should work on, or might work on, something like that. Vladimir Alexandrovich was slurring his words pretty badly and Oleg couldn't get a handle on what he was talking about, but from the bits and pieces Oleg was able to pick up, it sounded like it was something preposterous, like the fantasy of some third-rate analyst who had never left Moscow and had too much time on his hands. Not to mention, the more the guy talked, the clearer it became that it was something that Oleg did not want to know about.

Oleg nodded as Vladimir Alexandrovich went on, not really paying attention. He wanted to get away but was trapped. Although several people walked by, none seemed to be inclined to draw Vladimir Alexandrovich away. Moreover, Vladimir Alexandrovich wouldn't shut up about whatever the fuck he was talking about. As he talked on, poking Oleg in the chest now and then to make a point or to steady himself, it wasn't clear which, he pulled a sheaf of folded pages out of his pocket and made Oleg put them in his own inside coat pocket to read later. *Da, konechno*, yes, of course, Oleg had said distractedly, still looking around for a way to get away from this drunk.

Suddenly, Vladimir Alexandrovich stopped talking, spying something in the mirror behind Oleg. Oleg looked past Vladimir Alexandrovich and saw a statuesque blonde swaying slightly, looking lost, drink in hand. Vladimir Alexandrovich, leer on his face, winked at Oleg and turned away, heading toward what he obviously hoped would be his next adventure.

Oleg decided it was time to get home, so he made his way through the crowded room toward the door. He was stopped halfway by a friend who did something with the Foreign Affairs Ministry and who wanted to introduce Oleg to some of his colleagues—he had seen Oleg talking with Vladimir Alexandrovich from across the room. Oleg had to stop and have a drink with them and exchange business cards. Finally, he was able to push through the crowd of movers and shakers and their molls, out to the street.

He had to walk several blocks to the Metro, almost tripping on some uneven pavement, and then, finally, made it into his small apartment.

He let himself in and, as he was taking his jacket off, spied the papers that Vladimir Alexandrovich had pressed onto him.

What the fuck. He made some tea and opened the papers.

Once he started reading, he forgot about the tea.

The sheaf was a numbered copy of a highly restricted document outlining, in some detail, with names, dates, and other specifics, what had sounded to Oleg like a cheap movie plot from Vladimir Alexandrovich's prattling on. The document was pretty much crystal clear, other than what looked like an addendum at the end that consisted of a list of letter-and-number sequences. The list meant nothing to Oleg. As Oleg pored over the papers, a business card dropped out onto the floor.

Oleg picked up the card and read it. That was when he knew he was in real trouble.

Vladimir Alexandrovich Zhuravlev, whose full name and title were on the card, was no ordinary skirt-chasing bureaucrat. He was a senior security official in the ministry and likely connected to the Kremlin at a high level.

Very high.

Oleg read through the papers again. He poured out the tea and switched it for another vodka. This was serious stuff. As serious, he thought, as a one-way ticket to an unmarked grave after a quick stop in one of Russia's super-efficient interrogation facilities.

The whole thing was preposterous on its face. It outlined an effort obviously doomed to failure, but whose even partial execution could have cataclysmic consequences, particularly for Moscow. How would it affect other countries, he thought, such as China, now working hard to regain what it saw as its historic role as the world's leading power? Beijing was already flexing its muscles elsewhere in Asia and around the world. It might well want to get involved if word leaked out, and that would spell trouble for everybody.

More immediately, though, and completely separate from the intellectually stimulating global and geopolitical implications of the papers, Oleg knew he, personally, was now fucked. No one would want this out in the open, and a roomful of people had seen Oleg talking with Zhuravlev, who was presumably linked to the numbered copy of the document he was now looking at. Once it was discovered missing, Oleg would be easy to describe. Zhuravlev might not remember Oleg's name or even confess to having given it to him, but, no problem, because just to make sure he was absolutely and completely fucked, Oleg had handed out business cards to those staffers from the Foreign Affairs Ministry. Or wherever they were really from. And at least one of them, Oleg now remembered, had seen Oleg talking with Zhuravlev.

No doubt about it. He was cooked. And the sand, to mix metaphors, was quickly running through the hourglass.

He stared at his vodka, turning the situation over in his mind. No matter how he looked at it, he was in trouble. After thirty minutes of staring at nothing, he came to a decision. This wouldn't be easy, but it was the only way.

He stayed up for another two hours thinking about exactly what to do and how to do it. He was not without means and had experience traveling outside Russia.

Finally, in the small hours, he came up with a plan. He had no idea whether it would work, but it was the best he could think of.

What to do with this document, though. He would deal with that later. He had to get some sleep.

He arose after a brief, fitful rest and began to carry out his plan.

Oleg had remembered that his sister's musician friend's husband had strayed into drugs in a major way some years back, to such an extent that the husband had some hardcore drug dealer contacts, one of whom Oleg had met once. It was a tenuous connection, but it was his best bet.

Oleg called his sister and after surprising her with a hastily concocted and dubious story about having met a girl and wanting to hook up with the friend's husband for some drugs, got a name and phone number for the guy. Oleg's sister didn't quite sound like she believed the story, but she was running late for work and had to go. She no doubt figured she would shake the details out of Oleg later.

Armed with the number, Oleg put a call into the drug guy.

As he listened to the phone ring on the other end, he looked at his watch. He knew he might not have a lot of time, although Zhuravlev might be hungover or in the arms of the blonde from last night or panicking himself over the missing document.

The drug guy picked up finally and, remembering after a few moments who Oleg was, agreed to meet him shortly in a downtown park.

This was a risky step for Oleg, as he rightly figured they all would be from here on out. He only vaguely remembered the drug guy and wasn't sure he would recognize him in the park.

He did, though, seeing him sitting on a bench in jeans and a cheap leather jacket, smoking a cigarette and trying to look cool. He looked like a punk. Perfect.

Oleg sat on the bench next to him and outlined what he needed. The punk nodded as he listened, his eyes appraising Oleg, obviously figuring out how much to stick him for. Oleg passed him some cash, adding that there would be a similar amount after the transaction was complete. It had to be tonight, though, he said.

The punk looked in the envelope at the cash and back at Oleg. Wait here, he said, and walked a short distance away to make a call. When he came back, he told Oleg to meet his contact, "Ivan," at a well-known high-end bar that evening and told him how much cash to bring. Ivan would have a newspaper in front of him.

Oleg busied himself with other necessary tasks for the rest of the day, then, at the appointed hour, went into the bar the punk had mentioned. He found Ivan sitting at a reserved table at the back with a folded news-paper on the table in front of him. Ivan looked like a middle-aged slug, with a corpulent body, an overpriced suit, and too much jewelry. A few visible evil-looking prison tattoos marked him as part of the criminal underworld. As Oleg approached, Ivan gestured to the young woman of no more than twenty who had been sitting next to him staring off into the void. She wordlessly got up and went to another table, displaying her weapons-grade anatomy and footwear as she clicked across the floor.

The meeting with Ivan was short, no one was trying to make a new friend here. After a few brief pleasantries, Ivan looked at Oleg expec-tantly and Oleg passed another envelope to Ivan under the table. Ivan nodded—he didn't look in the envelope; he knew that Oleg knew what would happen if there were a problem. He slid the newspaper over to Oleg and then gestured to the girl. He looked at Oleg expectantly again, which Oleg took as a signal, and he left with the newspaper under his arm as the girl resumed her station next to Ivan.

Once on the Metro, Oleg found Micheletti's name, email address, and a codeword written on one of the inside pages of the newspaper.

He tore that part of the newspaper page off and put the scrap in his pocket. He waited a couple of stops, then got off the train and tossed the remainder of the newspaper in a trash bin. He left the Metro and went to a hotel popular with tourists and contacted Micheletti using the codeword Ivan had given him from one of the hotel's business center computers. Oleg was impressed when Micheletti wrote back immediately with instructions.

The next morning, after another sleepless night, he called into his office, ensuring that he was connected with a low-level secretary, and told her he would be leaving for a research trip for a few days and would then take a few days off. He knew the secretary was too junior to either be surprised that she had not heard of the trip or to raise any questions.

He now put the rest of his plan into action. He had a large amount of cash that he had stashed away and would leave some of it with his sister for the punk who had set him up with Ivan to keep him quiet, at least for a few days. Later, he went to the airport, carrying the sort of suitcase and briefcase that he would typically take for a business trip for his afternoon flight to Rome, which he had arranged that morning. Zhuravlev's papers were folded and sealed in an envelope among some innocuous-looking and mundane reports in the briefcase.

Which is where, now, they still sat, in his deluxe room, at the Mekong Dreams hotel. They had been preying on his mind and he had been wondering whether there was a way he could short-circuit events without getting himself in trouble. That was a laugh, he thought, he had probably already pretty much reached the limit of the amount of trouble he could be in and still be walking around.

* * *

It was a few days after his amorous adventure with Veronica. Guy hadn't heard from her other than a quick phone conversation, during which she confided that she was behind on her work and would be buried in that work for the next few days. Great, let's get together this weekend, he had said. She had said OK, she would call him, but she seemed slightly distracted. He wondered whether there was a problem.

He was pulled out of his reverie when his desk phone rang.

It turned out to be Peter, who, it seemed, was in the neighborhood and if Guy had a moment, would he like to meet for a cup of coffee.

Ordinarily, Guy's instinct would have been to brush Peter off, claiming to be snowed under with the important business of covering the news. However, since he was a little concerned about his chances of scoring with Veronica again, and since she seemed tight with Peter, making an exception seemed the smart move.

Guy suggested a nearby Starbucks and, when he had arrived and picked up his coffee, he spotted Peter waving at him from a corner table. Peter, it appeared, had been in some sort of meeting and had a series of financial statement-looking papers in front of him. He seemed relieved at the prospect of getting away from his work.

They chatted a bit about this and that, but then Guy was happy when the conversation drifted back to his work as a journalist. Peter confided that he had talked with his cousin, whom Guy, after a moment, remembered from the conversation at the Kennedy Center. The cousin worked at some hick Canadian paper and had been full of questions. The cousin, it turned out, had even heard of Guy from his network days.

Guy was happy to talk about his work, roaming from covering the State Department to presidential trips. He even threw in a few inside tidbits that everyone in Washington who mattered knew but would probably be news to Peter.

"I'm leaving in a week or so to head back home, this has really been interesting," Peter said after Guy had shared one such nugget with him.

Guy realized that this meant that if he had fucked things up with Veronica and wanted to use Peter to right the situation, he'd better move fast.

"Look," Guy said, improvising as he went along, "why don't I buy you a farewell dinner before you leave?" Pause. "Maybe you could join Veronica and me over the weekend." Veronica seemed unlikely to turn down a dinner with Peter, even if she were having second thoughts about Guy.

"That's quite generous," Peter said after thinking about it for a moment. He pulled out his phone and started tapping away. Then, after a moment, the phone beeped.

"Veronica says that's a great idea," he said. Then, adopting a conspiratorial mien and leaning closer, he added, "don't let her go, she likes you."

What a relief, Guy thought, now regretting having included Peter in the plans.

"I'll tell you what," Peter continued as if there had been no interruption, "I'll agree if you promise to let me buy you dinner if you're ever up in my Zip Code."

"Sure," Guy said. His own phone buzzed, distracting him with a text, and he realized he was late for a budget meeting.

Shifting his mental gears, he made his farewells to Peter and went back to the office.

Guy worked late at the office that evening before going home. He was exhausted when he got there, parking the Porsche in his driveway and heading in with an armful of mail from the last day or two. He made himself a drink and finished off a cold leftover Thai carryout chicken order from a few days back before turning in.

Just as he was about to go into the bedroom, he remembered the stack of mail he had brought in and decided to check it.

Something struck him while he was scanning the envelopes and brochures. He stopped and stared out the window for a moment. Then something else came back to him.

Probably nothing, he thought, and went to bed.

CHAPTER EIGHTEEN

BACK TO SCHOOL

Veronica and Peter were all smiles when Guy arrived that Friday night at a little Italian restaurant he knew on Capitol Hill, where he'd suggested they meet for Peter's farewell dinner. The food wasn't bad and now and then a House member or senator dropped in, which Guy figured would help him gain points in the Veronica department.

Peter had good news to share as they ordered drinks and appetizers—it seemed he would be around Washington for a few more weeks, so this wouldn't be a farewell dinner after all.

Gosh, that's great, or something like that, Guy said. The thought that had been nagging at him since the day he had had coffee with Peter had not left, and he didn't want to lose it, but he needed to see if he could fill it out a bit.

As the meal wore on, the conversation moved around from one topic to another. At one point, Veronica asked Guy about work. Guy started talking about a congressional story the paper had broken that morning but segued over to some work one of the reporters was doing on intelligence agencies. Usually, that was a winner with outsiders, but Guy noticed that Peter seemed to subtly, almost imperceptibly, shift the conversation in another direction. Veronica seemed not to notice anything.

The rest of the dinner passed uneventfully. At the end of the meal, Peter tried to split the check with Guy since, as it turned out, he wasn't leaving, but Guy would have nothing of it. Peter retreated, but not until they agreed to meet again. As they were leaving the restaurant, it turned out that Peter had driven Veronica over, but he was sure Guy wouldn't mind giving her a lift home. No, of course not, Guy said.

Then it happened so fast that Guy barely had time to react.

Just as they were about to split up and head to their respective cars, a young tough jumped out of the shadows, lunging at them with a knife.

To Guy's astonishment, and before he could even respond, Peter leaped at the attacker and had him pinned up against the wall with his hand, still clutching the knife, twisted behind his back.

Veronica was frozen as was, frankly, Guy. They heard Peter lean into the guy's ear and give him the choice of dropping the knife or getting a broken arm. The kid blubbered a bit but dropped the knife, which clattered onto the pavement. Peter pulled him away from the wall and shoved him in the direction from which he'd come. The whole thing had probably taken a minute.

When the kid was gone, Peter turned back and asked if everyone was OK, which of course they were. He picked up the knife and, after looking at it for a moment, tossed it into a storm drain.

"I grew up in a tough town," he said to Guy, who was staring at him, "you would know how to do that if you'd grown up where I did," he added, all Canadian modesty.

Then, as if nothing had happened, he said he needed to get back home and assumed Veronica could go with Guy. After wishing them both a good night, he headed off, presumably, toward his car.

Guy thought about offering to take Veronica back to his place, but he still wasn't on certain ground. It became clear, though, as they made their way back to her apartment that she did not intend for the evening to end quite yet.

And it did not. When they got to her place, she got out of his car and walked to her door, the unspoken message being that he should follow her.

In her living room, she proposed a nightcap before they moved on to the next order of business—her phrase—and poured them each some sort of brandy.

The mugger incident, of course, was hanging over the evening, and they managed to discuss it a bit over their drinks without, in Guy's mind, spoiling the mood for whatever was to follow.

It seemed Peter had shared some of his background with Veronica when they were both working in Canada. "Really quite an interesting guy," she said, "worked in Toronto but had been born and raised in someplace remote in the Canadian boonies and had made a name for himself in the big city."

"Does he have family in Toronto?" Guy asked.

"No," she said, "they were all back home."

"Does he ever get back there?"

"Not really," she said, "he seems to be something of a loner." She downed the rest of her drink. "Do you want to spend all night out here talking about Peter?"

The answer was no, of course, and a frenzied half hour later, Guy was lying on his back next to a lightly snoring Veronica, but his mind wandered elsewhere.

It all fit. Peter claimed to be a Canadian who had never been out of Canada, but Guy noticed he had said "sneakers," not "runners," as most Canadians in Guy's, albeit limited, experience said. Moreover, Peter had referred to being in his "Zip Code," but a native of Canada who had never traveled to the United States would be unlikely to use the American term rather than the Canadian "postal code," particularly when referring to where he himself lived in Canada. Neither of these slips was conclusive, but Guy had been beginning to suspect something fishy about Peter, specifically that he might be an American trying to pass as a Canadian for some reason.

Guy only knew one kind of American who commonly tried to pass as Canadian, but that possibility had seemed farfetched until tonight, when Peter had dispatched the attacker efficiently and effectively, hardly breaking into a sweat.

No one learns to handle themselves like that from bar fights with drunk hayseeds, Guy figured.

* * *

It was not surprising that Oleg would go to ground here in Phnom Penh, out of the limelight, Paul thought as he and Elise lingered over breakfast at the Royal's sumptuous buffet. That didn't make it easy, though. There were dozens of hotels and guesthouses where he could be staying. It had also occurred to Paul and Elise that Oleg might not even be in the city anymore—Cambodia's tourist boom had made much more of the country friendly to outsiders than had been the case in the past, so he might have headed to Siem Reap, a tourist haven and home of Angkor Wat, or even further afield. He might have even changed identities again or gone to another country; Laos and Vietnam were an easy hop away for starters.

Paul knew journalists here and had a list of contacts among diplomats, U.N. and World Bank staff members, human rights groups and the like, who might be expected to be among those who would hear of a visiting Czech first. It wasn't that Paul expected Oleg to march into some anti-trafficking organization and announce his presence, but these people all lived and worked in Phnom Penh and frequented the sorts of places a foreigner with more than tourism on his mind might go. Paul knew some of these people, others were friends of friends who would be likely to have heard of Paul or might even just agree to meet him because of a shared contact. It could be a long slog, but it struck Paul and Elise as the only way they might find Oleg.

Professor Eric Schiller, though, was someone Paul hadn't known, and it would turn out to be a good thing Elise had jumped on his offer the night before.

* * *

Paul and Elise had spent the evening with a dozen or so members of the surviving contingent of Phnom Penh's shrinking resident foreign press corps at a riverside bar called Ollie's.

The invitation had come in the afternoon from one of Paul's old buddies who Paul had alerted to his arrival. Come on down to this bar tonight, the old pal had said, someone Paul didn't know was taking a new job with the *Bangkok Post* and this was a farewell before he left for Bangkok. Everyone would be there.

Paul wasn't sure who "everyone" might be at this juncture—some mixture of reporters from the three local English-language papers, stringers from the wires or international services like Agence France-Presse or the BBC, a local freelancer or two, and maybe a drop-in by a visiting correspondent or stringer from Bangkok if things were slow out that way and they were in town trying to scare up a story. Not only that, but probably a few staffers from the U.S. or other embassies, one of the U.N.

agencies, or one of the local do-gooder NGOs might show up. Maybe even a spook or two masquerading as a commercial officer. So, sure, why not, he'd said—all good prospects for potential leads to Oleg.

A few hours later, he and Elise were talking as they made their way to the bar on foot; much of expat Phnom Penh was clustered along the river and made for an enjoyable stroll on such a pleasant night. They had come out of the Royal, through its elegant front doors and courtyard before turning left on Daun Penh and passing the foreboding fortress-like American Embassy, rumored by locals to be concealing all sorts of post-9/11 super-secret counterterrorism and surveillance facilities. They ignored tuk-tuk drivers' entreaties and continued to the circle at Wat Phnom, passing the site of a now-gone French restaurant that had just a few years back been popular with reporters, World Bankers, and similar members of the international herd.

It seemed a long shot, meeting these reporters, Paul and Elise agreed as they walked, once they were sure no one was around any longer who might want to eavesdrop, but the whole point of being here was to try to shake some trees.

The heavy afternoon air had been cooled by evening showers. As they made their way to Ollie's, the darkness was pierced by the sounds of passing motorbikes, *cyclos*, and tuk-tuks, as well as the lights from shops, stalls, and the growing number of tourist restaurants and bars. As they passed one such restaurant, Elise glanced down wistfully at the menus on display, showing an enticing array of Khmer and French dishes. Much more appealing than the crap probably available at what was no doubt a drunken journalist hangout.

"The clock's ticking," Paul said, ignoring the hostess waving them to come in and nudging Elise.

As Elise had expected, Ollie's was much like other bars frequented by resident expats; it was noisy and full of people speaking a variety of languages, although mostly accented English and a lot of really bad Khmer. The reporters were gathered at a table that was sheltered by an awning but open to the street.

At the bar itself, two Australians loudly argued about something while two Cambodian girls, apparently with them, obliviously chatted with each other in Khmer. The girls' eyes flitted appraisingly across Paul and Elise as they passed then back to each other.

Paul and Elise knew some of the group already and others were introduced as someone pulled two chairs from an empty table nearby. There were quick hellos and some catching up before Paul and Elise drifted into the table conversation, which hopped from local news to the guest of honor's impending move to Thailand to the sort of gossip you'd hear from overseas reporters everywhere—so-and-so had gotten a good interview with some big-shot Khmer official, so-and-so had left to shoot pictures and do a couple of pieces in Burma for a high-paying magazine, a Western network was looking for a stringer but they weren't paying shit, that Hong Kong editor is looking for someone to do a feature on how the poor are getting fucked by the developers here, plus he wanted good pictures and the whole thing by next week. That sort of thing.

Someone ordered more beers. Someone else passed a lit joint to Paul, who passed it on without partaking. He needed to keep his wits about him tonight.

As the bar became more crowded, conversation turned to the growing influx of tourists and how it was changing the formerly sleepy city into too much of a tourist center, and how the riverfront was turning distasteful, aspiring to Bangkok's level of vulgarity.

Someone saw a rat running along the curb, picked up a rock, and tried to hit it but missed. A couple of the reporters booed drunkenly, one cheered for the rat.

Seeing an opening in the conversation, Paul mentioned he and Elise were looking for an old friend, a Czech named Ivo Jezek he and Elise thought was in Phnom Penh, who might have popped up.

They told a completely fabricated version of what they were doing. They had been on vacation in Thailand, they said, and had heard from someone they knew in Chiang Mai that their old friend Ivo was hanging around Phnom Penh, they hoped to find him here. Sadly, they didn't have a current email address for him in Prague or know where he might be staying here in Phnom Penh, but they'd like to find him to say hello, and there probably weren't that many Czechs in town.

No one knew much about Czechs, although there were a fair number of Russians, probably especially in the sleazy nightclubs, everyone agreed. It was clear that Ivo Jezek's name wasn't ringing any bells with this crowd, but they'd keep an eye out. How long were Paul and Elise planning to stay? Oh, a while, Elise said breezily, noncommittally. Phnom Penh itself could be a little on the dull side but would be a good base, someone said. Maybe they'd take trips to Ho Chi Minh City or Siem Reap, somewhere like that, another piped in. Maybe, Elise agreed.

As the conversation drifted away, Paul and Elise noticed a member of the group they had not met yet—he had come in after Paul and Elise and sat not far from Paul.

"Eric Schiller," the man said, putting his hand out to Paul as the conversation drifted to the other end of the table. He was jug-shaped, with receding blonde hair, and had the eager look of someone not quite in with the group but anxious to make friends with new arrivals. He had adopted the uniform of the Westerner gone semi-native—khakis, loose sport shirt, and comfortable shoes. He seemed to know the waitress when she came by, and he spoke to her in rapid, seemingly fluent Khmer. She nodded, smiling, and responded, before leaving and quickly returning with a mixed drink of some sort.

Schiller turned back to Paul and Elise, who had watched the interchange.

"She's one of my students," Schiller said, sipping the drink. As he spoke, he looked around and nodded to others in the group.

Paul was about to ask Schiller something when Elise spoke, cutting him off. "Really," she asked, "what kind of student?"

"Well," Schiller said, turning to her, "I teach at one of the universities here for well-placed Cambodians—those with the pull and English skills to get in." He seemed pleasantly surprised at the attention.

"My, how interesting," Elise said, turning on the charm, "what do you teach?"

It turned out that Schiller, a former correspondent himself, had landed a spot running the journalism department of this university, which beat trying to flog stories to editors who didn't know where Cambodia was and thought the Khmer Rouge were a heretofore undiscovered French wine. He stayed in touch with some of these reporters and, on occasion was able to give them gigs teaching a course or two.

"That's really interesting," Elise said. Paul, who thought it wasn't, was glancing around impatiently as Elise elaborated on the made-up version of what she and Paul were doing in Phnom Penh.

Schiller seemed to mull over what she had told him.

"Do you think Paul—or you—could find the time to come by the school and talk with some of my students? Some of the upper-level ones?" he asked after a moment.

"It wouldn't take much time and they'd really appreciate it," he added.

Paul started to respond negatively. He had only been listening with half an ear and was anxious to leave. Before he could speak, though, Elise cut in again. "What kind of students do you have?" she asked. She leaned her chin on her open hand as she spoke, winning smile, really interested in the answer.

"Well," Schiller said, surprised and happy to talk about his world, "they're a pretty sophisticated lot. They follow the news closely, or as closely as they can from here on the internet and like to deal with me and the other foreigners here in town and on the faculty."

Paul started to listen more closely.

"They all speak pretty good English," Schiller continued, now realizing that Paul was paying attention as well as Elise, "although they are under the mistaken belief that they're fluent." Haha, he laughed, haha, Elise agreed.

"They're a very interesting bunch, I've learned a lot from them," he said, serious again. "In fact," Schiller continued, warming to what he expected would interest his audience, "one is really fascinating, he's the son of a tuk-tuk driver, so this is a big step for him."

"Uh huh," Elise said, not wishing to be diverted. "What would you like Paul to talk about?"

"Well," Schiller said, surprised, but abandoning what he'd expected would be an inspiring tale that these two would enjoy hearing, "and of course, you would be welcome as a speaker too but, you know, general international journalist sort of stuff. We don't get many outsiders here with Paul's—or your—background."

"I think that's a great idea," Elise said, before Paul could respond, "when would you like to do it?"

"How about tomorrow afternoon," Schiller asked, ignoring Paul for the moment.

Elise looked at Paul, now, having realized what was going on, fully onboard.

"More than happy to," Paul said, giving Schiller a winning smile of his own. "Maybe we could talk to a couple of classes."

Schiller lit up.

"Perfect," he said. Then, "Maybe you could meet with some of the other teachers and students," adding, "if you have time."

"It would be our pleasure," Paul said.

CHAPTER NINETEEN

SOCHEATA

This meeting with Schiller and his students might be a waste of time, Paul and Elise knew, but they agreed on the way back to the hotel that he might turn out to be a lucky link to another group of foreigners in Phnom Penh, which could lead them to Oleg or someone who knew him. Might as well take the shot, they agreed.

Besides, they were beginning to get nervous. They had made quick work of finding out that Oleg was traveling under an alias and had landed here in Phnom Penh, which was, truth be told, impressive. However, until they talked to him, they wouldn't be able to confirm that the document purportedly outlining a plan—and possibly one in progress—for the Far East to secede from Russia was kosher. If so, it was huge news, but if not, they needed to find out quickly before they or Gunther—or even Guy, for that matter—wasted any more time on it. Certainly, Paul's conversation with Doris Pollock in Bangkok had not been encouraging.

It could be that they were being played, for some reason, but neither of them could think of why that might be, so they had to continue on the assumption that the document was real. Certainly, the fact that Oleg had gone on the run, and under an alias at that, meant that something was afoot and he was somehow involved in whatever that something that was afoot was.

Curiouser and curiouser.

They kept their voices low as they walked, even though there were few pedestrians on the street, and those who they did see seemed oblivious to them.

They tried to dissect what could have made Oleg run. It seemed that if it were known that the document had leaked out, the Moscow authorities would be after him over it.

"However," Elise said, "if Moscow officials were concerned about a fledgling separatist movement in the Far East, they'd have bigger fish to fry than chasing after an academician who had spilled the beans."

"True, but they would probably want to keep the news quiet," Paul said.

They walked for a bit.

"We don't know," Paul said, "what Oleg was, or had been, actually doing in Moscow." There was no way to tell whether the document was related to whatever Oleg was doing or whether this was information he had come across by accident. "If it were the latter, Moscow might want to shake him down for his sources to find out who was talking."

"I suppose," Elise said.

Elise glanced at the American Embassy across the street as they approached the hotel. It seemed quiet, although some lights were on. A guard watching them from his post at the main entrance glanced at them, pulled out his walkie-talkie, and said something into it. He seemed to watch them as they turned into the hotel. Or he was just watching the street. No way to tell.

They passed through the grand entrance of the hotel forecourt and made their way up the sweeping driveway toward the doors. A few tuk-tuk drivers at the entrance had looked up briefly, but then turned their attention elsewhere when they realized that these foreigners were coming back to the hotel, not leaving, and were therefore unlikely potential customers.

Elise slowed her walk so she and Paul could continue their conversation before reaching the entrance and the small group of foreign tourists chatting there.

"The more I think about it," she said, "the more I think that if the Russians were actually onto Oleg's plot, they would have taken more dramatic action than just scaring Oleg out here to the tropics, there would have been signs of some sort of panic."

"Well, we might not be in a position to see those signs," Paul said.

Elise stopped walking and looked at Paul. She said nothing. Paul, also stopping, looked back at her. Then he remembered that she had stayed in Rome after he had left and that Serino wasn't her only tie left to her former profession.

"I see what you mean," he said after a moment. They resumed walking. He waited to see if she said anything further.

"The thing is, though," he said when she apparently had nothing to add, "we know about this paper, and we, or at least I, know Oleg well enough to know that he's not a nutcase. At least he wasn't before. If this is from him, there's something to it."

They were near the door now, but far enough away to neither be overheard by the tourists chattering away about their visit to Angkor Wat nor attract their attention.

"So," Paul continued, "there must be some reason why he's written this paper."

"And some reason why it somehow got into our hands," Elise said. "Someone wanted us or someone like us to see it," she said, "maybe Oleg himself."

A lizard ran up the hotel's wall, chasing a bug. As they watched, the bug became dinner.

"Let's see what we can find out from the Schiller thing," Paul said.

Paul wanted to finish the evening with a drink. Elise was tired but agreed to join him in the hotel's strikingly in-character Elephant Bar, with its vaulted ceilings emblazoned with pictures of elephants and faux period-appropriate tropical-motif couches and tables.

They sat at a table near the windows as Paul sipped his scotch. They made small talk, feeling they had exhausted the subject of Oleg and his report for the moment. It occurred to Paul that Oleg might decide to find his way here to the Elephant Bar for a bit of the colonial experience. That would be too easy, though, he thought. He looked around the room, just in case lightning had struck, but saw that the only other customers were a small group of tourists a couple of tables away. They were talking quietly and poring over a travel guide as they sipped cocktails. They kept looking at the ice in their drinks suspiciously, apparently wondering whether it contained the germs of some dreadful tropical disease that would cause a slow, excruciating death as, no doubt, they had been warned. Paul looked back at Elise, who was lost in her own thoughts.

"I guess we're not going to hear again from your pal, Serino, right?" he asked.

"No," she said, "he was out of touch on some sort of trip." She looked at her watch. It was time to go, she said.

"I think I'll stick around and finish this," he said.

She nodded and left for their room, still lost in thought.

It might have been Paul's imagination, but he thought he saw the table full of tourists, almost imperceptibly, pause their conversation for an instant as Elise walked by, as one of them seemed to quickly glance her way as she passed.

Paul took his drink up to the bar and made small talk with the Khmer bartender for a few minutes while he finished it. The bartender seemed happy to pass the slow night with a customer and they chatted a bit about the changes in Phnom Penh in recent years. When he'd finished his drink, Paul paid his check and turned to leave.

The tourists were gone.

* * *

The next day, Paul and Elise left the Royal in the morning. They skipped the breakfast buffet at the hotel. Instead, they walked down to Monument Books on Preah Norodom Boulevard, which served a good breakfast as well as carrying a solid selection of Western books, newspapers, and magazines. The plan was to use the bookstore as a base from which to call down Paul's list of contacts who might have heard of a visiting Czech. There was always a chance, they figured, that Oleg might drop into the store for coffee and a newspaper, as Elise had done most days when she and Paul had been there on one of his assignments a few years before.

In the event, though, Paul didn't make much progress with his searches, conducted over the course of three cups of coffee on his newly acquired Khmer cell phone. Everyone he called was friendly or glad to hear from him again, depending on whether they already knew him, and happy to offer to help, but no Ivo Jezek had turned up so far as they knew, and no one had noticed any new Czechs wandering around. Call back, though, they all said, and why don't we meet for a cup of coffee or a drink.

This was starting to become frustrating. "If only we could get in touch with Serino," Paul said, "we could find out where Oleg had checked in as Ivo Jezek, and we'd be home free—do you have any idea when Serino would be back on the grid?"

Elise shook her head.

"OK," Paul said, "let's go down to Schiller's school, maybe we'll learn something there."

The clash of the new and old Phnom Penh was plain as they made their way down the wide Preah Norodom and around the circle to cross Preah Sihanouk after lunch. The traffic was horrendous, with the buzzing motorbikes jostling with the increasing number of cars—including some pretty hefty and pricey SUVs—racing past the exploding number of new buildings. Crossing streets was an adventure requiring faith in a protective superior power. Traffic lights and regulations were apparently seen as merely providing interesting, suggested guidance for drivers, to be followed or ignored at their discretion. The only way to make it across a street was to look for a slight gap in the traffic and venture out, having faith that cars, motorbikes, tuk-tuks, cyclos, and bicycles would swerve to avoid a pedestrian.

Not far from the circle, they found the campus and walked through the main gate, surrounded by a crush of students chattering away to each other and on their cell phones. One of them directed Paul and Elise to a large, central building that seemed to house many of the school's offices and classrooms. Once inside, they found their way to Schiller's office, grateful for the room's air conditioner.

Schiller stood as they came in and, smiling, waved them to two chairs facing his desk. He handed them two welcome bottles of cold water. They chatted for a while, then, once they'd recovered from the heat, he took them around to meet some of his colleagues, finally escorting them into a staff lounge, where a dozen or so Khmer and foreign professors were waiting, eager to chat with the visiting American journalist. Paul realized that there were probably few such visitors, so he would likely be given something more of a celebrity welcome than he was accustomed to, with more professors showing up than might have been the case otherwise. The more the merrier, he thought, one of these academics might have spotted a new Czech visitor.

They spent about half an hour schmoozing with the gathered academics. Paul started to tell them that he and Elise were looking for a

Czech colleague, but it seemed that Schiller had already mentioned that and, unfortunately, none of the academics could be of any help.

After half an hour or so, Schiller shuttled Paul into a classroom, where, he said, a group of international affairs and mass media students wanted to meet him.

The classroom was in another building and had open-air windows, a flickering neon tube light, a blackboard, a fan, and rickety desks. There were about a dozen students, male and female, who watched him closely as he came in. After being introduced, he stood at the front of the room and began the quick presentation he'd conjured up on the way over. He didn't want to sound stilted or speak too long; after all, he was mainly here to see if he could learn anything useful. He spoke a bit about journalism and what was going on in Southeast Asia, some of the students nodded approvingly when he broached the subject of poor regional countries like Cambodia and Laos getting screwed by richer ones like Thailand and Malaysia as the countries of the region cooperated more. He had known that would be a winner with them and maybe loosen their tongues. Afterward, several asked questions about what he had said, and while under other circumstances Paul would have found the session enjoyable, now he feared he might be wasting valuable time.

Once he'd finished, he politely thanked Schiller for the invitation and the students for their time but said he had to run to another meeting. A few of the students followed him out of the room and out into the hall. One, a kid with long hair and a wispy beard, unexpectedly stopped Paul to ask him about his time in Moscow.

The question stopped Paul for a moment. He made some broad comments about working there but that had been almost an aside in his presentation. He asked if the kid had raised it because he was interested in whether Russia wanted to become involved in Southeast Asia, in competition with players like China and the United States, which Paul thought would be an extremely perceptive question.

No, that wasn't it.

The reason he was asking, the kid said, is that he had recently seen a man whose English seemed to have a Russian accent. He wasn't like some of the Russian gangster types who were sometimes seen around Phnom Penh, though.

"What do you mean?" Paul asked, feeling as if he might be about to get lucky.

The kid spoke English well for a Cambodian student, as the classes were taught in English.

"He wasn't," he started, searching, "flashy," he concluded, proud of having found the right word, "he was very quiet, almost as if he didn't want to be noticed or a brother."

"A brother?"

The kid thought again for a moment.

"Bother," he said, correcting himself, "he didn't want to be a bother."

Paul nodded. "Where did you see him?" he asked.

"He goes to the coffee shop where my girlfriend works and orders croissant and coffee."

"For too much money," one of the other students said, spurring a round of tittering and chattering in Khmer among the group who had come over with the kid.

"How do you know he had a Russian accent?" Paul asked.

"I saw him one day and heard him talk, he sounded like Russians in the movies," the kid said. Then a shadow of doubt crossed his face.

"Wait a minute," he said, his brow furrowed, "I am wrong, he's not Russian even though he talks like one."

Paul suddenly thought he could hear every tick of his watch.

"Socheata," the kid said, apparently referring to the girlfriend, "told me he was from somewhere else. He comes in most mornings around ten."

One of the others made what sounded like a snide comment, spurring another round of giggling. The kid started to turn to them, but Paul touched his arm.

"Tell me more," he said.

The kid shot the others a nasty look, then returned to his narrative.

"She told me he is from, ah," he seemed at a loss for a moment, then, "what country is in Prague?" More laughter from the others.

"You mean what country is Prague in?" Paul asked. This was looking too good to be true.

"Yes," the kid said, glaring at the others again.

"The Czech Republic," Paul said.

"Yes! That's it, Czech Republic!" the kid said triumphantly. He gave one of the other kids the finger. Paul wondered whether this was a Khmer gesture or also came from the movies. Or the internet.

"He just got here," the kid said, now ignoring the others, "he's some kind of professor."

"Can you tell me where Socheata works?" Paul asked.

* * *

Until now, Marina, sitting in her anonymous office building with her earphones and keyboard, had been beginning to feel like a secretary, albeit one with the highest of clearances and extraordinary linguistic prowess. The work wasn't demanding and pretty much consisted of listening to Americans speaking English, putting the conversations in the right format on the screen, and hearing the odd background conversation in another language.

Then, however, as she transcribed the second of the two conversations queued up on her screen today, it became clear why someone with her background had been needed for this assignment.

The first of the conversations sounded like it was in a bar, and most of the talking was in English with various accents but it was pretty straightforward stuff. The targets, Paul Girard and his wife, Elise, were being introduced around to a bunch of others, reporters it sounded like, who were all getting drunk in celebration of one of them getting a promotion. The recording started shortly after Paul and Elise had arrived, when the waiter, bribed by one of the embassy's purported consular officials, placed the microphone, hidden in a small rock, in the dirt not far from their table.

It was clear to Marina that the bar was in Cambodia from the Khmer chatter she heard in the background. She figured it was Cambodia itself rather than a Cambodian bar in California, say, or France, where contingents of Cambodians might be found, because she could hear un-Western-sounding motorbike and tuk-tuk traffic and she could make out some of the Khmer small talk in the background during pauses in the reporters' conversations. Two girls, bargirls maybe, were chattering with each other about the Australians they were apparently with, one of whom was apparently better-looking and more free-spending than the other.

The conversation among the reporters was pretty humdrum, nothing leaped out at her, although the assortment of accents was mildly interesting. Then, abruptly, she heard strange sounds very close to the microphone, as if someone had picked it up, then, a moment later, the recording stopped. Marina, of course, had no idea that one of the reporters had picked up the rock holding the microphone and thrown it at a rat. The rock missed but it crushed the microphone, so in the end, only the rat had come out ahead. One of the bar customers, leaving the bar shortly thereafter, absentmindedly kicked the rock into a storm drain.

Marina hadn't been surprised to hear Paul's voice on the recording. She had, after all, heard him tell Elise that he was going to Phnom Penh in pursuit of someone and had known that Elise would be meeting him there at the Royal Hotel.

She typed up a summary of the bar conversation and attached it to the transcript. She then emailed both to the senior official in a good suit who had given her this new assignment and who she now knew as Max. He was very good at his job and seemed very interested in helping her in her work. She was coming to enjoy working for him; he reminded her of some of her parents' intelligent, interesting friends and colleagues.

After typing the transcript and notes, Marina wanted to stretch, so she strolled down to Max's office, where he was sitting with his jacket off, peering at his computer screen. Max heard her at his door and waved her in. He was quite interested in these conversations, he told her, and he urged her to keep an ear out for anything interesting that might come out of the other conversation she had. Really good work, he said, smiling at her. As she left his office, she heard Max talking intensely with someone over his secure phone.

She stepped out a doorway into an interior courtyard just to get a breath of fresh air and then, feeling a little recharged, went back into the building and to her computer station to listen to the second conversation.

Most of the way through the next recording, though, she stopped abruptly and went back to the previous thirty seconds or so.

This recording was different than the first. She had heard Paul give what she frankly thought was a fairly interesting talk about journalism and Southeast Asia—she knew a fair amount about that part of the world from her work and had traveled there in her job once, under another name and nationality, naturally. To be honest, though, she wasn't overly impressed with the students' questions.

The recording was crystal clear, made by a student using what looked like an ordinary recorder to record Paul's lecture. The instrument was from a cutout, a fellow student who said it had been a discarded boyfriend's. It had actually come, along with a sum of money, from another cutout acting on behalf of the same embassy intelligence officer responsible for the bar rock-microphone. It looked exactly like those available at an electronics shop, which it had been until one of the embassy's technicians had modified it. Unlike standard models, it could shoot the contents of a conversation in an encrypted burst to a receiver in the embassy. There, a powerful transmitter relayed it instantly to a satellite, which then sent it down to an array of antennas on the roof of Marina's building.

Apparently the class ended and, as Marina listened, she had heard the student pick up her recorder and then walk out into the hall. Marina had expected the student to push the stop button and end the recording, which would automatically transmit the recording to the embassy. The plan was to have the cutout meet her later and covertly switch in a duplicate, but undoctored, recorder.

However, Marina had heard the student walk out to the hall with the recorder still running, and then apparently go over to catch a conversation Paul was having with one of the other students.

That's when she heard something that grabbed her attention.

Marina had been doing this work long enough to start to develop an instinct for the nugget, the odd phrase or reference, or even some sort of change in intonation or other clue that signaled something of intelligence value was being discussed.

This intuition she'd developed kicked in when she heard Paul answering the student's question about Russia. It wasn't Paul's answer, per se, but there was something in his voice, a change in the rhythm of his speech that told her to pay attention.

She listened closely for signs of stress as she typed out the words.

It was there, she thought, something in his voice changed, if almost imperceptibly. She suspected she was about to get confirmation that she'd hit pay dirt.

She listened to the Khmer kid stammering around trying to get the right English words but waited patiently for some hint as to why Paul was suddenly so alert.

Then she heard it. As the kid realized that he meant a Czech rather than a Russian, she heard a tell-tale pause from Paul. He'd heard something he'd been waiting for.

Paul was obviously the target of this whole exercise, she knew, and if this was important to Paul, it was no doubt important to her superiors.

Marina listened to the rest of the conversation, including where the girl, Socheata, worked and quickly typed a cover memo for the transcript. She particularly noted her sense that something critical was going on, pointing to Paul's interest in discovering that there was a new Czech academic in town.

Once she had sent the transcript and memo to Max by secure internal email, she went down to his office. She trusted her instincts on the change in Paul's manner but did not know Max that well yet and wanted to make sure he understood that she had picked up something serious that might not be conveyed by the transcribed words he would be reading on his screen.

As she entered his office, Max was looking at his monitor. He glanced up and motioned her to shut the door and sit down.

Ten minutes later, she left his office. He had again sworn her to secrecy and assured her she could expect substantial rewards in terms of promotion for discerning something of immense intelligence value.

She was beaming as she walked down the corridor.

* * *

Meanwhile, in Washington, Guy watched the Starbucks door from a table in the back. He was early, but he wanted to make sure he got there before Peter, whom he'd surprised that morning with a phoned invitation for coffee. He had then spent an hour on the internet and on the phone, time he now considered well spent.

Using the website on Peter's card, Guy had looked up Peter's firm and discovered it was a small—"boutique" one would assume would be the preferred adjective—investment firm with Peter listed as a principal. Further checking showed that the address was in a bland but respectable office building in Toronto with a large number of tenants, mostly dull corporate entities like Peter's company.

Guy called the number on Peter's card and was connected to a woman with either a Canadian or American accent, Guy couldn't tell from the short conversation. He asked for Peter and was told, sorry, Mr. Thorsen was "abroad again."

Abroad again? Peter had pointedly said he had not been out of Canada before. "Really," Guy said, "it's important that I reach him, is he out of the country much?"

"Now and then," the woman said, "mostly to Europe and Asia—Iraq, Pakistan, like that." Then she seemed to clam up a bit and asked who was calling.

"Never mind," Guy said and hung up.

That almost sealed it.

Peter arrived at the Starbucks, looking sunny, and came over and joined Guy.

Sipping his coffee, Peter asked politely about Guy's work. He seemed a little confused, but grateful, about their meeting.

Work is fine, Guy said, or something innocuous like that. Then he changed the topic.

"I was chasing a Canadian angle," he said.

"Oh?" Peter said. Guy thought he saw the slightest flicker of something pass across Peter's eyes.

"Yes," Guy said. "I've been working on a story on Canadian business and did some checking."

"Is this why you wanted to meet?" Peter asked. A little more focus showing, Guy thought.

"Uh huh," Guy said. He watched Peter for a moment. "I was in touch, actually, with your company," he said.

"Really. I guess you probably talked with Rebecca," Peter said brightly.

Slight tremor in Peter's voice here, Guy noticed.

"I suppose," Guy said. "She told me you travel around quite a bit, as it happens."

Peter seemed to think for a beat.

"Yes, that's true," he said.

"Even though you told me this was your first time out of Canada."

"What are you doing, a story on me?" Peter was smiling, but not that convincingly.

"No," Guy said. He let that hang in the air for a moment.

"I'm just not convinced you're Canadian," he then said.

"Really?" Peter said. Guy saw the flicker across Guy's face again, but only for a moment.

"Maybe I should be insulted," he said, seemingly amused at the unexpected and sudden turn of the conversation, "although, you know, we're famous for our even tempers."

"Your Canadianisms slipped a couple of times," Guy said.

Peter, watching him closely, tried to hide a smirk.

"Not the McKenzie Brothers, eh? Sorry," he said. The smile flickered just for an instant.

"Plus, you seem to have spent a lot of time in some interesting places." Peter was watching him, the merriment still in his eyes.

"You know, Iraq, Pakistan, that sort of place," Guy said.

Nothing from Peter.

"Not really the sort of place a small investment counseling firm would send people," Guy continued. He stopped to see if Peter reacted.

"OK," Peter then said, the smile fading just a hair, "let's ignore the fact that you probably know nothing about investment counseling, and let's accept, for the sake of argument, that you're right, so what?"

"Seems odd, doesn't it?"

"No," Peter said, "maybe I wanted to impress an attractive young American researcher but it didn't quite click that way."

"By telling her you were a yokel who made good in the big city? That doesn't seem likely." Guy was pretty sure he knew whereof he spoke when it came to pumping up his cred to impress women.

"Well, we all try what we can," Peter responded evenly, his eyes now steady on Guy.

"And, of course, you're married," Guy said, although in Guy's mind that didn't really disqualify Peter from trying for a little action on the side.

"I don't see how this is any—" Peter started, now a little hot under the collar, but Guy held up his hand.

"Listen," he said, "I don't really give a shit who you are, but I don't like being played with."

"Well," Peter said, an edge creeping into his voice now, "I don't really care what you think, and frankly, given the help I've given you getting Veronica into the sack—successfully, I might add—I'd think you wouldn't care who I am or am not." With that, he made to finish his coffee and leave.

Guy soldiered on without missing a beat.

"There's only one group of Americans that tries to pass themselves off as Canadians all the time," he said.

"Oh?" Peter's amused look was back. He had been going for a final sip of coffee, his cup was stopped midway to his lips.

"Yes," Guy said, as Peter then took his sip, "CIA officers."

Peter looked as if he were going to spit out his coffee like some vaudeville comedian.

"You're fucking joking," he said after swallowing the coffee, eyes aglow with the foolishness of the thought. "Me? I wish, but thanks for the compliment." He was actually chuckling now.

He looked at his watch and stood up.

"I really must go," he said, still smiling at the notion. "I need to get the ejection seat in my Aston Martin looked at," he said, "it's developed an irritating squeak." He was still smiling at the whole idea.

"You handled yourself pretty well with that guy the other night," Guy said, still sitting.

Peter looked at him for a moment, the jocularity now gone.

"Yes, I did," he said. And turned around and walked out of the Starbucks.

* * *

Oddly, when Guy took Veronica out to dinner a few nights later near the harbor in Annapolis—always a winner with the chicks, he'd found—there was hardly a mention of Peter.

"Oh," Veronica said when Guy broached the subject, "he's tied up with something. Besides, I think we're past the point of needing a chaperone, don't you?"

CHAPTER TWENTY

OLEG

The next morning, Paul and Elise left the Royal and, armed with the address of Socheata's coffee shop written in Khmer characters, hailed a tuk-tuk. The driver seemed to speak little English but nodded when he saw the address.

Paul and Elise talked about their plan as they sped through the streets, Paul reflexively glancing up at the driver's face visible in the mirrors on either side. Once or twice he thought the driver was watching him back, but he put this down to nerves.

The driver slowed as he passed a new hotel under construction and an obviously new and very large house with a Range Rover idling out front. Then, after checking both ways, turned a corner and stopped in front of a brightly colored café.

After Paul paid, the driver gestured, indicating he was willing to wait for Paul and Elise, but Paul shook his head. The driver looked disappointed but, seeing the large number of obviously well-off foreigners in the coffee shop who were probably too lazy to walk back to their hotels, he pulled over to the side to wait.

Paul and Elise surveyed the storefront.

The coffee shop was small, on two levels, with a waitress visible on the ground level, shuttling between tables. It could have been a Starbucks.

As they entered, the waitress smiled at them. Elise smiled back, very wide-eyed and touristy, and then, suddenly looked at the girl.

"Didn't you used to work at the Hotel Le Royal?" she asked.

The girl looked confused for a moment, then smiled again. No, she hadn't.

"Really, you remind me of one there, her name was Socheata," Elise said.

"Sorry," the girl said, still smiling. She looked like she was about to say something else but an overfed customer in a Hawaiian shirt started waving at her impatiently. She turned and went off to take his order.

Paul nudged Elise and pointed with his chin. Another waitress was walking up the stairs to the second floor.

Paul and Elise followed her up and took an empty table by the wall.

When the waitress came over, Elise, still playing the tourist, asked if they had café au lait. She said it slowly as if this were an exotic delicacy that would be unknown in such a remote place as Cambodia, its French colonial past notwithstanding. The girl smiled and said, yes, she could bring a café au lait, and what would Paul like? Just coffee, Paul said. This is such a pretty country, Elise said to the girl, all smiles and rich-tourist openness. The girl smiled back.

"What's your name?" Elise asked as the girl was starting to turn away.

"Socheata," she said with another smile. She then turned to the next table, where a lanky Western youth in a Singha Beer shirt was studying his phone.

* * *

The intelligence apparatus had swung into high gear after Marina had transmitted the text of Paul's phone conversation from Bangkok to Elise in Rome and her cover memo. With the bar conversation and Paul's conversation with the student after his lecture, the focus had increased exponentially. Others up the chain had now agreed wholeheartedly with Marina's conclusion that they had hit pay dirt, or something close to it. And they, of course, were better informed than she was and knew exactly what that pay dirt would be.

Although very closely held, away from most of the government's various intelligence agencies and fiefdoms, concerns among intelligence professionals about the contents of what was coming to be known as the "Oleg Makarov file" were rising. This certainly wasn't surprising, considering its contents—its disclosure could have cataclysmic consequences that no one relished the prospect of dealing with.

After the conversation with the student that Marina had transcribed, it seemed that quick action would be needed soon, and the machinery had to be put into place. Calls were made outside the small circle of those already read into the files as needed, but they were limited to those with a genuine need to know. No one wanted anyone from the outside, and certainly not any reporters—any more reporters—snooping around.

After a rapid-fire sequence of secure meetings, phone calls, and video conferences, officials were able to take the sorts of actions that show what dedicated professionals can do if a quick response is needed and the resources are available. Frankly, there weren't many intelligence bureaucracies in the world, especially if you eliminate those that could politely be called major adversaries, who could have so quickly set up such an operation, with its mobilization of a small cadre of specialists, arrangement for their transport into Phnom Penh from their postings or assignments far away under covers as innocuous third-country tourists, with carefully prepared fake passports and other documentation needed to complete the ruse. Having in-house capabilities and facilities, of course, they didn't have to go searching around for someone like Micheletti.

Then there was the forwarding of the equipment needed via diplomatic pouch. The operation was to be closely held on the ground, with the only member of the local intelligence unit in on any part of it being the head of that Phnom Penh unit, who would simply make sure the arriving operatives would be able to get the communications and other equipment being provided for the operation.

* * *

Paul saw Oleg first, although he didn't recognize him right away. All he'd seen was a European of some sort with a wide-brimmed hat and sunglasses—nice-looking ones like some Paul had seen in Rome, by the way—who came up the stairs at the same time as a group of tourists, although it didn't seem as if he were part of the group. He'd separated himself from the group when they came in and taken off his shades and hat when he sat down. As it happened, he was across the room from Paul and Elise and facing them. That was when Paul recognized him. It was Oleg Makarov all right, now passing as Ivo Jezek—and an Ivo Jezek looking quite different than Oleg Makarov had years before in Moscow and looking like he was at the end of his rope.

Oleg looked like he hadn't slept in a week, and after what could only be described as stealing into the restaurant, he had quickly scanned the upstairs seating area before finding a seat at a remote table. His gaze had swept by Paul and Elise without a flash of recognition, but that didn't mean anything; he hadn't seen Paul in years, and besides, Paul wasn't who Oleg was on the lookout for.

Paul waited a moment. He was trying to concentrate but the Singha shirt kid next to him had chosen this moment to call his girlfriend, apparently. Paul couldn't understand the words, but it sounded irritatingly lovey-dovey.

Across the room, Socheata was talking to Oleg. It was clear from her body language that he was a regular customer and one she was glad to take a moment to chat with.

That was enough for Paul. After a moment, he nudged Elise and he crossed the room to where Oleg was now sipping his coffee, Elise behind him.

Oleg looked up warily as Paul and Elise approached his table.

"Mr. Jezek?" Paul said quietly. He didn't know whether Oleg would recognize him, and he'd never met Elise. He didn't think it was a good idea to shout out a "Hey Oleg!" across the room to someone who was hiding in a Third World backwater under a false name.

"Yes?" Oleg said. He looked at Paul, then Elise. Then his gaze flicked back to Paul uncertainly.

Paul had one of his Washington business cards in his shirt pocket. He took it out and slid it across the table to Oleg.

Oleg stared at the card, then again at Paul, then again at Elise.

"What the fuck are you doing here?" he asked very quietly. The accent hadn't disappeared. Paul and Elise sat down, "And how the fuck did you find me?" Oleg asked, scanning the room apprehensively.

Paul glanced around the coffee shop. It was getting more crowded. Four backpacker types were now crowded around the table he and Elise had had, along with that of the Singha shirt kid, who was now gone.

"Let's go somewhere more private," Paul said.

Oleg looked at Paul for a moment, then nodded. He left a few dollars on the table and followed Paul and Elise out to the street with his coffee.

Out on the street, Paul saw the Singha shirt kid talking to the tuk-tuk driver who had brought Paul and Elise. The kid seemed to be about to get in when the driver, apparently seeing Paul and Elise and remembering their generous tip, waved the kid off and came over to pick up Paul, Elise, and Oleg. Three passengers, maybe a bigger tip.

* * *

Oleg had donned his hat and tough-guy sunglasses on the ride over to the Royal and had ducked his head as he, Paul, and Elise passed through the lobby, then through the lounge and pool to the back corridor where their room was.

He glanced up and down the corridor before slipping through the door into the room. Once inside he looked around quickly and then, pushing Paul aside, looked under the bed and through the closet and bathroom before coming out. He then made sure the heavy drapes were closed.

Paul and Elise sat down at a small table set away from the bed. Paul gestured to the empty chair, but Oleg stayed standing, keeping his back up against the door, and kept flicking his eyes across the room.

"What the fuck are you doing here?" he asked again.

He stared at Paul.

"*Tebya iz Moskvy prislali?*" he asked—did Moscow send you?

This was a surprise. Startled, Paul translated for Elise.

"You sent us," she said. Paul reached into one of his bags, pulled out the copy of the paper Archie Richter had shared, and put it on the table in front of the empty chair.

Warily, Oleg looked around the room one more time before sitting down in front of the document. He looked at the front page, obviously surprised, then looked up. Neither Paul nor Elise said anything.

Paul opened bottles of water and poured some into each of three of the hotel glasses on the table as Oleg began to read the document. Paul and Elise waited silently as Oleg read, sipping water occasionally but betraying no emotion.

Oleg looked up suddenly when he reached the end of the document, the page purportedly showing that he had written it. He seemed to be searching for some sort of clue in Paul's and Elise's faces for a moment. Seeing none, he then looked down at the page again as if to confirm what he had seen.

He put the pages back in order, tapped them on the table into a neat stack, and put it on the table to the side. He stood up and walked over to the curtained window and stared at the closed curtains for a minute, maybe two. It seemed as if he were staring through the heavy fabric and out to the hotel grounds and the city beyond, lost in thought. Then he turned back to Paul and Elise.

"I've never seen this before," he said.

It seemed then as if he were about to say something more but changed his mind.

The room was quiet for a moment. This was not what Paul and Elise had expected to hear.

"What do you mean, you've never seen this before?" Elise asked, breaking the silence.

Oleg looked at her for a moment before speaking.

"Just what I said," he replied, "I have no idea what this is."

"You didn't write this?" Paul asked.

Oleg looked at him.

"No. I've never seen it," he repeated.

The room was silent for another moment or two. Then Oleg sat back down.

"How did you get this?" he then asked.

Paul told him about being handed the document while covering a conference. He then had shared it with Gunther at the paper—you remember him, right? yes of course, Oleg said—who had agreed to bank-roll his effort to find Oleg.

And who was the person who handed it to you, Oleg asked.

A congressional staffer, Paul said, adding nothing more.

Oleg nodded. He seemed lost in thought.

"You don't know of any such move to break the Far East away?" Paul asked after a moment, adding that he could see the idea's appeal from Russian Far Easterners' perspective.

"No, this is preposterous, I've never heard of such a thing," Oleg said. He was thinking about something else, it was clear.

"None of this makes sense," Elise said. "Why would someone make this up in the first place? And attribute it to you?

"If this is true, the first thing that is going to happen is that Moscow is going to think about sending in troops, but if this is out, or even known to Western officials, the whole world will be watching."

"And whether it's true or not, why was leaked to the press? To us?" Paul said.

He thought for a moment.

"This doesn't make sense," he said.

"Maybe someone wants it out to head off some sort of Russian action that's in the works for some other reason, or, on the other hand, maybe someone wants this out to justify a planned Russian action in the outside world's eyes."

"Still, though, why attribute it to Oleg?" Elise asked.

Paul noticed Oleg wasn't listening but was lost in thought again.

"When did all this happen?" Oleg asked abruptly.

"Pretty recently," Paul said. When Oleg seemed to want more, he thought for a moment and gave him exact dates.

Oleg nodded. Something was clicking in his head. Another minute ticked by.

"And you said this came from someone who works for your Congress, not your security services."

"Right, at least to us—to Paul," Elise said.

Oleg nodded.

"And the member of the congressional staff," he said, "was this an experienced person or someone new?"

Paul glanced at Elise, who was watching Oleg closely now.

"He was pretty new," Paul said, "he latched onto a new member of the House and quickly made a name for himself. Sort of came out of the blue."

Oleg seemed to think that over.

"A Democrat?" he asked.

This was an unexpected question. "No, a Republican," Paul said, watching Oleg closely.

"Where did he get it, this staff member?" Oleg asked after a moment.

"We don't know," Paul said, "but given the document, apparently from somewhere in the national security community. He wouldn't say."

"National security community," Oleg repeated, emphasizing the last word. He seemed to be turning the phrase over in his mind.

"And this fairly new congressional staff member," he said, "would have access to such people?"

"Possibly," Paul said. "If he knew someone in the executive branch with such access or if they knew him, they might pass it to him, particularly if they were a Republican who didn't like the president."

Oleg thought this over, then nodded.

The three sat for a moment in silence. It seemed Oleg had no more questions.

"Why are you here and traveling under a false name if you didn't write this?" Elise then asked Oleg.

Oleg didn't answer her but was staring at the curtain.

"And it was our old friend Gunther who made it possible for you to find me," he said.

"Yes," Paul said, "the paper is paying me as a freelancer to do this in hopes of a story."

"Your connection with Gunther is pretty well known, I think," Oleg said.

"Yes," Paul said, "I think pretty much everyone knows we are friends."

"Yes, everyone," Oleg said, thinking. More puzzle pieces seemed to be moving in his head. Or chess pieces, more likely. He was Russian, after all.

Paul started to say something, but Oleg held his hand up. He went over to the window and moved the drape slightly to look out, then closed it. He turned back to Paul and Elise.

"We must leave," he said.

"What?" Elise asked, surprised, "Why?"

Oleg ignored her and looked around the room again.

"Leave your phones here," he said, standing, "and let's take one of the back entrances."

"What's going on?" Elise asked. Paul had gotten up and put their Blackberries in the room safe, for what that might be worth. He was now standing next to Oleg.

Oleg seemed to be looking for a phrase. He asked Paul something in Russian and Paul responded, but Elise couldn't hear what either of them had said. Oleg nodded and turned back to Elise.

"We've been set up," he said in his accented English.

CHAPTER TWENTY-ONE

WHEELS TURN

Washington

Gunther and Guy met in Gunther's office, away from the newsroom and any prying eyes.

Gunther looked as if he had not gotten much sleep the night before. He had had a late-night call from Paul in, of all places, Cambodia, who had given him shocking news. The paper now had a decision to make.

* * *

Paul, Elise, and Oleg had slipped out the back of the Royal and made their way over to busy Preah Monivong Boulevard. After dodging traffic to cross it, they had looked back to ensure they had not been followed before they hailed a tuk-tuk for a ride to an intersection a few blocks from the Mekong Dreams.

As the tuk-tuk disappeared in search of another fare, Oleg told Paul and Elise to stay where they were for a few minutes and to see if anyone had followed them. He then turned back to Paul and said something quickly to him before disappearing on foot.

After a few minutes, Paul motioned Elise to follow him toward another tuk-tuk they could see half a block away. As they were getting in, Paul said something to the driver, who nodded and, after checking the traffic, gunned his engine and headed up another street, past the cutesy guest houses, the shops with Western toiletries and batteries, and the foodie-friendly restaurants that had sprung up in recent years for the growing tourist trade, ultimately making his way to an imposing set of buildings at the intersection of streets 113 and 350.

Elise, realizing where they were, caught her breath but said nothing.

Paul and Elise got out of the tuk-tuk, and Paul paid the five-dollar admission fees so he and Elise could enter the compound.

While getting lashes or electrification you must not cry at all

Elise reluctantly followed Paul onto the grounds of what had once been a high school. The Khmer Rouge had turned it into an interrogation center, known as the S-21 prison, during their brutal rule in the late seventies, filled with cells, barbed wire, and torture chambers. Now it had become a museum, complete with the cells, torture instruments, and depictions of interrogation sessions. There was a set of ten regulations for prisoners now posted in Khmer, French, and English—the English, at least, had obviously been translated without regard to some of the finer points of grammar or formatting.

Do nothing, sit still, and wait for my orders. If there is no order, keep quiet. when I ask you to do something, you must do it right away without protesting.

"I hate this fucking place," she said quietly. Paul nodded but kept walking.

Don't be fool for you are a chap who dare to thwart the revolution.

S-21 was not for the faint of heart.

If you don't follow all the above rules, you shall get many lashes of electric wire.

Elise, who had been glancing at the prisoner regulations, followed Paul toward one of the buildings.

"Where are we meeting him?" she asked.

Paul pointed with his chin at the building they were approaching.

"There's a photo gallery in there, former prisoners," he said, "we'll wait for him in there."

Elise said nothing, resigned. She took one last look at the sign.

If you disobey any point of my regulations you shall get either ten lashes or five shocks of electric discharge.

One of the prison's blocks had been converted to display row after row of photos. Paul and Elise found two Western tourists gazing at the photos solemnly. They wore shorts and flip-flops. The woman wore a halter top, the man wore a T-shirt saying he had visited the Golden Triangle. After a few moments, they noticed Paul and Elise and left wordlessly. A minute later, Oleg came in, looking around to make sure the three were alone. Then he gazed at the photos for a moment before turning to Paul and Elise.

"Nice place to meet," Elise said, as they then walked along the banks of photos of victims of the torture center. Dozens, doomed to a grisly death, stared out at them wordlessly, their backs to walls, numbers pinned on their chests.

"I needed someplace I knew Paul would know where we could meet quickly that wouldn't be crowded with loud tourists," Oleg said. "I remembered having read about it online before I came," he said, examining their surroundings. "It seems to have been a good idea."

Paul looked around. There wasn't time to contemplate the ghosts on the walls.

"You said we'd been set up," he said to Oleg.

Oleg looked at one of the walls of photos. The faces of the dead watched silently.

It had been a Saturday night in Moscow, Oleg said, not much to do, and he did not feel like being alone. A new contact from Saint Petersburg had invited him to a party with some friends. Why not, he'd thought.

It was a sleazy affair, he said, not at all what he'd hoped for. There were some respectable types, but the room was mostly full of loud, boorish men wearing gaudy jewelry and clothes and their girlfriends spilling out of tattooed-on short dresses, all very *nekul'turnyy*, uncultured, if emblematic of what Russia had become, he said. There was a smattering of hard-looking men in tight suits keeping an eye on the proceedings and staying away from the vodka and the girls. He would have left, but he didn't want to offend his new friend.

While he was trying to figure out a way to discreetly escape, Oleg said, some big shot he'd never met came up to him, mistaking him for someone else, and started talking about a crazy-sounding scheme that no one in their right mind would believe could succeed—or was even necessarily a good idea.

"But it wasn't about Far Eastern secession?" Elise asked.

"No," Oleg said quickly.

"You didn't know who the guy was?" she asked.

"Let me get to that," Oleg said. Impatient to get on with his story.

He then went on to describe the scheme Vladimir Alexandrovich Zhuravlev had outlined at the party.

Paul and Elise stared at him when he had finished. Neither spoke for a moment.

"This is ridiculous," Elise then said. "It might make sense to a drunk, but even if it were what they wanted to do, they could never carry it out."

Oleg pulled out the sheaf of papers Vladimir Alexandrovich had handed him, which he had retrieved from his hotel room at the Mekong Dreams, and gave them to Paul. Paul scanned the papers and then looked up.

"This can't be real," he said.

Oleg pointed to the official seals on the papers and showed him Vladimir Alexandrovich's business card. Paul looked at the Russian-language card for a moment and nodded before handing it back to Oleg.

Elise, not speaking Russian, she hadn't read the document. Paul quickly filled her in on the details in the paper. She looked at him for a moment. "This is preposterous," she said, "it can't be true."

Three backpackers came in, chatting to each other. After glancing at Paul, Elise, and Oleg, obviously in the middle of something, they made their way down the line of photos before leaving silently.

"What would be the point?" Paul asked when he was sure the backpackers were safely gone, "to throw our election?"

"Well," Oleg said, "that might happen, if it went that far, although it seems unlikely. Just causing confusion and doubt would mean they come out ahead, though. That would be enough. The point would be to cast doubt on your country and the whole notion of liberal democracies and the world they have created.

"Payback, in part," he said, "for the humiliation of the collapse of the Soviet Union."

Paul looked at the photos on the wall, nodding. Of course. It all made sense.

"If they were to, somehow, win the election, though," Oleg resumed, after thinking for a moment, "that would just be the start. You'd really be in *terra incognito*, and so would the rest of us, given that you're the world's only remaining superpower and the model for democracy.

"For as long as that lasted," he added.

He paused for a moment to let that sink in before continuing.

"Ideally, I mean from their point of view," he continued, "once Washington was neutralized, they could continue with their grand plans to recreate the old order unimpeded."

The whole thing was so ludicrous. Paul looked at the papers again.

"We're talking more of Ukraine, I suppose," he said.

"Sure," Oleg said, "but why stop there? It's what your military calls a target-rich environment, including Moldova and a few other easy pickings among the former Soviet republics. Including, of course, the Baltics, maybe the old Central Asian ones."

"What they'd really like," he continued, "would be to defang NATO. That would be the ultimate coup in their minds."

Paul started to say something, but Oleg continued, ignoring him.

"They see the United States as a declining power—as do the Chinese and a few others—and this would exploit that progression and help move the process along, in their minds," he said.

Elise looked at the wall of black and white photos of people who never knew what was coming, then looked away. Suddenly, she remembered the conversation Paul had told her about with Bob, the guy in Texas who wanted new leadership and said he was tired of Americans getting kicked around by the rest of the world. She thought of accounts she'd read of Europe in the thirties—and of some Americans then, for that matter.

She looked over at Paul and realized he was thinking about the same thing.

"It's brilliant," she said, "I mean, if it would work."

"I suppose it's possible," Paul said.

"But," he added, "it would tear the country apart."

Paul thought for a moment.

"This scheme," he said, "even if it didn't come out right away, it would eventually, and the country would unite against it. It would never succeed, certainly not in the long run."

Oleg looked at one of the mugshots for a moment. A man looked out, petrified by fear, a number tag pinned to his shirt. He had no doubt not realized what was coming at first, but by the time the photo was taken, he had figured it out.

"Really?" he asked, turning back to Paul and Elise, "It would never succeed? The Soviet Union was invulnerable until it wasn't.

"Your country is no different—you should have learned that half a century ago when your president was murdered in the street in Dallas. He was vulnerable like any other political leader and your country is just as vulnerable as any other. You're not special. You've just convinced yourself you're different, special, immune from history, and you've had an easy run since World War Two to convince you you're right."

He let that sink in for a moment.

"Ultimately," he said, "as long as they're not discovered, they'd keep stirring the pot and rouse the population. Moscow has some experience in rousing populations. And that would just be the beginning; roused populations can be full of unpleasant surprises."

Paul thought about the Houston conversation with Bob again, suddenly remembering Bob's reference to hotheads with guns and training. "You wouldn't want to set them off," Bob had said—but Paul said nothing to Elise and Oleg.

The more he thought about it the more sense this plan made, given what he knew about Russia and Putin.

"We don't know whether they're thinking of a candidate or a group of candidates at this point, but they're probably looking around," Oleg said.

"They're interested in confusion and doubt. They want someone, or some people, running the government who would start smashing government institutions and conventional wisdom like a bull in a china shop. That would not only sow chaos in Washington and the Western alliance but validate their claim that your so-called democracy is no more high-minded than their system. Authoritarian governments and even nonauthoritarian governments would find it easier to cozy up to Russia and China for investment and protection—and for help quashing troublesome dissidents—with the busybodies at the U.N., the World Bank, and elsewhere silenced, now that all the West's talk about noble, pure democracy had been shown to be the hypocrisy Moscow and Beijing had claimed they were. Moscow and Beijing, for their part, would crawl all over Africa and Asia, waving aid contracts and deals shorn of any troublesome labor-rights, environmental or other inconvenient provisions. The West, being weakened and fragmented, wouldn't be able to do anything.

"The topping on the cake," Paul then said, "could be if there were some sort of crisis. It doesn't matter what—an earthquake, a disease outbreak, a terrorist attack, we know all the possibilities—they know that that sort of leadership would bungle the response. Maybe so badly that other countries would be called in to help deal with the emergency, irreparably puncturing the image of the United States as not only a champion of liberty and democracy but as an invincible superpower immune to the sorts of crises that can hobble lesser nations but can always be counted on to bail the rest of the world out in emergencies."

Oleg nodded. "This will be easy for them," he said, "from their point of view, your country is ripe for this kind of operation. They'll watch your politics closely—as I'm sure they're already doing—and see what opportunities present themselves. They'll find someone or some group of potential candidates who want the same things Moscow wants."

"What do you mean?" Elise asked.

"Moscow likes autocrats and autocratic officials, and it likes the resurgent racist nationalist movements it sees around the world, including in your country. They no doubt watched the whole birth certificate controversy with glee," Oleg said. "My guess is that there are plenty of Americans who would love an America led by nationalists with autocratic tendencies, as much as Moscow would."

The three sat for a moment, watched over by the photos.

"All I'm saying," Oleg said, breaking the silence, "is that's the plan. Nothing's been done yet, at least so far as we can tell from this document. There is no indication any approach has even been made yet.

"However," he said, "it looks like there are serious preparations being made.

He pulled the papers back toward him, turned to the last page, and pointed to the addendum he had noticed when he had first seen the paper in Moscow. It was apparently a column of identifiers of some sort, each starting with two letters. He rotated it around so Paul and Elise could see it.

"These are bank account numbers," she said after glancing at the page. She knew what she was talking about; this had been her world as an investigator. "They look like the numbers used by the international bank account numbering system, IBAN, coded by country," she said.

"They could be accounts where potential candidates they are looking at have money stashed away, unknown to the Internal Revenue Service. They could be accounts where money for this operation is sitting. They could be something else; we don't know."

"They're apparently important to this plan, though," Oleg said.

"We don't even know what banks they are, though," Elise said, nodding, "I might be able to find out online when we get back to the hotel."

Paul turned the page so he could see it and looked at it for a moment.

"I don't think we have to wait," he said, reaching for his phone.

He looked at his watch, then dialed a Washington number from his contacts list. It was Warwick, the oil reporter. When Warwick answered, Paul told him what he needed and read the list of numbers into the phone. He listened for a moment before thanking Warwick and clicking off.

"Warwick wasn't hopeful, but he agreed they sounded like IBAN numbers," he said.

"The first two letters in each sequence identify what country the bank is in, and he said about half were in Germany, some the same bank. The others, he said, are in other places like Liechtenstein, Andorra, Cyprus, like that. He'll get back to us."

"This could be the proof we need," Oleg said.

"Well, a lead anyway," Paul said, "if my friend can tell find out who these belong to."

"OK," Oleg said, "but let's not forget the massive effort referred to in the paper, in social media. That is what would convince people in America to go along with the whole thing."

"Huh," Paul said, looking at Elise, then Oleg, "social media. That's like LinkedIn, right? That sort of thing?"

He and Elise looked at Oleg blankly.

Oleg looked at both of them with a disconcerted expression.

"No," he said, "not LinkedIn."

* * *

An hour later, at the Royal's front desk, Elise, putting on a sunny tourist smile, asked for a second room. Her husband, she confided conspiratorially to the thin desk clerk with manicured nails, snored. She made a comical snorting noise as she said this, just to drive home the point. The desk clerk tittered, putting his hand in front of his mouth in embarrassment, and, after manipulating his keyboard, told Elise the number of the new room and where it was. She put her finger to her lips, asking him for silence on the matter. Still embarrassed, he nodded.

While Elise was entertaining and embarrassing the desk clerk, Paul and Oleg had taken a tuk-tuk to the Mekong Dreams, where they quietly retrieved Oleg's luggage to bring back. They managed to do so without any of the Mekong Dreams staff seeing them, so that, as far as the Mekong Dreams would be concerned, Oleg would not have left. On the way out, they made sure the bedsheets were in disarray and rumpled the towels in the bathroom so that when the maid came in the next day, she wouldn't realize no one had been there overnight.

Back at the Royal, Paul and Oleg snuck back into the hotel. Elise gave Oleg the key to the newly acquired second room, where Oleg decided to go and stay out of sight.

As soon as Oleg was safely in his room, Paul went out to the lobby and arranged for a second Khmer phone and SIM card, which a smartly dressed bellhop brought to him shortly. Then, back in his and Elise's room, he checked his watch and called Gunther at home.

* * *

Gunther was alarmed when the phone rang in the middle of the night in Washington, particularly when he saw that it was an international call from whatever country had the code "855." When he answered the phone and heard Paul's voice, he unplugged the charging cord and carried the phone into the office he'd set up in a spare bedroom so he wouldn't wake his wife.

Ninety seconds after Paul had started to talk Gunther was wide awake and reaching for a pad to take notes. Paul gave Gunther the story in outline, leaving out names or details he didn't think were necessary, but including enough to make it clear what he had found out. They talked for forty-five minutes, with Gunther raising the same objections that Paul and Elise had. This must be complete bullshit, he said. In the end, though, he reached the same conclusion that Paul and Elise had, that this could not be ignored.

Now, for the third time in twenty-four hours, the gist of Oleg's memo was being explained to an incredulous audience, this time an audience of one. As Gunther recounted his late-night phone conversation with Paul to Guy in his office, Guy initially dismissed it, as Gunther, Paul, and Elise had each done, but he came around as he learned more and agreed that, whatever their doubts, this had to be followed up.

The question was what to do. Gunther, of course, could talk to Archie, on the Hill, who, after all, had been the original source for the story, but that idea was quickly disposed of—this was way above Archie's level. Not to mention that Archie had had the wrong story, having thought this was all about Far Eastern secession. This would require bigger-gun sources.

Which, of course, spurred a loud pissing match between Guy and Gunther over which of them should take the lead and contact his super-duper national-security-insider sources, but in the end, Gunther had to yield to Guy, who was higher up on the totem pole, and let him contact his big-shot sources first.

Once Gunther had left, Guy picked up his phone to call Caputo at the CIA's press office but could not get through. He tried a few other numbers among those of people around Washington he considered his primo spook sources but had no luck there either.

Gunther, stewing, went back to work in his own office. He finished the day's stories before leaving the office at around eight, typical for an editor on the day shift. On the way home, he called Paul in Phnom Penh and told him to stand by; wheels were turning.

Paul pressed him for further details. The line was scratchy, they could barely make each other out.

"Guy's handling it," Gunther said.

There was a pause before he heard Paul's voice intermittently through the static on the line.

He didn't hear most of what Paul was saying but he did hear the phrase "up shit creek."

CHAPTER TWENTY-TWO

THE REAL DEAL

Meanwhile, in her sterile office building, earphones in place, Marina listened to conversations the computers had yanked out of the air for her. What she heard made her forget about the tea and *Times* crossword puzzle next to her keyboard.

This was the real deal, she realized as she listened first to the call Paul had made to Warwick from Cambodia about the bank numbers, then the call he had made to Gunther, then the call later that Gunther had made back to Paul after his meeting with Guy.

What she heard was unbelievable. She was shaken, but the professional intelligence officer in her took over—this, she knew, was why they had wanted someone like her for this assignment, and she knew this was the sort of moment for which she had been preparing her whole life, not to mention one that would make her career.

It was clear that these transcripts would need to go to Max and his team fast. She sent Max an electronic message alerting him that she would have something urgent for him in a few minutes, then worked quickly, but carefully to avoid missing any nuance that might be important for her background notes. She sent the transcript and notes to Max, flagging them as urgent in the subject line just to be sure, and then rushed to his office to ensure he was there and saw them.

When she got there, he was on his secure telephone, holding the receiver with one hand and gesticulating frantically with the other as he kept his eye on the computer screen in front of him. He didn't notice Marina.

The transcripts, of course, spurred a flurry of activity, although it was a very quiet flurry. Completely away from the public eye, and even the eye of many officials who thought they were in the loop—and certainly the eye of anyone who might blab to the press—more phone calls were made by encrypted links. Then an urgent meeting spanning a number of time zones was held by secure video conference.

The intelligence professionals, as had been the case with Paul, Elise, and those at the paper, realized that Oleg's revelations required immediate and decisive action—although since Marina and her colleagues had different functions than did the journalists, they had somewhat different concerns and would take somewhat different steps. Fortunately, most of the preparations had already been made by now. A final call was made, and the operation, along with a second, ancillary one, was given a go.

CHAPTER TWENTY-THREE

VISITORS FROM FINLAND

The clerk at the Mekong Dreams was happy when, as he watched the computer screen, he noticed that three deluxe twin rooms had been booked on a Finnish credit card for a set of arrivals that afternoon. That wasn't surprising, the clerk thought, they were probably tourists in Siem Reap to look at the temples at Angkor Wat and thought they'd pop into Phnom Penh for a day or two to see the Killing Fields and S-21. There wasn't a whole lot else for casual tourists to see in Phnom Penh.

The clerk checked the system and saw that three rooms were available on one of the nicer corridors, one whose rooms offered a pleasant view of the street.

He made arrangements for the new guests to get those rooms.

Just down the hall from the quiet Czech professor.

The Finns arrived that afternoon and, although friendly, they seemed anxious to get to their rooms. They were burly men, athletes maybe, the clerk thought, and had no trouble carrying their bulky cases. The clerk tried to tell them about nearby sights and restaurants, but the Finns seemed impatient. They'd been out drinking the night before and needed their sleep, one of the Finns confided to the clerk slyly—is it quiet up there? Oh yes, the clerk said, all the guests were no doubt out sightseeing or shopping, the hotel is very quiet this time of day.

Excellent, the Finn said, smiling, before he and his friends rushed to the elevator so they could sleep it off.

Five minutes later, most of the Finns searched Oleg's room while one of their number stood lookout in the hall. There wasn't much to find, except it was clear that Oleg had tried to make it look as if he'd spent the night there when he hadn't. The bed looked as if it had been slept in, but the sink was spotless, the little bars of soap were all still wrapped, and there was no sign the shower had been used. Fucking amateur, one of the Finns said to another, although not in Finnish since neither of them had actually ever been to that country. He pulled out an encrypted satellite phone and spoke into it for a few seconds. He then listened to the response from the secure facility thousands of miles away. He reflexively nodded as he acknowledged his orders, clicked the instrument off, and turned to tell his teammates what they would do next.

CHAPTER TWENTY-FOUR

AN INCIDENT IN THE CORRIDOR

The blood had been the frightening part. So much of it.

It was late night. Bopha, who had spent the day serving coffee to tourists in the lobby bar at the Royal as usual, was shaken. She was recounting the story to a desk clerk she knew from her village as they walked out of the hotel after their shifts. Both were glad to have jobs in the hotel and sent money back to their parents upcountry, but Bopha was now wondering whether she should quit and go back home.

She had stumbled onto the body in a corridor while stretching her legs after her shift, she said. The throat was slit and the man, obviously European of some sort, was staring up at the ceiling with dead eyes. His dead hands were clutching his dead throat.

There was blood everywhere.

She quickly called the manager, who called the police, and soon, the corridor was swarming with them. It seemed, from what she overheard before she was shooed out, that the man was not registered in the hotel, maybe a guest's visitor. He was carrying a Czech passport but, one of the policemen said, there seemed to be some sort of problem with it. While shaking his head, someone from the Czech Embassy was staring at the passport and consulting with someone on his iPhone.

Where was this, the desk clerk asked. When she told him, he remembered the woman with the snoring husband and wondered.

The next day, though, when he began his shift, he discovered that the woman and her husband had checked out suddenly.

CHAPTER TWENTY-FIVE

A DEAL IS CUT

Guy had thought he had taken control of the story when he strong-armed Gunther into backing off, but now he was concerned it was slipping away from him.

It was a day after that meeting in his office and now he had had to rush into the paper early for yet another goddamn conference with Gunther after receiving an overnight text from him saying they had to meet first thing in the morning.

Once they were both in Guy's office, Gunther told him he had received another call the evening before from Paul, now suddenly in Bangkok. He—Paul—had been calling from the airport where, for fuck's sake, he was about to take off for Washington. He had told Gunther a harrowing story about Oleg having been killed at the hotel in Phnom Penh. It was crawling with cops. He and Elise had hightailed it out and were bringing with them a document from Oleg that would confirm the story. It laid out the whole thing in lurid detail, he said.

Guy and Gunther had to decide what to do on the story, and quickly. Oleg's killing added urgency, and they decided that the thing to do was to verify this new Oleg document as soon as they could and then publish the story. This, of course, was easier said than done.

Guy, trying to regain the initiative, had volunteered to pick Paul and Elise up at Dulles when they landed that afternoon. Gunther paused for a moment before pointing out that his cramped, if sexy, Porsche was probably not the best choice to pick up two adults and their luggage, particularly after such a long flight. He would go instead, leaving Guy back at the paper.

Guy assented reluctantly and went back to his office.

Late that afternoon, Guy looked up to see Gunther standing in the doorway of his office, a manila envelope under his arm. It was the document Oleg had brought out of Moscow. Gunther placed it on Guy's desk.

"This is the key to the whole thing," he said.

"Without this, we don't have a story," Gunther said. "Verify it and we're on our way to a Pulitzer, not to mention maybe saving the country."

He looked at his watch pointedly, then looked back at Guy.

"No time to fuck around on this," he said. He watched Guy for a moment, appraisingly, before turning and heading back to the newsroom.

Guy picked up the envelope and examined the pages. They meant nothing to him; he didn't speak Russian. He put the pages back in the envelope and put it in a desk drawer.

He was beginning to wonder whether he'd bitten off more than he could chew. Gunther, that prick, was right, the document was the key to the story. If he could get it verified, he'd be a hero. None of his spy pals were calling him back, though, and he didn't have much time.

Saving the story wouldn't hurt his situation with Veronica either, he mused. He'd tell her about it one night, inflating his own role, of course. Over a nice dinner.

Dinner.

Veronica.

Suddenly, he had an idea. It was a long shot, but why not? He picked up the phone, dialed a number, and had a short conversation. He took the envelope out of his drawer and put it in his briefcase. He looked at his watch. He'd head out in half an hour or so.

* * *

Paul and Elise were at home. Elise, hit harder by the jetlag, had gone to bed and dozed off. Paul was thinking about the story. Things were moving quickly.

It occurred to him that Archie was still working away in his congressional office, unaware of what was happening. Maybe, Paul thought, he should at least give him a call.

He was half expecting Archie to be in some sort of meeting when he called his cell phone, but he picked up right away, sounding happy to hear from Paul.

He had to be careful.

The story had reached a "milestone," Paul told Archie, having puzzled over phrasing before he made the call. Really, that's great, Archie had said. He sounded a little anxious but maybe that was Paul; Archie still had his good ol' boy accent. Yes, Paul said, he expected to have some news soon, maybe in the next couple of days. That's great, Archie said. Suddenly it seemed there was another call for him; he'd get back to Paul.

* * *

Forty minutes after having made his own call, Guy was facing Peter across a table in a near-deserted Starbucks not far from the paper. He hadn't spoken with Peter since their conversation over coffee. That had not ended well, and he hadn't even been certain Peter would talk to him.

In the event, though, Peter seemed to have forgotten their confrontation when Guy called. In fact, he sounded almost happy to hear from Guy and he agreed to meet for a cup of coffee.

"Sounds urgent," he had said over the phone, "what's the emergency?"

"I'll tell you when I get there," Guy had said.

Peter certainly wasn't who he said he was, but Guy was only about fifty percent certain at this point that, as he'd supposed, Peter worked for the CIA. This was urgent, though. If Peter were with the CIA, or anywhere in U.S. intelligence—the U.S. *intelligence community*—he would be a good place to start in terms of verifying the document. At least Guy hoped so. He was out of options and running out of time.

They were sitting at a table far from the few other customers.

"We are working on sort of a tricky story," Guy told Peter, "and we may need your help." Peter looked up at that as Guy carefully began to outline the story in bare bones, hoping he sounded in control of the situation. As he spoke, a subtle change came over Peter, who watched Guy closely and then cut him off mid-sentence.

"Phnom Penh," Peter said. Guy had not mentioned Cambodia.

Guy looked at him. His jaw may have dropped, he later thought, but he wasn't sure.

"I think you know where I really work," Peter quietly said after a moment. He looked steadily at Guy. Any past traces of humor or past lightheartedness were gone.

Guy nodded.

Peter was still watching him. He seemed to think for a moment more, then resumed.

"We've been following your colleagues' activities in Europe and Asia," he said.

"In fact," he continued, "that's why I'm back here in Washington from, ah, overseas."

He glanced around the room.

"I'm afraid I need to ask you a favor," he said. "We do," he corrected himself.

A favor. Guy said nothing. Despite all of his customary bluster, he was, in fact, out of his depth.

"A big one," Peter said.

Guy nodded mutely.

"We need you to back off this story," Peter said, adding, "at least for the moment."

Before Guy could react, Peter continued.

"This document of Oleg's makes some fairly preposterous claims, I think you'll agree," he said, then adding, "at least we think they're preposterous. God help us if they're not." Hint of a smile there, but only a hint.

Guy nodded, wondering how Peter knew about the document.

"This is a matter of extreme sensitivity across the river, as you might imagine," Peter said, flicking his eyes suggestively toward the Potomac and, on the other side, Langley.

Peter paused for a moment.

"You need to keep this completely to yourself, of course," he said.

Guy nodded—of course—but Peter let it sink in for a moment before he continued. He seemed to be considering how to proceed, whether to share something sensitive.

"We're following this in real time," he said. Guy listened attentively. *Real time.* This was the sort of military phrasing Guy knew was common among special-ops and intelligence community—*IC*—types. His types.

"If you keep digging into this story now," Peter continued quietly, "you will put an operation and one of our sensitive human assets and his case officer in grave danger." He looked around for a moment again before continuing. "The gravest sort of danger, if you get what I'm saying," he added.

Guy looked at Peter for a moment. Sensitive human assets. Case officer. He felt like he'd died and gone to heaven.

"If we follow it up now?" he repeated.

Peter leaned back a bit.

"Right," he said. "We know it's an important story, and we know someone else might get it if you keep it to yourselves, but we just need you to hold off for a bit. I'll let you know when it's safe to go after it, and it won't be long, I promise." Two colleagues, cooperating for the greater good.

"I guess," Guy said. He was really in unknown territory, he now realized. He didn't know what to do. Plus, he still needed to get some sort of confirmation.

Then, suddenly, he had a thought. Maybe he could kill two birds with one stone.

"I have the document with me," he said.

"You do?" Peter looked up, seemingly surprised to hear that.

Guy leaned toward Peter, conspiratorially.

"Do you have the ability to verify a document purportedly written by a senior Kremlin official?"

Peter was wearing an expression Guy hadn't seen before. He seemed to be processing the question.

"Yes, of course," he said after a moment.

"I thought so," Guy said.

"How about," Guy said, "if I let you have the document to verify—without attribution by us, of course, we won't mention your team—and in return we'll hold off the story for a while until you get back to us." He thought the reference to "your team" would strengthen the feeling of comradeship in Peter.

"It's a deal," Peter said.

Guy felt as if he had taken control of the conversation. He reached into the briefcase by his feet and passed the envelope with Oleg's document to Peter under the table.

He watched as Peter discreetly slipped the document into his shoulder bag.

The two finished their coffee in silence and then got up to leave together. Peter, who was heading in a different direction than Guy, shook his hand. We'll get back to you as soon as we can, he said. Guy thanked him. As he watched Peter walking down the street, Guy congratulated himself on parlaying the situation to his advantage. This would pay off in the future, he knew.

* * *

It was good, Guy thought as he made his way back to the paper, to operate—and successfully one might add, in all modesty—as few journalists could, in the rarified world of high-level CIA spooks. The world of *sensitive human assets* who risked being put in *the gravest sort of danger*. Fuck Gunther Schroeder, he thought. And fuck that asshole Paul Girard and his stuck-up, full-of-herself wife as well.

Back at the paper, he stopped in Gunther's office and, after closing the door, told him he was in the process of getting the document verified. He said this with the solemnity befitting such a significant piece of news, but not so much that it would sound as if he weren't accustomed to the sorts of journalistic tasks that obviously required deep, dark, well-connected sources in the most secret corners of the covert world. He did not tell Gunther who was doing the verifying or that he had agreed to delay the story. He certainly did not tell him that the story was being delayed to protect the identity of what he assumed must be a deep-cover agent in Moscow or that he, Guy, despite all their sneering, now had a solid contact with a covert CIA officer. Maybe, he thought, he could figure out a way to hustle a story on the deep-cover agent if he played his cards right with Peter. That might even be his ticket back to the glam world of TV.

For his part, Gunther realized that everything was now on hold. Without the document—which Guy had apparently given to his mysterious contact—there was no story. He called Paul and filled him in before going back to work while he waited to hear from Guy.

It occurred to Paul while he was working that it might make sense to let Archie know that things were developing quickly.

He called Archie again and told him the story was working and he might have something soon. Archie sounded gratified but somewhat rushed. Paul could not, of course, tell him that the story had nothing to do with the Russian Far East. He didn't want to blindside him, though, so he started to say that he would give Archie a call just before it came out, maybe they could meet. That would at least give him some warning, he figured. Archie said that would be fine except, and his good ole boy accent seemed to be growing stronger, he had put his notice in; he'd had enough of Washington and wanted to get back to Real America. You know, he said, where people are honest and talk to each other about important things, he said, like the PTA and the local high school football team.

That surprised Paul, but it certainly made things easier. OK, let me know how to reach you, he said.

I surely will, Archie said. Then he hung up.

CHAPTER TWENTY-SIX

WIRE COPY

Gunther had had to put his spat with Guy aside momentarily for the mundane business of running the foreign news section of the paper.

He was staring at his computer screen on the newsroom floor trying to concentrate and not think about Guy when one of his assistant foreign editors woke him from his reverie from his desk at an adjacent workstation.

It seemed, the other editor said, that a stringer piece from Africa was going to end up too short. It was on a railroad project being funded by China, as it tried to increase its global role at the expense of the West. The story had to run today to beat a World Bank announcement on the project scheduled for the next morning. Now, however, the editor had found a couple of paragraphs that didn't fit and needed to be cut.

What's the problem, Gunther asked. He really didn't give a shit about the Africa story just now. The editor looked at his watch and pointed out that they were almost on top of a deadline and would need to fill the space.

Find some filler on the wires, Gunther said absentmindedly, going back to trying not to think about Guy.

The editor switched his screen to the wire services and found something that would fit. Go ahead and put it in, Gunther said, without looking at it. Later, he saw it when he was looking at the day's stories, but it didn't mean anything to him. Some Russian official named Vladimir Alexandrovich Zhuravlev had apparently had a fatal heart attack before a well-covered conference he had been supposed to address. Fortunately, he had been rushed to a government-run hospital, and a substitute speaker filled in for him. The news was regretfully announced by the Foreign Affairs Ministry, but no further details were available.

had been a joy to government and hospital, and would have been killed in jail had... The news was respectfully announced by the Prime Minister, but no further details were available.

CHAPTER TWENTY-SEVEN

THE WRONG NEIGHBORHOOD

He shouldn't have been there, the cops all agreed. Even the new guy, although, to be honest, he was just going along; he didn't know what he was talking about.

The body was hidden from the street, barely, behind a trash can in an alley off Fourteenth Street in Northwest, one of those areas that hadn't yet made up its mind whether it would remain loyal to its funky, impoverished recent past or succumb to the opiate of gentrification.

The Spanish groceries and the liquor stores were still hanging in there on the nearby commercial strip along with a check-cashing joint, but they were being replaced by restaurants serving artisanal hamburgers and by bars for the newly arriving kids in their twenties looking for cheap rent, cheap beer, and hookups. One of the bars had now just started taking credit cards, which everyone agreed was an inarguable sign that the neighborhood was about to go to hell—by which they meant the middle class would be arriving soon, with their minivans, foodie cookware and designer strollers full of white children.

Apparently, though, that day was still a ways off, as indicated by the body.

It was a middle-aged man, wearing a nice suit and nice shoes.

Probably looking for drugs, one of the cops said.

The guy had been clocked, but good, on the back of his head. It looked like whoever had done the clocking had gotten scared and dragged the body into the alley before fleeing the scene, although it wasn't clear where the clocking itself had actually occurred. Who cared?

No watch, no wallet, no money though.

Seemed pretty clear. This guy was in the wrong neighborhood, the new guy said. The others gave him a look for belaboring the obvious. The new guy looked at his watch, embarrassed. He just wanted to get home. His girlfriend had had promised him "something special" tonight, which was his birthday. Since she was a terrible cook, and very self-conscious about it, he expected the something special would not have anything to do with dinner.

Then one of the cops shouted out he'd found a wallet and brought it over.

No money of course, but some ID, anyway.

"Andrew Warwick," the cop intoned.

"Looks like some kind of reporter," he said, pulling a few business cards out of the wallet, "some sort of hot shit oil newspaper."

"Man, he shouldn't have been here," the cop said, now about the twentieth time someone had said that. The others glared at him.

OK, one of the cops, the senior officer present, said after a moment. She looked at her own watch. She'd let the others handle this. It was the end of the shift; she wanted to go home, have a drink, and watch a little TV with her husband. This was just another rich white boy trying to score some drugs. She didn't give a shit. The guy should have been smarter; he'd been in the wrong neighborhood. Nothing to be done. She'd let one of the others file the report, and they'd all be done with it.

They all packed their stuff and went back to their marked and un-marked cars. The new guy hung back, something on the ground had caught his eye.

He picked it up and looked at it. It was a matchbook. Man, you don't see many of those anymore he thought, someone must have dropped it. He turned it over and looked at it. It had a swastika printed on it and a toll-free phone number. Certainly odd in this neighborhood, he thought, staring at it.

One of the older cops yelled at him to stop fucking around and get in the car.

He dropped the matchbook back on the ground and went back to the patrol car. He was thinking about his girlfriend and the adventures he expected tonight, not some matchbook, swastika or not.

CHAPTER TWENTY-EIGHT

AN IMPORTANT MEETING

Langley, Virginia, three days later

This couldn't be. Yet, there it was, on the screen. As plain as day. If only, she thought . . .

Evelyn Kilgore, of the CIA's Russia House, went back to work on her keyboard, then looked at the display and swore again. Quietly. Under her breath. She rarely swore. Even quietly. Even under her breath. It was unseemly. Unladylike. *Nekul'turno*, as she would say in Russian. This was different though.

She sent a flash alert to several of her colleagues telling them to be ready for a meeting in the SCIF near her office as soon as she called them. Put everything else aside, she said. She copied the seventh floor, the director's office—the director's executive assistant personally, the message flagged as extremely urgent.

She looked at the information spread across her two computer screens.

There it was, on the screen. Hidden in plain sight.

She looked at her watch and then at the time zone clocks along the wall.

She swore yet again.

If only, she thought . . .

* * *

It had started a few hours earlier.

Evelyn had, at this very desk, participated in a routine liaison meeting, the sort of meeting that was held among intelligence community senior managers or specialists, as needed, to share intriguing but uncorroborated, and not earth-shaking, reporting. A low-level informant thought he'd heard a vague rumor about an unlikely plan to attack a U.S. embassy in Africa, a North Korean military official was said to be secretly meeting in Macao with a Pakistani thought to be flogging nuclear weapons gizmos, an Azerbaijani trucking company's profits were maybe being skimmed to finance Islamic terrorists, a long-missing illegal arms dealer thought to be dead had apparently risen from the grave and checked into a hotel in Sofia for three days under a false name. That sort of thing.

Evelyn had been in this meeting because it dealt with Russia and specifically Russian intelligence. It had been spurred by an uptick in coded message traffic that had been detected overnight among elements of Russia's network of spy agencies. The increase had appeared suddenly, and while not huge, it was discernible—even though the contents of the messages remained unknown so far.

This sort of comms jump was not alarming, or even unusual; it happened periodically. Evelyn hadn't been particularly concerned about it when she saw the reports, it seemed more or less routine to her. As one of Russia House's senior analysts, though, she agreed to represent the CIA in the meeting, which was held via encrypted videoconference.

So, she had cleared her desk, metaphorically speaking, made herself a cup of black Russian tea, and joined the meeting, using one of two large screens hooked up to her computer for the session, while keeping an eye on the other one, monitoring incoming cables, internal messaging and emails, and other routine business.

The National Security Agency had called the meeting, so the NSA representative began the session, outlining what had been picked up. There had been, he said, a slight increase in message traffic among several Russian intelligence components in Moscow and elsewhere, including some in the United States, the Russian mission to the United Nations in New York among them, as well as some in Asia and several points in Europe.

The NSA representative flashed a map onto the screen with details of the communications blip. Could be something, could be nothing, Evelyn thought, quickly scanning the map. Nothing to panic about.

She sipped her tea, listening with half an ear to the NSA representative.

Her eye flicked to her other screen. There was a message from the CIA's security office on updating passwords on classified and unclassified email accounts. She scanned farther down the list. A former case officer now teaching at The Farm, the CIA's training center near Williamsburg, Virginia, was retiring and a party would be held near the facility for all who were interested. A block of rooms at a nearby hotel had been booked, ostensibly for a friendly Richmond law firm's management retreat, for those who didn't want to drive back to Washington afterward. Please pick up a packet of legal-looking files from the security office to leave in the hotel room during the party if you want to stay in the hotel, just in case, the email said. They thought of everything.

Her mike muted, Evelyn looked back at the NSA rep, now on the screen, who looked to be about twelve years old. He was anxious, visibly nervous as he spoke. Evelyn knew he had just been promoted and this was his first time in one of these meetings. Had he been a little more seasoned, she thought, he probably wouldn't have asked for this meeting but just sent a memo around and kept his eye on the situation.

Something was beginning to nag at the back of her mind, though.

The NSA kid was growing more nervous and was starting to repeat himself. On her other screen, Evelyn saw that one of her friends in the meeting, an FBI counterintelligence analyst, had sent a snide private message about the NSA kid needing to go back to middle school. Evelyn ignored it, she remembered when she had been green. The FBI analyst too, for that matter.

With one ear following the polite discussion of the NSA kid's pretty unremarkable information, Evelyn pulled up the kid's profile on her second screen from an HR database she had access to as a senior manager. He had an impressive background and probably a solid future in intelligence; he was just new. Evelyn decided, as had the others in the now-finished meeting, to let him go on. The information wasn't earthshaking, but it was a slow day.

What was it that was lurking back there, just at the edge of her consciousness?

After the presentation, there was a certain amount of polite discussion among the analysts from the smorgasbord of agencies—Evelyn from the CIA and the FBI analyst, as well as others from Homeland Security, the Treasury Department's terrorism and financial intelligence people, State, the Pentagon, the National Security Council staff, and more, even the Transportation Department's Intelligence Division. It was a slow day, and they were all responding encouragingly. There was an unspoken agreement among the big dogs to help this kid along.

Something was nagging at her, still, she just couldn't put her finger on it.

As the discussion of the new Russian messaging traffic wound down, one of the Homeland Security analysts, who hadn't been in her own position that long, signaled electronically that she had something to say. When the NSA representative was finished, she came on the screen and said that a video had come along that she wanted to share. It had come from an allied country's version of the Transportation Security Administration through Homeland Security's own TSA, she said. Not really a problem, but she wanted to share it to be on the safe side. Evelyn, her own camera off, looked at her watch, as she assumed a number of her colleagues were doing, and hoped this wouldn't drag out much longer.

Evelyn could see the analyst lean toward the screen, apparently punching some keys on her keyboard, and then the video came up. It showed normal surveillance of airline passengers coming off an airplane. The video had been routinely passed through a facial recognition algorithm, and a red flag had gone up for one of the passengers caught on the video, the analyst said. She seemed gratified to report that TSA was doing something other than making life miserable for traveling U.S. taxpayers.

Evelyn watched the screen as a line of passengers came off a plane. As the algorithm kicked in, the image froze and darkened except for a square around one of the deplaning passengers, who actually seemed to be avoiding eye contact with the camera as he passed in front of it.

The computer then superimposed a mapping grid over the passenger's face, scanned it, and, within seconds, dozens of potential matches flashed by at the side of the screen until a match popped up, with identifying information in the originating country's language, translation into English conveniently below, like a movie subtitle.

The analysts on the call were silent for a moment until Evelyn's FBI friend spoke, saying, yes, this was interesting, but probably not important. People like this make trips all the time and we certainly can't be seen as trying to keep an eye on them.

But they don't spot security cameras and then do their best to avoid the cameras' gaze, Evelyn thought.

Chastened, the Homeland Security analyst agreed and apologized for bringing it up. No problem, someone said, before, by apparent consensus, the meeting broke up and everyone forgot about the TSA video and went back to the rest of their day. Evelyn left the frozen image of the passenger, just as he was about to look the other way, up on her screen.

The originating country, out of deference, had taken no further steps when the passenger had been identified. Evelyn, however, felt no such constraint.

Tapping into the same airline networks that Serino had in Rome, she quickly checked the airline's flight manifest on her second screen and discovered that the passenger was not traveling under his own name. That definitely set off a siren, and a loud one—there was nothing surprising about him traveling, but doing so under an alias definitely meant something was amiss.

Evelyn stared at one screen and the face frozen on it then at her other screen with the incriminating information in clear, 12-point lettering.

Moving her mouse to an icon not found on your average home or business computer, she opened a new window and entered her name and password. She then clicked on the passenger's face again with the new program engaged, allowing her to link the video to her own, infinitely superior CIA facial recognition program, which was tied into the agency's highly classified and much more extensive image library.

When the computer displayed the results, she stared at the screen. It couldn't be, but it was. Rather than the identifying information the scan from the TSA analyst had revealed, or even the false ticketing information Evelyn had found, there was a completely new set of data on the screen in front of her now. Data that set off the highest alarm possible for her.

This couldn't be. Yet, there it was, on the screen. As plain as day. She had an unwelcome thought, a very unwelcome thought. She swore, uncharacteristically.

Using her electronic CIA credentials, she logged into a series of databases and, starting with information on the passenger who had been flagged, ran a series of comparison and pattern-matching algorithms through the system, which produced another series of passenger records, as she had feared. Then, using credentials that masked who she was, and, in some cases, even that she was searching from the United States, she looked at other airport surveillance videos, online purchases, traffic monitoring videos, and satellite shots, all from the previous forty-eight hours. She also examined customs and international entry databases, looking into the records of passports scanned into various countries' ostensibly secure records systems during the previous day or so. The most recent video she looked at had been made at an airport ticket desk less than two hours before, as the passenger first flagged by the Homeland Security analyst now checked in for a flight, under still another name, to a destination that definitely should have set off alarms.

She looked at the display and swore again. Quietly. Under her breath. She rarely swore. Even quietly. Even under her breath. It was unseemly. Unladylike. *Nekul'turno*, as she would say in Russian. This was different though.

She sent a flash alert to several of her colleagues telling them to be ready for a meeting in the SCIF near her office as soon as she called them. Put everything else aside, she said. She copied the seventh floor, the director's office—the director's executive assistant personally—the message flagged as extremely urgent.

She looked at the information spread across her two computer screens.

There it was, on the screen. Hidden in plain sight in the morass of computer records shooting from computer to computer and around the world.

She looked at her watch and then at the time zone clocks along the wall.

She swore yet again.

If only, she thought . . .

If only . . .

If only she'd seen any of this the day before.

CHAPTER TWENTY-NINE

THE DAY BEFORE

Philadelphia

They had come here by disparate routes.

Veronica had awoken early, but not so early as to attract attention, then walked out of her apartment and looked around, taking in the details of this lovely morning. She had then gotten into her Porsche Boxster, started up the engine but did not put the top down, and headed up through Georgetown and Northwest Washington into Bethesda, then on to the Beltway. She drove against most of the morning rush-hour traffic, so she made good time and, as she could see as she frequently checked her rear-view mirrors, no trucks or other worrisome vehicles seemed to be threateningly bearing down on her from the rear.

What a beautiful day for a drive.

She drove north from the Beltway on I-95, around Baltimore, and north toward New York, keeping up with traffic but never speeding. She frequently checked her mirrors.

She stopped at a rest stop just over the Delaware line for a Starbucks, sitting and watching the tourists as they came in and out. Then, seemingly suddenly tired of the coffee, she dumped the cup and went back out to the lot to resume her drive. She then continued on her way, up the Interstate, past Wilmington, Delaware, then Philadelphia and Trenton, New Jersey, and finally to a commuter lot near Princeton, where she locked the car and went into the train station. She bought a ticket using cash and then took an NJ Transit train back down to the Thirtieth Street

Station in Philadelphia. There had been a middle-aged man lingering on the train platform with her while she was waiting in New Jersey, but he seemed to pay her no mind and did not seem to notice when she got on the train at the last minute.

She had a seat to herself on the train and, although she had a book open in front of her, her eyes frequently flicked up to scan the inside of the car and the few other passengers.

Once in Philadelphia, she dawdled over a magazine in the station souvenir shop, then went out to the waiting room, her eyes darting around as, apparently, she checked the departures board and the various gates to see if the line for her train had formed.

After half an hour, she turned as if heading to look for a ladies' room but instead went through an exit and to the cab stand. There, again paying cash, she took a taxi to a spot several blocks away from here. She then walked the rest of the way, periodically glancing at the reflections in store windows as she went.

* * *

Peter had also awoken on the early side and taken the Washington Metro to Union Station, where he bought a Greyhound ticket for Philadelphia, using a credit card and U.S. driver's license identifying him not as Canadian but as an American from Idaho, the documents specially prepared for this occasion. He was the last to board the bus and scanned his fellow riders as the driver motioned him to hurry up and find a seat. Fortunately, he spotted an aisle seat toward the rear after sweeping the passengers with his eyes. None of them really noticed him, just another guy with a baseball cap and large aviator sunglasses, both of which served to hide much of his face, and a nondescript jeans jacket. They would have been hard-pressed to describe him further should the need have arisen. He put his gym bag into the overhead compartment and spent the trip leaning back in his seat, dozing, maybe. It was hard to tell with his eyes hidden behind the big shades.

When he got to the Philadelphia bus station, Peter took a cab to the Downtown Sheraton hotel, where a trade show occupied much of the mezzanine level, as he had known it would. He walked past the front desk, apparently a guest on his way to his room, and took the elevator up to the mezzanine level. The hall was full of corporate types milling around the free coffee and snacks between sessions. Peter eased through the crowd to an empty area of the corridor, pulling out his phone, apparently to make a call. As he spoke on the phone, his eyes flicked around the corridor at the crowd of visiting managers and then, seeing no sign of trouble, he went into the men's room.

There, in a roomy handicapped stall, he opened his gym bag and changed from his Idaho duds into tailored slacks, a well-cut sport shirt and a sport jacket, all of which had been neatly folded in the gym bag. He then took the last item from the gym bag, a large black plastic trash bag, put his old clothes and the gym bag itself into the plastic bag, and secured it with a twist tie. He stuck his head out of the stall and, seeing the room was empty, took the now full plastic bag out into the corridor and left it in a large rolling trash bin under some discarded papers.

He left the Sheraton and walked to another hotel a few blocks away and ordered an espresso, lingering over it as he watched that hotel's lobby and entrance. Satisfied, he had then left the hotel by a rear entrance and come here on foot. Like Veronica, he had periodically checked store windows to ensure he had not been followed.

* * *

In Alexandria, Virginia, that morning, the promotions department at a trade association for the aircraft industry was understaffed. It wasn't really a problem because although this was a small trade association with a limited staff, it wasn't a particularly busy time. Meanwhile, Gwen, who helped out in the association's president's office, had called in sick. She was a good worker who was unfailingly cheery and hardly ever took time off. Well, there had been that sudden request for a couple of days off a few weeks ago, when she had to go home to New Hampshire to help her sick mother for a few days. Otherwise, she was always there, toiling away in her cramped cubbyhole office, alone, always willing to digest the minutiae of the changing needs of the industry's customers. When there were lunches or other functions, and someone was needed to hand out badges or put on a smiling face for the visiting dignitaries from industry or the nearby Pentagon, you could always count on Gwen to volunteer. She was really a gem.

Nothing like that was going on today, though, so it wasn't a problem that she'd taken a rare sick day. She had really come down with something, she had confided over the phone to Kat, her best best friend at work. It might be a couple of days, and she wondered whether Kat could cover for her. Omigod, Kat had said, of course, take all the time you need. Gwen had covered for her on more than one occasion. Not to mention all the times the two had gone out together after work to gab about who was up and who was down in the aircraft industry, or what was coming up at the next annual conference, that sort of thing. It was fun talking to her about that stuff. No one else paid that much attention to them at the office and certainly no one outside the office cared to hear about that sort of insider gossip. Last week, Gwen had said she couldn't go out for drinks because her cousin was in from out of town, and she had to show him around. Bring him along, Kat had said. She didn't have many friends other than a few from college who lived far away, and who never seemed to write or return her calls or emails anyway, and her neighbors, and she always loved to meet new people. Turns out Gwen's cousin was a nice guy, a little pudgy, but funny, and good-looking in a sort of bashful schoolboy way. Moreover, he had seemed a little taken with Kat. The next day, Gwen had snuck over to Kat's desk to confide, *sotto voce*, that the cousin had asked Gwen for Kat's number. Kat said, sure, give it to him, and they'd both had a giggle over it. Gwen was like the sister Kat had always wished she'd had. So, Kat was more than happy to help her friend out today.

In truth, though, Gwen had been feeling perfectly fine when she called in that day from her apartment in Arlington. Well, a little tense, but who wouldn't be? She had been expected to stay where she was, working her way up the trade association ladder, for a few more years, insinuating herself further into that world, but now that had all changed when she got an innocent-looking invitation on LinkedIn. It was seemingly from an insurance salesman in nearby Olney, Maryland, who wanted to join her network. The salesman's message included a mention that he was a Little League "croach"—the occupation and misspelling were the emergency signals.

Gwen took an elevator down to the ground floor of her apartment building, walked to the Metro station, and took a Metro to Reagan National Airport. Once there, she walked around a bit, taking in her surroundings before making her way to a car rental agency and picking up a car using the new identity documents and credit card that had been in the expected spot outside her building. She started up the rental car and, making sure she was not being followed, headed for I-95, which would take her to Philadelphia. She stopped on the way to change her clothes and get a snack. While changing in the ladies' room, she took a cell phone out of her purse and removed the SIM card with the Canadian number Guy had called for details on Peter and his company, which she had answered as "Rebecca." She flushed the SIM card down the toilet and tossed the phone—wiped clean of prints—into a trash bin before continuing on her way. The rental car was now in a pay lot a few blocks away, from which she had taken a circuitous route, being careful to make certain that she was not under surveillance.

*   *   *

Archie Richter had the longest trip.

His first leg, by a car, also rented under a flag of convenience identity, took a couple of hours, being longer because of traffic at the Chesapeake Bay Bridge. After crossing the bridge to Maryland's Eastern Shore, he continued driving, stopping in a McDonald's to switch to another car waiting for him. He then followed Route 50 until he cut off onto Route 301 toward Centreville, making sure, as he had been since he had left home, that he was not being followed.

He stopped on the way at a burger joint, where he was joined by a young officer who had driven the junker he had been using for a couple of weeks, now left by the side of the road a mile or so away. Had he been there, Paul might have recognized the young officer as the scraggly kid in the Ocean City pizza joint—although the tattoos, acne, and sideburns were gone—and he might have even remembered him as having been in the bar near the hotel in nearby Berlin, Maryland, when he and Elise had had a drink there, but he'd had his back turned, and probably not anyway.

The pair walked out of the burger joint together and, after ducking behind a liquor store to a spot under the building's sheltering eaves that could not be seen from the road—or from above—they had gotten into yet another car that was waiting, hidden, with a driver. After thirty minutes, it pulled out and took them to the Centreville compound.

There, Archie had then spent almost an hour talking with his bosses many miles away on a heavily encrypted channel from a secure room. He then handed one of the other officers, who had diplomatic status, his shoulder bag with the document Oleg had brought to Cambodia from Moscow in it. It would travel out of the country by protected diplomatic pouch. Archie had been incredulous when Peter told him what a dope Guy had been—not only handing the document itself over to him without a second thought but coming up with the idea himself. What a fucking idiot.

Archie and the young officer had then taken a clean car that was waiting for them and driven up 301 and then to Philadelphia, where they were able to ditch the car and meet the others, taking countersurveillance precautions, of course.

Veronica smiled at the young officer when he arrived. She had trained him, and he had done a very persuasive job with the knife outside the French restaurant with Guy, particularly since he had managed to be convincing without actually stabbing anyone.

It was risky for them to meet, even here, in an alley in Chinatown, but Archie, a name he was no longer identifiable by, brought congratulations from headquarters on an exceedingly well-executed operation. He also brought new identities and travel documents so the five could leave Philadelphia and the country surreptitiously.

It was a risk, but Archie had also brought a small bottle and paper cups. He poured a shot out for each of them, and they toasted before tossing the bottle, cleaned of any prints, and cups into a sewer drain.

There was no one around, but the toast was nevertheless whispered, so quietly that no one else could possibly have heard it, even if they could have understood it.

* * *

They went their separate ways. A flight to London, a train to New York for a flight to Frankfurt, a flight to Boston and then Montreal and Vienna, a bus to Baltimore for a flight to Rome. A flight to Chicago and then a flight to Paris. In each European intermediary city, they would change their identities again with the help of local colleagues and catch onward flights. No expense had been spared in this operation. It was that important.

Bidding each other farewell in the Chinatown alley, they moved quickly. They knew they would see each other again in a few days in the same anonymous building where Marina, working in a different section, had toiled away listening to stolen conversations. They would be congratulated on a job well-done by Max and some of the very few others cleared to know about them and their operation. They had, together, neutralized a danger to a critical covert action operation, possibly the most important in the history of the country, and had done it well. They knew they would be feted, if only in secret.

It was said President Putin himself would be there.

It was his project, after all.

He was very proud of them.

EPILOGUE

CHAPTER THIRTY

NO HARM, NO FOUL

It went like clockwork.

Not surprising, of course. It was an easy set of tasks that the organization had carried out elsewhere many times. Its forte, one might even venture to say.

The first part was easy. Being both Paul and Elise, though, it had to be done in a way that would not raise suspicion, other than the obvious—and intended—sort, of course.

Their neighborhood was still evolving back to its previous glory, to what it had been before urban blight had brought in the drug dealers and the street crime. It was making progress, of course, that was clear from the coffee shops and trendy restaurants edging out the 7-Elevens and low-rent liquor stores.

Nevertheless, it was still a dodgy area and, everyone said later, Paul and Elise should have known that when they moved in. They certainly should have known to keep their eyes open walking home one night from one of the new restaurants on Eighth Street.

It was kids, one assumed, from the other side of the river, maybe, probably a pack of them. They'd shot both Paul and Elise and, it appeared, taken their money. By the time anyone in the neighborhood had gathered the wherewithal to look outside and then, ultimately, call the police, the attackers were long gone.

The neighbors, professional and mostly white, were shocked that this still happened in this neighborhood, what with the housing prices skyrocketing as they were. One or two resolved to write to the city council or, in a couple of cases, talk to colleagues in congressional offices. Big shots. They'd show these thugs. Nothing, of course, came of it, either in the D.C. Council or congressional offices. Eventually, everyone shook their collective heads and went on with their lives.

The second was much simpler.

Gunther had been shopping in a Whole Foods, looking for the kind of pasta his wife wanted for that evening. He had been distracted while working on the Oleg document story and she had put up with it without complaining. Tonight, they were going to have a nice dinner, just the two of them, maybe go for a walk in the park near their house. Glass of wine or two. No talk about work.

He'd proposed going out to dinner, but she wanted to make it an intimate dinner at home, so he had volunteered to go out and do the shopping.

He had no idea what he was doing, though—pasta was pasta as far as he was concerned. As he was consulting on the matter with a clerk, a woman trying to talk on a phone cradled against her shoulder while she wrestled with an overfull cart as she walked by, knocked into him. She turned to apologize and slightly lost her balance grabbing his shoulder to steady herself. Embarrassed, she apologized again and made her way down the aisle.

There had been a slight sting on his arm when she grabbed it, Gunther thought, but that was one of his last thoughts before the poison took effect. There were no blisters, no screaming or vomiting onto the floor or pasta shelves, none of that sort of drama. It was all very quick and quiet. The point was to solve a problem, not make a statement. Older men had heart attacks or whatever. It happened.

The final step not only addressed a potential problem but also strengthened a growing working relationship.

Guy had been moping around since the apparent disappearance of Veronica. She had left a phone message that she had to go out of town and hoped to be back soon, but something didn't sound right. He had tried to call her cell phone several times and left messages, with no response.

Guy, though, was not the sort of man who placed undue emphasis on monogamy or loyalty to sexual partners, Porsche Boxster or no Porsche Boxster. After a few days, he started nosing around some of his old haunts and kept an eye peeled for new action.

He took one of his habitual drives up into Potomac and back in his 911, newly waxed, by the way, and then, as always, went into Mr. Henry's for a hamburger and a beer—ironically, in Paul and Elise's neighborhood.

That's when he saw her. She was the perfect antidote to the now-disappeared Veronica. She was tall, with long blonde hair, wearing a silk blouse and short skirt, plus heels slightly higher than necessary. In her hand, she nursed what looked like a wine spritzer or some other girly, lightweight bullshit drink. Intern, Guy thought, or first-year staffer on the Hill.

He thought she'd caught his eye as he'd walked by her on the way to his table, and it turned out he was right.

As he was looking at his menu just in case he wanted to try something new, he caught a whiff of perfume and saw she had approached his table.

"You're Guy Lynch?" she asked, standing close and brushing some of her luxuriant blonde hair away from her face. She was giving him a shy smile.

"Why yes," Guy said. This might turn out to be a pretty good night, he was beginning to think.

She said she was a grad student from USC studying broadcast journalism here on a class trip and had seen videos of many of his shows, could she join him? If it wouldn't be a bother, of course.

"Absolutely," Guy said, catching a glimpse of cleavage as she sat down, "be my guest." No bother at all.

"My name is Ingrid," she said, extending a long, elegant, manicured hand. *Ingrid*, Guy thought. This was getting better and better.

She asked him about his work. The TV work, that is. She listened, rapt, as he began to discuss, with appropriate modesty, his role in covering some of the big stories of recent years. She accepted his offer of another drink—just tell the bartender the same again, she said. When it came, her hand carelessly brushed his as she took it from him.

"Ingrid," of course was not actually named that, her name was Sarah Cutler, and she was the daughter of parents in Indiana who were ardent Klan members and had raised her on a steady diet of white nationalist and neo-Nazi literature, surrounded by like-minded people. Her striking beauty, particularly in a Nordic—Aryan, that is—way, ensured that people remembered her. She was very athletic and had embraced the paramilitary training offered by some of the movement's local allies, demonstrating remarkable skill and fearlessness, according to her instructors.

She had met some new friends from Russia, a country she knew had shed its Godless Communist past and was now ruled by an admirable leader who believed in Christianity and traditional, family values. She had spent time with these new friends and gotten to know them, even going out with one of them a few times. She was in heaven.

She had been a little surprised when she had been asked to undertake this mission and, frankly, found it a little distasteful. However, they assured her, she wouldn't have to actually do anything, if she got their drift, just follow the script. The troops would show up before anything really happened.

And follow the script she did. The perfume, the blue eyes, the inviting smile did the trick, as expected, as Guy droned on about his boring work. She concluded he must be a Jew, he was so full of himself.

After a while, following the script, she feigned amazement that such a famous journalist would be so open with her. She let slip that she had had a boyfriend who was in the business, but he had dumped her recently. "Too bad," Guy said, sympathetically. She could see the gears turning in his head. He was so obvious.

After another drink, she shyly asked him if he might walk her home. Not far, she said, a place the school had found for her. It was just that she wasn't from around here and was a little nervous walking alone at night. "Maybe a little tipsy too," she added.

"Of course," Guy said.

Men are so stupid, she thought.

Guy paid the check, got a wink from the bartender, and left, gallantly holding the door open for Ingrid on the way out.

She was staying, she told him, in a carriage house in a nearby alley. This made sense, a common sort of dwelling on Capitol Hill, converted into compact and comfortable abodes behind what had, in bygone days, been their main house.

The two walked together into the alley toward the darkened carriage house she had pointed out from the street, Guy thanking his lucky stars. She was a little unsteady on her heels and brushed against him once or twice as they walked.

Then, as they entered the alley, two men jumped out of an idling car, one smacking Guy on the head with a brick. The other shot him twice in the forehead and then they bundled his body into the trunk of the car before pulling out, past the carriage house, owned by a lobbyist they had known would be out of town.

"Ingrid," had asked the bartender for nonalcoholic drinks and so she was, therefore, stone-cold sober. When the men jumped out of their car, she had turned and left the alley, heading for her nondescript rental Toyota rented under another false name, parked nearby behind an apartment building. Once in the darkened car, she changed into jeans and a hoodie that would cover her hair and pulled on a pair of sneakers before pulling onto the street.

A block away she pulled to the side and, using a burner, checked in to report the mission had been a success. She used a number inside a matchbook with a swastika on it that she'd left in the car, then she drove out to a motel on Route 50 in Arlington where she was actually staying under her real name. She was set to fly out the next morning on an early flight.

The killing of three, maybe four, people connected to the paper in such a short time was, of course a shock to the paper, the Capitol Hill neighborhood and the city, raising a hue and cry. The paper's editors, local citizens and officials demanded and got an investigation but ultimately it got nowhere and, given the overall crime situation in the city, it petered out for everyone except for a few malcontents and activists.

* * *

Evelyn Kilgore was the last piece of the puzzle, and her actions were either a double tragedy or a double stroke of good luck, depending on which side of the former Iron Curtain you might be watching from.

When the TSA analyst had flagged the image of a congressional staffer going through airport security, that, of course, had not been something that would have raised any concern among the spy agencies on the conference call. The staffer's identification as Archibald Richter, who worked for an unknown first-term House member from the boondocks, would have meant nothing to any of them—even if they had had dealings with Congress since the member was such a backbencher.

That included Evelyn; Gunther had not mentioned Archie to Guy when he had initially briefed him on what he thought was a document from Oleg. As a result, Guy did not mention Archie when he visited the CIA, triggering the Russia House investigation of the purported Oleg document.

In fact, after some snooping around and exchanging some information with allied services in Asia and the Pacific, tapping into a lot of supposedly private conversations, and mobilizing some of the American arsenal's impressive armada of space assets, the CIA had pretty much discarded the whole notion that there might be a Far Eastern separatist movement, either already extant or in the works, and moved on to other business.

However, in the intel agencies' meeting, something had struck Evelyn as off—subconsciously, like a hunch, from the kid's presentation about the Russian communications uptick. There was something amiss, but she couldn't put her finger on it. Those suspicions had really been raised when Archie, seen onscreen, had avoided eye contact with the security camera. That suspicion had led her to the extremely disconcerting discovery that Archie had been traveling under an alias, which was definitely not standard operating procedure for congressional staffers, particularly those who were working for obscure members no one had ever heard of and probably never would.

Then, of course, she used her more advanced CIA facial recognition program and discovered, to her shock, that "Archie Richter" matched the image of a Russian the CIA's Moscow station had had their eye on. The Moscow station had stumbled onto him by accident during a routine surveillance of a Russian woman who had taken up with a now-gone low-level code clerk formerly assigned to the U.S. Embassy's back rooms.

The station's watchers had eyes on her one afternoon as she walked toward Novodevichy Cemetery near the Metro Sportivnaya station in Moscow when she seemed to run into an old friend the watchers didn't recognize. They then, though, identified him as a probable intelligence officer when he had been picked up by a nearby agency officer with a long-range mike, stupidly speaking to her in American-accented English. The Moscow station opined in a flash reporting cable back to Russia House that he was probably headed for duty as a deep-cover operative masquerading as an American—known in the trade as an "illegal"—in the United States, given the American-flavored English.

He had, though, dropped out of sight after that.

Until now, that is.

Identification of Archie as a Russian asset, of course, was a blockbuster find, and Evelyn took the necessary steps to ascertain the damage he might have caused, including whether he had recruited any of his fellow congressional staffers as agents or used them as sources. Highly classified emails were distributed on a strictly need-to-know basis to a very small number of people in the agency, up to the director, as well as the White House national security adviser and her chief of staff. Heavily scrubbed—"redacted" being the favored sterile bureaucratic term *du jour*—versions were also sent on an eyes-only basis to the heads and senior minority party members of the House and Senate intelligence committees and their chiefs of staff, unavoidable given the circumstances, it was reluctantly agreed in Langley.

Archie had not, as it turned out, caused any discernible damage, and the member for whom he worked not only never made much of a splash, but she lost her reelection bid in the next cycle.

It seemed to be a puzzle why Archie had been placed in Washington in the first place. Evelyn and her CIA colleagues were not only unaware that "Archie" had spurred Paul and Elise to chase down Oleg on the basis of the phony Oleg document. They were also, of course, ignorant of the actual document Oleg had snuck out of Russia that would have spilled the beans on Moscow's plans, and which Archie had effectively used Paul and Elise to recover for Moscow, using a concocted Far East separatist movement memo.

Evelyn ultimately filed an internal final report on Archie's infiltration of a congressional office. The incident was among several other episodes outlined to the new administration in Washington when the new management took over in 2017, but was not even the most significant of them, so was effectively forgotten, along with much of the rest of that report to the new team. Evelyn left government service right after inauguration and formed a very quiet consulting firm with some of her former colleagues that worked for the U.S. government and trusted allies.

From Moscow's point of view, everything went according to plan, despite Oleg's discovery of the document.

No harm, as one might say in English, no foul.

On to the next step.

CHAPTER THIRTY-ONE

A NEW LIFE

Washington, December 2016

On the Georgetown University campus, most of its students, professors, and the rest, were, like much of the rest of the United States, especially the liberal, MSNBC-watching, *New York Review of Books*-reading United States, stunned at the results of the just-finished presidential election.

It was all they could talk about. How could it have happened? What will happen next? Should we move to Australia? Sales of Sinclair Lewis' *It Can't Happen Here* and George Orwell's *1984* got a bump. People made nervous jokes comparing the situation to having Tony Soprano in the White House. *Sopranos* fans among them retorted that Tony Soprano would have been a better choice.

Meanwhile, in other parts of the country, the people were ecstatic.

Those conniving bicoastal globalist elitists—fuck them—with their condescension toward anyone who wasn't in their club had been beaten back and America was safe from the Deep State. Did they even know what it was like to run a dry-cleaning business or a farm or anything else about what it was like to actually work for a living?

Plus, now, the country would be able to regain the stature it had had before, when it was respected, if not feared, around the world. Protecting freedom and liberty. The country would stop apologizing for itself all the time.

And, the government would get back to the business of staying out of people's business with its nanny-state regulations and stop listening to every whiny minority group who found a way to get its hands on taxpayers' money and use it for some scheme that would enable its lazy members to sit on their asses all day instead of work for a living. Plus, stem the immigrant throngs, pull the courts back from the extreme left, protect gun rights, and the rest. It was a great time to be an American. Finally, the country would be great again.

Not far from the Georgetown campus, some graduate students were sipping designer coffee and getting ready for the morning's classes in a Starbucks.

At one table a few were comparing notes.

This was a somewhat cosmopolitan group, the sort one might not find on campuses elsewhere. There were a few students who, as was the case at any prestigious graduate school, had gone right from undergraduate work into graduate school. They knew that Georgetown, like Johns Hopkins and the other Washington-area schools, provided the connections and networking opportunities that would enable them to get good jobs in the government, the United Nations, the World Bank, or other bastions of the International Establishment.

Some others in the group, though, were already in that establishment, pursuing their graduate work in area studies, national security, economics, or other subjects while they held government jobs as congressional staffers or in State, Defense, the Fed, or elsewhere. Even the CIA.

Plus, in addition to these Americans, there were a few of the school's many international students at the table. There was a Chinese student from Guangzhou, a Saudi who was—not surprisingly—studying energy economics, and a few others, including a French girl and a guy from Brazil, all studying various high-minded and arcane subjects. All of these foreign students had brought an intensity to their studies that was lacking in some of the American students, but they also seemed fascinated, as one would expect an outsider to be, by American politics and what had just happened.

Among the Americans was a quiet, attractive girl from someplace remote, Alaska, maybe or one of the Western states, some small town out there that was pretty much unknown to the rest of the students.

Like the rest of the climber student body at Georgetown and the other go-getter Washington-area graduate schools, she did her best to make as many contacts as possible in official and quasi-official Washington. She also connected with interesting international students advancing in their home countries' power structures as she pursued her studies.

The group all knew each other pretty well; they met here almost every morning to compare notes and share observations.

The small-town girl from out West looked a little tired. She had told the group she had been working on a long paper for the last week and had been up the night before, late.

This was in character. She was a bookish girl who kept to herself a lot. The Saudi, who had a flair for the ladies but had not been able to crack this particular nut, wondered whether maybe she had a special friend she had not mentioned to the others. He probed a little, as he had in the past, but she just smiled at him and changed the subject. This was well-trodden ground for them.

As it happened, there was no special friend. Or demanding paper, for that matter.

Having spent her year in the United States aggressively making contacts through people she met at Georgetown, including some congressional staffers and think tankers, she had a pretty good network within what, surprisingly, was about to become the new Washington elite. She had fortunately established a reputation as a solid believer in the traditional values of hard work and independence, although she was fun and vivacious, even if the Saudi and a few others had had to give up the battle in frustration.

The previous night, she had not been with a beau or working on a paper.

She had, as most nights, gotten home on the late side.

She dropped her keys by the door and her backpack on a nearby chair.

She looked around the apartment for any obvious signs of an intruder but saw none. She did not check the alignment of loose change on her dresser or check a talcum powder film around the keyhole of her front door for signs of intrusion. That stuff was for paperback novels. She reached up to a pewter Georgetown University beer stein. It was on a high shelf, aligned with miniature motion-triggered cameras that were camouflaged around the room. She tripped a hidden switch and saw a tiny pin light in the seal glow green. No intruders

She then did what she did most nights. She paused in front of a wall mirror and stared into it, mentally shedding her cover. Then, in a weekly ritual, she retrieved an apparently discarded laptop from beneath soiled laundry in a closet, inserted an electronic key that rendered the machine operable, and sent a burst message to her superiors in Moscow.

She was passing that day's trove—predictions for who the new administration might appoint to be secretary of state and head of the CIA. She was predicting how Congress would work with the new administration. She even had an idea who might be given a couple of key Pentagon spots, but she wanted to keep that under her hat until she was more certain. At this point, that would be a big find.

She looked at her watch as she finished the email. It was 2 A.M. in Washington, already work hours in Moscow. She'd let them read the message and would read their reply in the morning after she got some sleep.

She was a little wired, so she poured herself some vodka—Stoly, not that French crap the Americans were so enamored with—and called up another page on her computer. Once there, she did what she always did when she couldn't sleep, easier online now.

She did the day's *New York Times* crossword puzzle. The weekday ones were different than the Sunday ones and this one was easy. She knocked it off in seven minutes.

She finished her vodka and went to sleep.

In the morning, she read the response from Moscow, which included congratulations for her habitual excellent job, and instructions for the coming week.

After that, Marina—Marina Viktorovna Golovina—put on makeup and fresh clothes and left to meet with her graduate student friends. She was confident the relationships she was cultivating with them and others would pave the way to more access and contacts in official Washington, the kind Moscow was most interested in cultivating and exploiting,

And she was right.

КОНЕЦ — THE END

AUTHOR'S NOTE

I owe a lot of friends, family members, and colleagues in the United States and elsewhere for their help and encouragement in writing this book and getting it published, most of whom must remain anonymous. I can pull the curtain back slightly on two, though. The first is my wife, who was unflagging in her support in this project—in fact less flagging than I was occasionally. This book would never have been published if she had not been there encouraging me. The second is my sister, who has always been my pal and showed so again in her support and encouragement all the way through this effort. To her great credit, she not only read the first draft of this book but, knowing that no thriller works unless the clues are there in plain sight, read it a second time to confirm they were. Thanks to all of you.

ABOUT THE AUTHOR

PHILIP LAZAR lives in the Washington area. His work has taken him periodically to Europe and Asia over the years. This is his first novel.